DELTA: REVENGE

CRISTIN HARBER

PROLOGUE

Rio de Janeiro, Brazil

"IT BEGAN LAST fall in the woods." The drunk lady's slurred words were as irritating as the cloud of smoke circling her head. Cigarette after chain-smoked cigarette, she told the same story to each customer that walked into the dirty tattoo shop. Her orangey-pink lips puckered, wrinkles crinkling with each cigarette draw. "Last fall…"

Javier's temples pounded. His two black eyes reminded him of his recent fight each time he blinked. His busted lip hurt when he drew it into his mouth, so he did that whenever the lady began her story again. He lived for the pain, and at the moment, the biting buzz from the tattoo needle wasn't enough.

Tonight had been big. He'd been unbeatable, untouchable, and he'd taken down the fool who'd tried to best him.

"Done, yeah?" Suarez, his man with the golden gun, wiped down the inside of Javier's forearm.

Javier looked at the design. He hadn't given a picture of it but had only described what he wanted. And his boy had come through just like he had every time before.

"Done." He nodded, biting his lip and relishing the burn on his arm while the basics were taken care of and wrapped.

But without the hum and sting of the needle, the lady and her story tried to push into his head space. Problem was, there was no room. That was why he fought. Why he drank. Why he inked and pierced and trained and tortured his body—to drown his thoughts.

Brazil was a tourist haven, a slice of heaven that didn't hide its hellish side. The TBA—the tri-border area at the junction of Argentina, Brazil, and Paraguay—sank to the dark side with each sunset. There was evil in the land, in the air, in the people who'd come from overseas to make their money and fund their jihads. Once upon a time, all Brazilians had needed to worry about were drug cartels. But now, with the barely understood partnerships between al Qaeda, ISIS, and Hezbollah—and with the nonindigenous mafia syndicates representing every country in the world—Brazil had problems, and because of those, Javier had nightmares. And a goal that kept him alive: revenge.

Suarez nodded. Javier nodded. Their unsaid conversation meant nothing more than *Good-bye until the next time.* Javier's muscles itched and twitched. His mouth salivated for the next fix of adrenaline, and he bounced on his toes, ready to throw down the bills he'd earned that night—bare-knuckle, surrounded by barking, betting men. The drunken, smoking mess sat there. Her skin was brown leather. Her teeth were nicotine yellow. The dress she wore was too tight, revealing too much, and her lazy drunken lull drove him to the point of wanting to punch the cinderblock wall.

But he wouldn't tonight. Breaking bones in his fists would only feel good until he couldn't fight, couldn't *breathe.* Not to mention, how else would he buy what he needed if he didn't have his winnings? He had to pay for seedy *churrascaria* visits and beer to wash down the smoky barbequed meats—neither of which he could identify and both of which he needed. Protein and alcohol. They were his tickets to survival and to fighting another night.

The orangey-pink lips started moving again. Same story, too much to ignore. "Began last fall—"

"Stop." No more. He could take no more. The fix from the tattoo must have worn off. "You want to tell stories? About the fall, surrounded by the evil reaches of tree branches? Their deceptive, shadowy blanket?" Javier planted himself in front of her and watched her take him in. He knew what he looked like, especially after winning in the underground: battered and bruised. "Here's a *história* for you. My father's a *criminoso.* My mother's a whore. But my sister, see, she was an innocent, my guardian angel."

The drunken eyes trembled, waving him away, but he didn't care. He had listened to her, and now she had to listen to him. Not even Suarez stepped in; the tattoo artist knew the story of Javier's sister and the *Primeiro Comando*. Many people did, though most thought it was an old wives' tale.

"Alone in the woods when my father thought he'd left me at our shack of a home. I was just a boy with a whore for a mama. No one to keep me in place—no one besides my sister, my angel. He took her—*my protector*—and sold her as I watched from where I was hidden behind a car like a"—*child*—"coward."

Bile churned in Javier's gut. Raw hatred flowed in his veins—for himself and for the Primeiro Comando cartel. Many years had passed, and he was a man. Still, the pain of the past ate him alive as the stench of cheap rum sweated from the woman across from him. It seeped from her pores and burned from her breath, its sickly scent making his nostrils flare.

"Never, never mind—" orange, smoker-cracked lips stuttered.

He took a step forward. "Under the watchful eyes of my father, my sister walked away—shaking and sobbing in cheap lingerie, crying for a mama that did not care. A mama who probably had a dick in her mouth and a needle in her arm while her daughter was sold. Never to be seen again."

The wrinkle-lined skin around the woman's lips pulled tight when her foul mouth gaped.

The room inched closer onto Javier as it always did when he recounted the story. A PC auction was simple and commonplace, and that one had forever changed him. "*That's* a story that should be told if we're telling awful tales of a cold night, surrounded by trees."

He threw the paper bills on the counter and walked out, letting the shabby door slam. Humid heat slapped across his body. Javier wrapped his hand around the freshly bound tattoo and squeezed, hoping for enough pain to quiet the rage building deep in his soul. The familiar bite didn't work to ease the monster that ate him from within.

Skin vibrating, blood racing, adrenaline coating his tongue, he rushed through the familiar back alleys, head down and fists balled. He needed to fight. To focus. To channel the rage that could make him blackout mad. Javier headed to the flophouse where he boarded, across from a PC whorehouse. He liked to keep an eye on the girls there. If a girl didn't make it, if one wasn't able to walk after a John was finished, Javier took care of the bastard. He was a teenage-vigilante presence who lurked in the shadows of Rio, hunting down the men who'd sold his sister.

He might not be able to go back in time and save his sister or rescue the girls from their whoring lives, but he sure wasn't going to let them get the worst of it without doling out punishment.

His skin prickled for attention. Instinct was his survival, the only thing he could trust. Javier clenched his fists, put his head low, and stalked around the corner. There, he readied for war as he heard a slick, soft step on the damp sidewalk.

Javier lunged for his shadow, and it attacked him back. His adversary was stronger, a white guy with street moves—good ones—but with a decade on Javier.

Fists flew fast. Javier absorbed punches and ducked around cheap shots. They fought dirty, fought hard. It was the kind of brawl that Javier craved and few knew how to give, with jabs and gut shots.

"Enough." The white guy stepped back smoothly, and his fists stopped swinging. He slowly clapped as though he were impressed, giving a head-shaking chuckle. "Nicely done, Javier Almeida."

"You know me?"

"Everything about you."

There was no trusting a white American in a Brazilian alley. Double that when they knew his name. "What do you want?"

"I have a proposition for you."

"No, thanks." Javier bounced to his toes, ready to fight again and more than ready to beat the man unconscious for making his skin crawl. *Knows everything about me?* That didn't sit right.

"There's a lot of money involved, Javier."

"Don't swing that way." He gave the American a hard eye. "Stop using my name."

"All right, Brazil. No names." The man shook out a fist but didn't seem to be in pain. He was no stranger to a street fight.

"What do you know about me? What do you want?"

"You're an underground of Rio de Janeiro legend. A street fighter. A watchdog who gives no fucks." The man took a step back to assess him the way a boxer's manager might. "Pretty impressed with what I just saw."

He shrugged. "Don't care."

"You're obsessed with Primeiro Comando."

"Careful of what you say and who you say it to down here, *americano*."

Narrow eyes assessed him, mocking his warning. "I have a job offer for you."

"No." *Simple.*

"It's not wise to say no before you have the terms. Of all the things I've learned about you, jumping to conclusions was not one of them, Brazil."

"Don't care about the terms." Javier wouldn't turn his back on an attacker, but he was done with this conversation. He *had* a job: fighting, protecting, hunting. Those were as much a passion as they were a living. And a means of survival.

"Then"—the man stepped closer—"you'll care about what I can offer."

Javier smirked. "And what's that?"

There was nothing a white guy with an American accent could offer him that would be of interest.

He caught Javier's arm, ripped the plastic wrap off the fresh tattoo in a smooth move, and nodded toward red, swollen, newly inked flesh. "That."

REVENGE

Unnerved, Javier stared at the letters that meant so much. "Who are you?"

"My name is Brock Gamble. I am the Delta team leader for Titan Group."

Whatever that means. "You can guarantee me this?" He lifted his arm.

"Without question. If you want the Primeiro Comando, work for me, and eventually, I will give them to you."

As Javier stared at the inside of his forearm, all of his hesitations were gone. Brock Gamble had just offered the only thing he'd ever wanted. "Job offer accepted."

CHAPTER ONE

Five Years Later
Chester County, Pennsylvania

*O*H GOD. THE pressure was too much. Everyone said cold feet were normal. Sophia Cole wiggled her pedicured toes in her silk, peep-toed heels. Her feet weren't cold. This was a warning light. Or bell. Maybe a siren? Whatever it was, it was loud. Clanging. Blaring, *Jump off this train before it dives over the cliff.*

Her heartbeat hopped from worried to alarm. Not one to have a panic attack at the altar in front of God and a guest list worthy of a who's who of Washington, DC society pages, she casually shifted her stance and wiped at her cheeks. Seriously—she was sweating. Her warm cheeks were moist as though the air in this stifling church were humid. But really, it couldn't be humid and stifling. The air conditioning was likely blowing. An event planner had probably picked out the perfect room temperature for the ideal church wedding.

Sophia adjusted her gaze from her peep toes to Josh, who looked the all-important part of adoring and handsome groom. He was so perfect. *On paper.*

Oh, God.

The corset tie at her back itched. Had she moved that much just now? Had it tightened? Could she get married? To Josh? In this dress? *Of course I can.* Was it nerves? She'd spent years with him and was now standing at the altar *hyperventilating.*

Sophia forced her lip-lined smile into place and swallowed away a wave of white-hot warning signs, taking as deep a breath as her dress would allow.

She had questions; Josh was always so smooth with his answers. *Too smooth?* She'd caught him in a lie or two or twelve. He was a reformed cheater. But that was behind them—right? Her stomach churned with a nauseated knowing. *Think!* Wow, this was a mental moment she could have had before the minister started doing his job…

Josh was perfect. They were friends. The sex was fine. His body was great. He made a killer soufflé. He was a pediatrician—the world's greatest job, according to everybody. Particularly her mom.

Shit. That was not a list of husband-like qualities. When was the last time she'd swooned? Had she ever melted against the man who'd have her for forever?

"Oh, God," she whispered, positive the church tilted at an angle. Had she *ever* melted with him—swooned to the point that the world didn't matter? Even when they were dating?

Josh's eyebrows went up.

Adequate sex and a good soufflé? Seriously? Seriously! She'd never swooned over him. Never. Not once. Sophia's mouth rounded, unsure—

"*Oh, God.*" That guilt-soaked whisper did not come from Sophia.

Nor did it come from Josh or the minister.

It didn't come from her mom or a little angel sitting on her shoulder readying to spit wisdom that might sound something like *run.*

Sophia spun in the mermaid-style wedding dress that her mother insisted was famed designer Paul Lang's gift to the female form. The dress *was* heaven for the right person. It really was perfect. And gorgeous. And tight—very tight—except where the skirt whooshed out at her thighs. Turning, Sophia caught a glimpse of her best friend, also known as the maid of honor, whose mouth continued to hang open after the profession of *Oh God* in God's house.

Sophia's questioning, semisuddenly knowing eyebrow crept up. "You okay, Liz?"

"Oh God." Liz's bottom lip trembled.

"What the heck?" Josh mumbled, low and quiet and guilty as all hell.

Sophia pivoted back to her groom. "I… can*not* believe you."

But his eyes were slits, evilly studying the shit out of Liz and totally bypassing his bride. Sophia spun back, ridiculously, as the silent church dropped a notch quieter.

"Liz?" Sophia asked.

Her watery eyes said way more than her mouth did. "Soph—"

Josh made a noise like a growl. Sophia might end up with a broken heart, maybe a moment of embarrassment of epic proportions, but what she wanted to do was bum-rush him and knee him in the nuts.

Mom wouldn't approve. Dad would do so privately. Colin, her brother, would cheer her on. The event planner would somehow make a magical PR drape fall from the cathedral ceiling and end the show.

None of that would actually happen, though, and did she seriously think he was never going to change? Maybe or maybe not. But an affair with Liz?

Her mother was likely having heart palpitations that very second. Lord knew that when her parents had to play the role of the ambassador and his wife, they didn't have drama, especially when the press was in the room.

Sophia was losing her mind and focus in front of pews of people…

"I'm—" Liz's colorless face brought Sophia back.

"*Lizzie,*" Josh cut her off. "Shut it."

Sophia twisted back to Josh. "Lizzie? Since when is Liz Lizzie?"

"I'm so sorry," Liz whispered to Sophia's lace-and-corseted back.

"You're kidding me. Josh?"

The minister cleared his throat, glaring at Josh but also at *Sophia* as if she'd had an idea the affair would come to light *at this moment.* "If you're ready to continue."

"Really?" *Screw him and Josh.* Sophia turned again to her maid of honor. Liz hid her face with the bouquet that she'd helped pick out. Tabby, the bridesmaid behind Liz, leaned forward in a way that indicated that if Sophia gave the sign, she'd take out the wayward bridal-party member with a right hook and a body slam.

The minister cleared his throat again. "Perhaps you need a moment in private."

Stunned, Sophia ignored the minister and turned to Josh, who mouthed, *Please.*

She should be hurt. But Sophia was angry and channeling all her fury. She pulled her long skirt around, took in the full church—all watching the altar in rapt attention—and slowly found her parents. Dad's eyes and firm jaw said the same thing as Colin's death glare. Mom was a moment away from clutching her pearls or maybe passing out.

Dad and Mom had very different outlooks on life. Mom was very much concerned with her role—the events, the society, blah, blah. She was great and loving in her own way but still uptight. Dad looked the part of the man who'd done time in Benghazi, Afghanistan, and Kirkuk. He was very much about country and honor, a former marine who bled red, white, and blue. But he also did a poor job of hiding the fact that he was okay with Sophia being a daddy's girl.

Behind her family were a few close members of Colin's Delta team. That was when her disbelief-turned-anger morphed into embarrassment. Colin and his friends were like superheroes. They were willing to sacrifice their lives for a greater good. There was Grayson, the good guy, Mr. All-American, sitting with Emma—his wife—and their child. Next to him sat Trace and Marlena.

Then there were the guys Colin ran around the world with, likely breaking hearts. But at least they were up-front about it, not cheating and lying like Dr. Josh. They were *the boys*—Ryder, the guy with the golden smile, and handsome, focused Luke, who seemed as though shadows sometimes chased him. And Javier. She couldn't look away from him. He could've been the poster boy for Calvin Klein, exotic edition. He was tall, dark, and handsome. And now, he looked like a… killer.

They all did. *All for one and one for all*—that might have been the Delta motto, because each of the chiseled mugs matched Colin's. They all wore looks that said they were ready to protect what was theirs: her.

Josh's hand reached for the Paul Lang original, and she stepped out of reach as though the good doctor were covered in something contagious. An audible gasp swept the church. Out of the corner of her eye, she saw Colin stand up in his pew as if he might side tackle her asshole of a groom. But there was no need for that. Sophia was strong like her brother. Like her father. She was tough in her own right, strong and brave, and didn't need this bull crap. Throwing on a smile as fake as her marriage would have been, she spoke only to her mom. "Time for the reception."

And that was that. The smile was still there. Maybe she was strong like her mother, too.

For all the risk she'd lived through, for every fight she'd waged overseas to help women and children in the parts of the world that didn't value them as people, how had this happened to her?

"Sophia—"

"Shut up, Josh." She squared her shoulders, held her chin up, ignored her mother's pained expression and her father's homicidal one, and walked back down the aisle. The only sound was the swishing of the spectacular skirt that wasn't very Sophia Cole to begin with.

CHAPTER TWO

A S SOON AS the heavy church doors shut behind Sophia, the loud explosion of gossip quickly fired up. Three inches of carved wood was no match for wedding-day gossip. Any second now, one of her girlfriends would race behind her, but if she had to bet money on who would make it out the door first—

"Sophia Marie!"

She smiled because she'd known it. The money would be on her brother every time. But she kept walking with pounds of white fabric in hand. Colin was by her side, matching her power stride before she could mumble, "How mad is Mom?"

"Soph?"

She angled around the sidewalk, heading toward the parking lot. "Got your car keys on you?"

He chuckled. "Shit, girl. Yeah."

"Well, let's go."

"Stop a sec." He pulled her to a standstill, both hands on her shoulders. "Seriously, you alright?"

Quickly taking inventory of her feelings, it was shocking how she was more upset with being pissed and publicly humiliated than cheated on. She'd spent too much time on the other side of the world doing what she could to make sure lives and feelings were valued for this to happen. "I'm ready for cake. Lots and lots of cake. And to get out of this dress." She was literally sewed into it and needed to escape.

"Soph?"

"Seriously. If Josh and *Lizzie* want to bump uglies, good for them."

Colin tried to hide a laugh with a hand rubbing his face then brushing into his close-cropped hair. "You're not alright."

"Probably not. But I'm ready to have a drink and eat a lot more than I've allowed myself in two weeks. Okay?"

His fingers flexed on her shoulders. "You were always too good for him."

"What, Dr. Josh? Who's too good for that guy? Mom couldn't have the invitations engraved any faster than she did."

Voices of well-meaning bridesmaids neared them, but she didn't want to see them. She didn't want to know who knew, who might've guessed, or who'd been as oblivious as she was.

Colin wrapped an arm around her lace-covered shoulders, and they hit the church parking lot. A minute later, he had her and several pounds of lace and silk in the passenger seat of his Wrangler. A rev of the engine and a slam of gas, and they were headed to their parents' estate, also known as the site of the reception, the location of cake, and the home of the open bar.

"Yeah?" Colin's phone was pressed to his ear. "Ten-four." He laughed in a way that told Sophia her mother had done something that would make her want to pull out her perfectly coiffed hair and veil—God, she was still wearing the veil.

"What?"

Colin dropped the phone in his lap. "Nothing you can't guess."

Sophia dropped the visor and opened the mirror to see what could be done about the veil. *Not much*, at least not until they were out of the car and in a bathroom with someone dexterous with hairpins.

"Mom announced the party is to continue. Both sides are headed over to enjoy dinner and dancing." He shook his head. "Fun times."

"Of course she did."

"Really, you announced it first. Think Josh will show?"

"No way. He's scared to death of you."

"As he should be. I'll track his ass down if Dad hasn't got to him first."

Sophia grumbled and leaned her head back. "This is Mom's nightmare."

"No, sweetie." Colin gave her a sad half smile. "It's Dad's."

"What?" Dad's nightmares were about middle-of-the-night phone calls and stuff like nuclear weapons.

"His little girl hurt like that? Josh better run."

She let Colin's point of view take hold. True enough. If it wasn't her brother being overprotective, it was her dad. Either way, she wouldn't want to be Josh with the family bulldogs loose. "Just take me to my party. I need champagne and fondant."

THE LINEN-COVERED TABLE matched the moneyed elegance of the Coles' estate. The extravaganza made Javier's skin crawl. He'd grown up in a hut in the *favelas*—the slums—in the overcrowded, stacked neighborhood of Complexo do Alemão. Back then, he hadn't known palaces like this existed. His world had been military police, cartels, traffickers, crisis, and occupations. Life was hell, but hell had been normal.

He wouldn't have comprehended this if he hadn't been yanked from Brazilian poverty, from the money-making hustle of street fights in Rio de Janeiro, and trained as a mercenary and a solider. *As an American.*

Titan's Delta team claimed him as one of their own. It'd worked out well. They wanted talent with local intel and a hatchet to bury, and Javier wanted a means to his revenge-fueled end. There was an added, unexpected bonus: he would travel the world, see beautiful things—beautiful *people*. Like Sophia Cole.

She set the bar. She was the one unattainable woman whose face he pictured when he flirted with other *available* girls. Sophia, after years of coloring his dreams and starring in his fantasies, was now *single*.

Maybe it was wrong to fantasize about his buddy's sister, especially when Javier knew how protective Colin was over her. But some things could not be helped. There was plenty enough to pay attention to. Her mouth had the perfect pout with full cherry-stained lips. Brown eyes warmed the sweetheart face that softened her steel Cole-family backbone. Sophia had grace, yet there was a rawness about her that added color to his black-and-white world.

Javier ran a hand over his mouth, hiding his smile. A wedding apocalypse shouldn't have been fun to watch. Yet with Sophia, it was hard to look away, not because of the disaster but because of how she'd handled it.

Again, he hid the smile that he didn't want to explain to the world, appreciating her from afar. But his stomach dropped. He wouldn't make a move on a woman in her wedding dress. There were some lines even he didn't cross. What was he thinking?

Javier's gaze swept the room, searching for the ambassador. Nowhere to be seen, much like Colin. If Javier could guess, Cole senior and junior were having a moment with the wannabe groom.

At least the reception was still a go. Free booze and food—and hopefully good news from Brock, Delta team leader.

"Hi, sexy." Trace's wife, Marlena, joined him at the table, smoothing her dress and pushing back her bright, newly red hair. He liked Mar; her edginess and intelligence made him comfortable. "I'm surprised to see you sitting down."

"Why?" he asked, even though sitting alone, staring at his phone and waiting for a phone call, was unusual. Or maybe not. All he did anymore was chase intel.

"This many pretty girls in the room, all watching you boys like you're a wedding-reception one-night stand waiting to happen—"

"Isn't that the point of weddings?" He joked to cover how distracted he was.

"Yet you're sitting at the table alone."

"Waiting on a phone call." Brock had important Primeiro Comando intel, and as soon as Javier found out if Delta was a step closer to the PC, he could relax. The closer they moved in, the better he felt. Tonight, Javier *wanted* to party with his teammates and booze it up, stare at a single Sophia, and maybe make a stupid mistake. Say something he shouldn't. Get hell from the team. Any minute after his call with Brock, he could—as soon as good PC news rang from the phone.

The screen lit, and as if Brock could read Javier's mind, a text message appeared.

Need another thirty minutes or so. Not looking like the break we need.

Javier grumbled. Actionable PC intel would happen that night; they were *so* close. Maybe one day he could live without craving revenge. What would it be like to wake up and not want blood?

Marlena cleared her throat, an eyebrow lifting as she stared at his phone. "Not good news?"

He lifted a heavy shoulder, questioning the hope he was trying keep ahold of. "It'll be okay."

Trace came over with two drinks, handing one to his wife. "Yo, man."

"Hey." Javier checked his watch. Not even a minute had passed. Another thirty minutes would drag like the first few bites of a tattoo's needle.

"What's wrong with him?" Trace asked Marlena.

Javier answered for her. "I'm waiting on Brock. He's at Titan, digging through Primeiro Comando BS with Parker."

"Oh, gotcha." Trace sat down. "If it doesn't happen this time, we'll learn more next."

"Right…"

In his peripheral vision, the unmarried bride and a few bridesmaids walked across the corner of the dance floor. Her white gown covered her from neck to toe yet left nothing to the imagination. Javier needed to look anywhere but at that skirt swaying tight on her ass, surrounded by a giant poof of fabric he would dive face-first into. Sophia was *gostosa*. She'd always been hot, but with a booty like that and that dress putting it all on display? Whoa.

"Down, boy." Marlena laughed into her wine.

Javier shifted back in his seat as heat flashed up his neck. "Just waiting on a phone call."

"You're staring."

At the bride was left unsaid, and Javier thought he could make an argument for any of the bridesmaids. "Lots of things to look at, Mar."

"A ton of ladies, that's for sure." Marlena clucked at him. "But probably not *her*."

It would be in poor taste because Colin was his boy. And because he needed to focus on the PC.

"Javier?" Marlena pulled him out of his guilt-tainted thoughts.

"Yeah?" His eyes dropped to the phone then back to the dance floor. What a woman…

"Still staring."

Trace gave a low laugh, throwing his arm around his wife. "Maybe that's what little Sophia Cole needs to forget about the day: a good night with Brazil."

Javier swallowed the knot in his throat, partly ignoring both of them and glancing up, not taking his eyes off Sophia. "Just waiting on a phone call. That's all."

"Then look out, ladies." Marlena giggled. "South America's finest is in a mood."

He tore his attention away from the bride, who was making the rounds with a vacant smile on her camera-ready face, playing the part of the diplomat's daughter very well.

Colin sauntered over to the table, beer in hand. "Hey."

Trace and Javier welcomed him with chin lifts, and Marlena gave Colin a nosy glance.

"Kill the groom?" she asked.

"Nah. Not worth it." After pulling up a chair, Colin nodded to Javier's phone on the table. "Have you heard anything?"

It seemed that word on possible intel moved as quickly as wedding-day gossip. Javier tilted his head, hating the answer. "No. Soon, though, I think."

"Good. If not today, then soon."

"Yeah, yeah. You guys can stop saying that already." The truth didn't help. Who knew what would?

"There it is." Marlena shifted onto Trace's knee. "When Javier gets worked up, that accent of his sounds like an orgasm waiting to happen. Take that onto the dance floor, Javier. That will be a good distraction for whatever you're waiting on." She crossed her heart. "I promise."

Javier rolled his eyes. "*Pare.*"

"Holy butterflies, if I weren't already—" she started to say, but Trace clamped a kiss over her mouth, and she dissolved into a fit of giggles.

They were cute enough to make a man puke.

Ryder walked over with a girl under his arm, laughing at Trace, who was kissing Marlena as though they were still the one-night stand they'd started as. "Hey, now. Are you getting an early start, mate?"

That made Marlena laugh harder. Trace flipped Ryder the bird, not stopping what he was up to.

Colin slugged back his beer. "Can't go wrong with an open bar. I'm going to need it to deal with that"—he pointed at the Trace-Marlena love connection—"and that." Then he pointed at Ryder, who grinned at the possibilities. "And *you*."

"Me?" That one caught Javier off guard.

"If you don't hear what you want to hear, you're going to be *pleasant*."

"Nah. Won't faze me." Lying, Javier let his gaze roam. "Your sister okay?"

Colin dropped the beer bottle to the table. "With her it's impossible to really know. Teflon tough. But this whole thing?" He tossed his hand toward the soft woman working the room. "That's to be nice to our mother."

"Yeah?" Interesting…

Colin shook his head. "Mom means well."

"If I were Sophia, I'd need a drink. Or five."

Colin nodded. "That's what's in her head. She'll have a straw in a champagne bottle at first opportunity."

Marlena giggled. "Trace said she needs a night with Javier."

Colin rolled his eyes. Trace's laughter bled into the music as he tickled Marlena in punishment. Ryder threw his head back, pulling his girl-for-the-evening into his chest. She laughed. Everyone was laughing and happy, making out and drinking. But Javier's mind stayed with Sophia, thinking about Marlena's joke of spending the night with her and of all the times he had thought about her like that before.

"Go say hi," Marlena squeaked.

"*Cristo*." He wouldn't put himself in that position. "I'm not going to hit on Colin's sister in her wedding dress."

"Or ever." Colin slugged back his drink. "She needs nothing from Delta."

Javier laughed in agreement, but the gesture was more defensive than amused.

Trace laughed. "Everyone needs a little Brazil."

Javier smiled to torque the hell out of Colin. "Her innocence is safe from me."

"Innocence, come on." Colin shook his head. "You guys are killing me."

"I—" The phone's screen lit, and this time it read *Brock* calling. Not a text message. This was the intelligence Javier needed. "I'll be back." He swiped the phone to answer. "Yeah, boss. Give me a minute to get somewhere quiet."

He *needed* this phone call to go well. Delta needed info, a simple break of information in their hunt. But Javier needed more intel to keep functioning, to keep his focus from going haywire. They were so close. He could taste it, feel it. All that was missing was a piece of information.

He headed into an empty hall, leading away from the party. The noise died as he put the phone back to his ear. "Alright. I'm here. Good news?"

A second ticked by. "Sorry, Brazil."

His head dropped back as disappointment, again, flooded him. One step closer; one step back. In the end, they might never find the fuckers that had hurt his sister. Every dead end was a reminder of how empty he felt, how bad he hurt.

"Javier?"

"Yeah, boss?"

"The break's coming. I promised it to you. It. Will. Come."

"Yeah, I know." But the inevitable heartbreak had already hit hard. He could go back into the reception, find himself a good time, and forget tonight. Or he could sulk. "Thanks."

"Chin up."

"Yes, sir." And as Javier's chin went up, a bartender wheeled out of a back room, pushing a dumbwaiter stacked with champagne bottles—like a sign from God that he should sulk and drink. Javier grabbed one, ignoring the surprised response. "Thank you very much."

"Hey—"

He wandered down the hall of a house that was so big it was a museum. A quick tear of foil and pop of the cork, and Javier was one sip closer to a buzz.

CHAPTER THREE

T HE WALLS OF a house she hated were closing in on Sophia. The bridesmaids, sans one very noticeable maid of honor, were doing their best to make her forget the awkward day. The effort was thoughtful even if the whole concept was uncomfortably weird.

How many people in the room did she actually know? Not many. Which was fine because her mother had transformed the reception into a fundraiser. Donations and charity could fix most situations, and while she'd rather not have had to be publicly humiliated to help raise awareness for women's rights around the world, it was a cause that she'd dedicated her career to, and her mother *did* have an entire press corp there.

"Soph, honey?" The oldest and sweetest of the bridesmaids, Tabby, bumped elbows with her playfully. "Doing okay?"

"It's a great day to raise money and awareness." For what cause? Whatever Mom had decided. *Raise money. Raise awareness.* Four perfect words that could shut down any uncomfortable small talk.

Tabby *phffsh*ed. "Give that BS line to someone else."

Thank God for real friends. "I need cake."

"And a drink."

Oh, yes. A drink. A big one with bubbles that comes with a warning. Something like, *Too many will make you hurt in the morning, but for now, you'll forget. Drink responsibly.* "Your suggestions are one of the many reasons why I love you, Tabby."

She preened to the point that they both laughed. "I think we've crossed everyone off the list you have to say hey to."

"Affirmative. That's why it's also cake time."

Tabby's light-green eyes narrowed as if working out a strategy. "So, how does that work?"

"Hmmm." Sophia did a small spin around the room in search of the wedding planner. No dice. The only ones working—on payroll for the event—were a few assistants, the caterers, and the DJ. "I think I'm just going to get a piece of cake."

"I don't know about that. I'm pretty sure there is protocol. There's an engraved keepsake after all."

"Do you want it?" Sophia asked.

Tabby laughed, trying to hide it unsuccessfully with a bite to her bottom lip. "Well, no."

She shrugged a lace-covered shoulder. "Think anyone will say something?"

"Yes. Your *mother*, for one. And—"

"My mom is in public-relations crisis management. My stealing a slice of cake is the least of her worries."

"Sophia…" A haughty, feminine voice edged close, and Sophia caught sight of the editor in chief of *DC File*.

Shit. Now was the time for a Bat-signal to the bevy of helper bees that were on Cole family payroll. The tall, assuming woman in a power suit was *not* what Sophia would consider *friendly* if she was thinking about strategic enemies the way her Dad would. But her mom would consider the woman barreling into their inner circle an *asset*. Mom was socially strategic. Tactical even.

"Sophia, how are you doing, dear?" Her voice screamed that all conversation would be on the record.

All eyes within a three-foot radius went from Sophia to *DC File* lady and back to Sophia. The enemy-asset woman had *tabloid headline* written all over her face. She was clearly not interested in anything to do with the plight of women's rights abroad or raising awareness in the US, both of which Sophia knew had been pitched to and rejected by *DC File*.

"Thanks for being here today." Sophia's back molars ground while she squared her couture-covered shoulders.

"I haven't seen Josh."

Well, no shit, lady. Colin and Dad probably had him strung up where no reporter or editor would find the body. "I'm sure he's around. If you're looking for him, someone can—"

"Rumor has it that you were working with the Saudis, brokering discussions between them and a Yemeni women's rights activist. That is where you were while Josh and you...*were apart.*"

Oh, hell. Forget the jab about her and Josh. That bit about her with the Saudi-Yemen partnership was serious insider knowledge. Not to mention *classified.* "It's great to have the opportunity to raise awareness tonight." *Instead of celebrating my nuptials to a cheating do-gooder.* Sophia gave her best, most innocent smile. "Though obviously you know that I have spent a great deal of time in both areas of the world, and the rights of women and children are particularly important to me."

DC File lady scrunched her in-the-know face. They were in a standoff that none of her bridesmaids knew how to handle, and she'd handled the Liz-Lizzie problem flawlessly. National security and actual public relations? This was her, who she really was outside the walls of the glitzy mansion and the too-tight dress.

Sophia wouldn't lose a simple staring contest. After her day at the altar, there was no backing down as seconds were strangled.

DC File lady blinked. Once. Twice. It was a white flag. "Alright, then. Just a rumor."

"Thanks for coming." Sophia gave a big, fake smile with lots of teeth like a shark dressed in couture.

"Of course." Then the woman sauntered out.

"That was weird." Tabby's eyebrow rose.

"Yup, totally." But where Tabby was confused, Sophia was unnerved. She'd deal with it later, but the woman had given a very accurate guess of a potentially dangerous classified piece of information.

The music shifted, and the DJ gave a shout-out to all the single ladies in the room. Sophia rolled her eyes, but a couple of the girls took that as a moment to wander toward the dance floor. She couldn't blame them. If she were in a better mood, she'd be out there too.

"Nobody cares. Put it away," Tabby hissed at another girl.

Sophia turned to Tabby. "Hm?"

"Nothing."

"I heard. Spit it out."

Tabby rolled her lips, staying silent.

"Tabby?"

"Nothing." She relented. "Just Liz texted."

"You're right." Sophia shook her head. "Not today. Tell me tomorrow. I'll deal with her then too."

"I shouldn't have said anything. We were trying to be quiet. Sorry."

What should she say? "I get it. It's weird."

"It's messed up."

Sophia laughed quietly. "Yeah, but…"

"Hm?" Tabby pushed her hair off her shoulder.

"I don't know." How could she put into words the confusing back-and-forth of emotions she'd experienced, none of which would be classified as expected?

Tabby stepped closer to her. "What?"

"What if I'm more pissed about Josh and Liz's betrayal than… I don't know."

"Than about not getting married?" Tabby offered.

Sophia nodded.

"Then I'd say everything happens for a reason." She put an arm around her and squeezed. "I was wondering if you were thinking something like that. I know you've got brass balls and all, but I just wanted to make sure you're as okay as you pretend most times."

"Sophia!" Another voice that she didn't recognize was calling.

"More of this?" Leaning into Tabby, she whispered, "I thought all the smiling BS was over."

A face Sophia didn't recognize came front and center, the salivating need for precious gossip almost dripping down her chin. "Oh my God! Did you know?"

She'd never seen the woman before in her life. "I did! Crazy, isn't it? Thought it would be best to end things with a bang. More fun this way—"

"Excuse me!" Tabby snagged her arm. "We have to use the restroom." She firmly yanked Sophia away. "You need a breather."

"Yup. I think I do." She had to get out of that room with all the lights and decorations and busybodies. The faces of the guests all said they either pitied her or they knew. "Not once, but *three times,* with my *three* overseas trips in the last year."

"We need out of this room before we start dissecting it."

"I was risking my life *in Saudi Arabia and Yemen*"—since *DC File* lady knew, what the hell, Tabby could know too—"while Liz was screwing my fiancé." Josh didn't know exactly what Sophia had been doing overseas, but he did know it was a project that her father had set up, that it wasn't the safest situation, but that she was doing something that mattered. "Glad he was worried about my safety…"

A love affair with the two people who said they were most concerned about her travels. That was BS.

"Screw him," Tabby promised.

"Yeah." Sophia's stupid-expensive dress swooshed with each step as they passed her mom, who waved as though it really were any old fundraiser. "You know what? I'm not going to hide."

"We're not hiding. We're breathing. In a bathroom. Or hallway. *Away from people.*" Tabby gripped her elbow. "Let's go breathe elsewhere."

"I'm done following the party line." She stopped, lace and fluff and silk anchoring her in one spot.

"Shit, Soph. Party line? You're not a politician. But you can't… I don't know." Tabby inched close. "Please don't do anything insane."

Sophia grabbed the white layers of the mermaid skirt. "This *dress* is insane. My mother turning the reception into the *must-attend* function of the year—that's insane."

The *conversation* her mother had started when Sophia arrived was *really insane*, but Tabby didn't need to know the embarrassing details. Her mom's prissy voice had pleaded with her over Colin's phone. *Couldn't you two wait to do this later?* Yeah, sure, Mom. Go through with a wedding and then have to deal with the divorce just to make her party go off without a hitch. Very Mom.

Tabby relented, knowing that the dress and the festivities were over-the-top and not very Sophia at all. "Point proven."

She dropped the skirt, feigning heartache. "God forbid a party falls through."

Tabby failed to stifle an appreciating laugh. "So, what do you want to do?"

"This." Sophia turned and headed toward her mom. She forced on a happy face. "That was everyone I needed to say hello to, so my duties are officially over."

"Sweetheart." Mom's discomfort would never be obvious, but the ladies standing with her had pinched expressions.

The DJ started another song, and the dance floor was reinvigorated. Sophia could dance but had to get that awful dress off. The corset choked off her circulation and, more importantly, wouldn't allow much room for cake and champagne, both of which she was going to sample—several times—if it was the last thing she did. And by *sample,* she meant *gorge.*

"I appreciate what you've done, Mom." It certainly should have been scary how quickly her mother and her bevy of assistants transformed the wedding reception into a fundraiser.

Actually, no, it wasn't scary. This was Mom's calling. Sophia tried to understand it—really. Mom's effort was how she showed love. The attention and PR ridiculousness were her mother's way of showing she cared. Some people hugged. Her mom created espionage-worthy illusions.

"Thank you," Sophia told her.

Mom's perfectly lipsticked lips opened, but Sophia turned, grabbing Tabby, and walked away gracefully before another word could be said.

"Awkward." Tabby giggled. "We need a drink."

"Amen." Sophia beelined straight to the closest bar, cutting in line and grabbing the bartender's attention. "Hi. Can you hand me that bottle, please?"

"Um, Soph? A drink." Tabby touched her arm. "Maybe not a bottle?"

"Um." The bartender's confused expression didn't help the speedy getaway that she was planning. Maybe she needed cake first.

"Definitely a bottle."

"Um." Tabby glanced at the bartender. "Maybe a *glass.*"

"Tabby, really, I'm good." Or not. "I'm grabbing *the bottle* and some cake."

Her friend's eyelashes batted indecisively. "You're sure?"

Sophia nodded and pivoted toward the bartender. "I'll be back in two minutes. I want *a bottle* of champagne." Still no reaction. For the love of all that was holy… "See the dress? It's my *fundraiser*. And my champagne. I'll give you a minute to figure it out."

Tabby nodded, finally showing solidarity. "Just give it to her."

"He'll figure it out." Sophia turned and headed toward the cake. It sat on a lonesome table, waiting for its shining moment, which would never come.

How was she going to do this? Hmm. Sophia grabbed the engraved spatula—wow, heavier than she expected—and knife, then she cut the first slice as large as the waiting plate would allow, not looking to see if anyone noticed.

Alright then, cake in hand. Next up, champagne. She swooshed the skirt toward the bar, heading for her bottle.

"Oh, I will definitely need this." She grabbed a silverware roll from a table on her way, unable to ignore that people were staring. A few eyes followed her, their gossiping gazes burrowing into the poor Paul Lang number, but mostly, she could feel her mother's stare. Alcohol was needed more than ever, certainly more than she'd needed it at the altar.

Sophia cut ahead of someone she didn't know. "My champagne, please."

The man produced a linen-wrapped bottle. "Would you like a glass, ma'am?"

"No, thank you." With the cake plate and silverware in one hand, and the bottle in the other, she grinned at Tabby, who had rejoined their friends at a nearby table. She mouthed, "Cake *and* champagne."

Tabby raised her glass and smiled. "*Salud.*"

With the senior bridesmaid's blessing, Sophia left the reception—*um, fundraiser*—and wandered into the hallway, taking in the vastness of a house that she was mostly unfamiliar with. In theory, it should have felt like coming home, but neither she nor Colin had actually grown up in this monstrosity.

Sophia leaned against the wall. Her elbow trailed the chair rail molding of the ornate hall. Once the voices had faded from the grand ballroom, the quiet played with her mind. A tear slipped free. Sophia had let her life become this: a wedding that required a press secretary and a fiancé who couldn't keep it in his pants. What if she'd stayed home or hadn't had those lofty save-the-world goals? Nope. A cheater would cheat, regardless; it stank that it took her wedding day to realize it.

Time for cake and a drink. She ducked into a dark and quiet study, a refuge where she could down the cake. She swished to the desk and plopped behind it. The good thing about a mermaid skirt was her butt fit in the chair, but pushing the bottom of the skirt under the desk? Eh, not so much.

Oh well. Sophia unrolled her silverware and stabbed the fork into the cake. Ah… heaven.

Drunk giggles warned her before the door bounced open. One of her brother's teammates, Ryder, and Sophia's friend, Stacy, were lip-locked and completely oblivious to her.

Shit. "Hey. I'll just get going."

The startled hookup froze.

"Oh! Sophia. I'm, um, sorry." Stacy's scarlet cheeks could almost match her dress.

They both looked unsure of what to do. God, it was awkward. "I'm heading out. You two just… stay."

"No, really. Are you—" She smoothed her dress. "Are you okay?"

"I really am. You guys should continue…" Sophia bit her lip. "Talking, or whatever. I was just leaving."

She gathered her cake speared with a fork and the bottle of champagne, nabbing a pair of scissors off the desk in a last-minute dress strategy, using her elbow and hands to hold everything, and headed for a bedroom where she could change, eat cake, and drink responsibly—which meant alone in her pajamas.

"Scissors?" Stacy asked, a twinge of concern trilling her question.

"I need to fix a snag." Or rather, she was sewn into the corset top, and the seam ripper had been packed into her overnight bag. Lord knew where that was. The ribbon that ran along her spine would be a goner as soon as she could figure out how to pull off such a flexible feat. "Bye, guys."

Sophia hustled as fast as her dress would allow. Conversations like this were hell. She went up a back staircase to the second floor, south wing, holding her cake and bottle of bubbly. A row of guest rooms that were likely unused—because while Mom loved a party, she wanted folks to leave at the end—were up ahead. Sophia doubted even her parents would spend the night in this house. Surely there was some fancy diplomatic event they had to scoot off to somewhere in the world.

Pushing through a door, she forked a huge bite of cake into her mouth and walked with her eyes shut, mouth full, and was the closest she'd been to content in about a day. "Peace at last."

"Sorry."

A low masculine accent that struck her as amazing raked from across the room.

"Oh," she mumbled, eyes now open, pulling the fork from her mouth. She slapped a hand over her mouth, clattered the plate and champagne onto the dresser, and dropped the scissors. Oh. My. God. Holy crap.

"Just leaving."

"Sorry," she said, desperately trying to swallow the cake without looking like an oaf dressed like an elegant marshmallow. "Didn't know anyone was in here."

Her eyes adjusted to the dim light, focusing on another one of Colin's teammates from Titan Group. Javier. *Javier.* Okay. Not a big deal. It didn't matter. He was the most attractive man at the wedding even if she counted her ex-groom. Not that she'd noticed before. Well, she hadn't *not* noticed. But it was more like inventory. Colin's teammates were, as a general rule, hot. Javier, in her opinion, was at the top of that list.

There was just something about a Delta boy. Physically, they were as good as men came. But add the whole warrior, protector, save-the-world attitude. Yeah, it worked for her.

She had met Javier in passing a couple times and knew that he had a bit of a wild reputation. But that was not the guy in front of her, sitting on the edge of the bed, hanging his head and holding the phone as if he'd just received bad news.

"Are you okay?" She wiped the corner of her mouth, sure there were icing smudges. He looked broken and alone, and she wondered how long he'd been there, lost in thought as night drifted by.

But he laughed, transforming whatever hung over him with a flash of his gorgeous smile. "Wow. Yeah. I'm okay. *How are you?*"

"I hate that question."

"Why?"

"Does anyone ever answer it truthfully?"

His dark eyes tightened with the hint of acknowledgement, but it was the cut jawline and olive skin that made her take notice. "Answer truthfully. What do you have to lose?"

The accent and the low pitch of his voice urged her to trust him as though he were genuinely interested in whether she was okay, even if he didn't know her from Adam. Her head tilted toward the dresser where she'd placed her post-reception creature-comfort plan. "I'm gorging on enough cake for four people and ready to cut off my dress and drink a bottle of champagne by myself."

He laughed and tilted his head toward *his* champagne bottle on the nightstand. "Feel you on the bubbly."

She smiled, taking a step closer. "So, you're about as okay as I am."

His smile wavered but came back. "Your day is worse than mine."

Her eyes bounced to his opened bottle. "Good bubbly?"

He nodded. "Not bad."

"Good. Think I'll join you." Sophia grabbed the scissors and the bottle, sawing at the foil. She could go into a war zone and covertly try to change the world, yet she had no flipping idea how to open a bottle of champagne. Her mother would have died. Surely that had been taught in a cotillion class or something. Or maybe not.

"Hey, hey, stop." Javier stood from his perch on the bed. "You're going to slit your wrist or lose a finger." In a few strides, he took the bottle and blade, shaking his head. "Have you ever seen someone open champagne with scissors?"

Well, no. "That's not why I brought them with me."

He pulled off the foil and popped the cork, giving her a look before handing her back the bottle. "Drink the whole thing, and you'll have a hell of a hangover."

She shrugged. "I'm operating without a plan. We'll see how the night goes."

"No plan, no problem?" That accent was intoxicating, far more so than the pricey alcohol. "Doesn't work like that." His thick arms crossed over his broad chest. His eyes were the deep color of coffee, and his hair was long enough she could have threaded her fingers into it, but not a strand was out of place. And the dress pants and a button-down shirt? Wow, the whole look fit in a way that made her delusional. "Are... you okay?"

"Um." Shit. She was staring at the massive man, silently studying what proved God might've been a woman, because to make a man that chiseled and perfect? Oh boy. Sophia was still staring. "Cake?"

He laughed quietly. "No, thanks."

"You don't eat cake?"

He gave a nonanswer with a slight turn of his head.

"Then you should go." She nodded, taking the scissors back from his hand. "I don't trust people who won't eat cake."

"I eat cake, Sophia. I just... you obviously came up here to have some quiet, so I'll go and let you have that."

"You were up here first."

His curious eyes narrowed. "But it's your house."

"Is it?" Sophia twirled, taking in a room she might not have been in before. All these rooms resembled the glossy photographs in *Southern Living*. They were beautiful but, in her opinion, lacked personalization. "Guess it is." She stopped her slow spin and tugged at the dress that was still making her miserable. "You know what?"

An amused eyebrow rose. "Hm?"

Even his questioning noises oozed sensuality. It made her mind wander. If a simple question sounded like that, what would happen if he said it closer, quietly? Against her ear? Between her legs—wait, what? She snapped her head back, aware of the sexy, slippery slope she could go down and how her nipples seemed to have perked and jumped to attention already.

She licked her lip, forgot anything about him being close or between *anywhere,* and focused back on their conversation.

"There's—" Her voice cracked. "A very small contingent of people who've genuinely asked me if I'm okay. Colin probably being the most direct and most interested."

Javier stood silently. His dark eyelashes fluttered. Maybe he was deciding how best to escape. Who cared if she'd just bared her soul to essentially a stranger? It was true that people's reactions to her crisis said a lot about them—which she already knew—but she realized it was also telling how quickly she'd become interested in *another man.* Not that she was *interested* in Javier, just that it was *possible* to hear an accent and stare at the living definition of sex appeal and forget about one's ex-fiancé. So. Very. Possible.

"Colin's a good guy," Javier offered.

"The best," she agreed, her heart pattering a beat faster as he stepped, enacting his escape plan. Her chest panged for a nanosecond before she ignored the absurd reaction to his abandonment. But Javier's next step came closer to Sophia, as though he waffled, not stalking directly toward freedom.

As though maybe he felt what she felt: a seriously questionable, very uncertain desire to inch together. She felt an unexplainable spark that might've been more interesting than champagne and cake, the kind that could make heat bloom in her chest when it hadn't flickered in a very long time.

"Oh boy." But that couldn't have been loud enough for him to hear, and she suddenly didn't want him to leave. He'd quieted the buzz that she hadn't realized had been ringing in her ears. Everything was quiet. Except her heart, which pounded in her lace-covered chest more than it had in years.

"So, are you?" he asked, scratching her with a tone that hit in all the right spots.

"Am *I*? What? Um...?" Her mind spun fast, trying to remember anything that might be conversationally appropriate.

His quiet laugh made her smile. "Are you *okay*, Sophia?"

Sophia. Her name rolling off his tongue made shivers roll down her spine. She liked her name, but the way he said it made one word come alive. "I am right now."

Their eyes locked. There were sparks; it wasn't just her. The idea was absurd. This had to be some psychological coping mechanism, but every nerve in her body had awakened and tingled for her to touch him.

So… simple. Just a touch. Her palms on his cheeks. The pads of her fingers sweeping down his neck if she leaned in, and their lips—

"Good." Javier nodded, breaking their connection.

Her cheeks heated, and where electricity had shot down her spine, now it was a one-sided sexual awareness. She'd had quite the day. Sophia pushed her shoulders back and tossed the scissors onto the bed, and Javier handed her the bottle of champagne.

She took it and the cake then sat on the edge of the elaborately covered queen-sized bed. Setting the plate down, she took a sip straight from the bottle, and the bubbles tickled her tongue and her nose, making her squeak out a laugh. "I'm gangster, right?"

"Total."

His chuckle and smile made her take another sip again because she couldn't quite look at him without broadcasting how attractive he was. Javier reached onto the bed, where he had abandoned his suit jacket.

She couldn't help it; she offered again. "No cake? You're sure?"

He returned the stare, eyes raking over her in a not-so-benign manner. It did amazing things for her insides. Wow. If she was going to marry someone, she should at least have felt a tenth of the excitement that Javier caused with a single smoldering look.

"Yeah. I'll take a bite." His large strides ate the space between them, giving her a show of just how powerful his thighs were. Before she could fathom cutting a piece off for him, he joined her on the edge of the bed, confidently picked up her fork, and took a man-sized bite.

Holy mother of snack shares—he used her fork. Who did that? Gah. That was a far cry from, basically, their first in-depth conversation.

He nodded his appreciation. "Good stuff."

Javier speared another piece, and before she knew how to process his movements, the cake was pressed to her lips, and she ate the decidedly smaller bite. Which was just as good as the first tastes, *but he had fed* it to her, so it was infinitely better.

Nerves and nutso thoughts rambled in her head, and fortunately, she managed to mumble her thanks. Her insides were scattered, her mind numb. Had hottie Javier *just fed her cake*? Why yes, he had. Along with his accent replaying in her head, she could pretty much check off every fantasy she'd ever had. And he was still next to her. *Still.*

Holy shit, she needed that bubbly. Pronto.

They both reached for their matching bottles. Apparently, Javier needed his bubbly too. That made her smile, which made *him* smile. What a smile. What an amazingly dangerous smile…

"Okay, so it was nice seeing you." He turned. "Shitty circumstances, I guess. But still, I needed a moment like this."

Gah! That pang of disappointment coiled in her chest. Needing a subject change to shield her heart, Sophia switched her mindset as fast as she could, away from killer smiles to why he'd been hiding in the first place. "You know my problem. What about yours?"

His dark brows tightened, and the light in his eyes dulled. "Excuse me?"

"Your face is so expressive. It's honest with me even if you won't tell me."

"Yeah?"

"Well…" For the thousandth time, her cheeks heated under his watch. "I'm blaming the champagne on an empty stomach on that. Maybe the stressful day. I don't know. I'm blabbering."

He stared a moment too long. There it was again—that intensity that was so delicious. Javier cleared his throat. "I had hoped something would work out on a job."

"It didn't?"

"No. Not this time. Trying not to get used to the disappointment."

She took another sip, definitely feeling a tiny buzz, but more, she was feeling as if she didn't have to conform to standards of polite conversation or appropriate jilted-wedding-day topics. "It's happened before?"

He sucked a long breath through his teeth. "Yeah."

"So, you're disappointed and… sad?"

His expressive face faded to unreadable. "A little."

But between the simple answer and the loss of his easy-to-read honesty, *a little* was bullshit. There was only one way to treat that. "Then you need more cake, Javier." She tapped a manicured finger on the overfilled plate. "Cake is always the answer."

He rolled his lips into his mouth, shutting his eyes for a moment longer than a blink as if trying to decide something bigger than icing and calories. "I have to head out."

Her heart dropped, and she *wanted* him to stay. "Of course."

"It was an absolute pleasure." His dark eyes let the truth slip, and his words matched his feelings. "Enjoy the rest of your evening."

She might be able to if only she could get out of this dress, gorge, and get a little buzz. Tomorrow, she could start life anew. But first priorities first: she needed to ditch the dress that she never would've picked. "Wait. Before you go?"

"Sure. What's up?"

She grabbed the scissors and pressed the handle into his warm hands. "Cut me out?"

He coughed, and the man who'd seemed bombproof had eyes that were back to expressive, evocative. Even surprised. "Excuse me?"

Ignoring the stutter in her heart rate, Sophia pressed. "Please. Just a snip, top and bottom. Nothing scandalous, I swear." Though the fact that she was babbling and heat crawled up her neck said otherwise.

His hand closed around hers, gripping the scissors. Her stomach dropped; her mind froze. Or raced. She didn't know which. The electricity from his touch was far past unexpected. It was a tsunami of oh-my-gawd. The sizzle was more intoxicating than the uber-expensive champagne that'd given her nerves of steel.

His hand stayed over hers, and her breathing just stopped. She was completely lost in the moment of feeling alive and dizzy from his touch.

"Sophia…" He pulled her off the bed, and he was so much taller than her when they were hip to hip.

Dropping her chin but looking up through her eyelashes, she swayed. "Please? The back is sewn in."

Their hands were still attached. She was able to talk, so she was still breathing, but each lungful burned shallow and heady. "They sewed the top and bottom so nothing would move."

"Sewed?"

"Just snip the top." She touched the back of her neck, then her hand dropped to the base of her tailbone, where the back was secured. "And here."

His chiseled face twisted, amusement breaking the trance. "Seriously?"

Sophia rolled her eyes. "Please don't make me explain the secrets of women's wedding wear."

His lips curled. "Okay…"

"I can't get out of it. I mean, I could tear it, or just start at the bottom and work my way up. But you helping would go a long way. I don't love the dress. It's not me. But, really, it's a work of art. I don't want to destroy it, but if I don't get out of it, I'm going to *die*."

He tossed his head back and stared at the ceiling.

"What are you doing?"

He laughed loudly before facing her again. "Praying."

"*What?*"

"I'm from Brazil. My people pray for everything. Lost keys. Holy days. Everything."

"You're religious?"

He gave her a playful grin that was more devilish than a question about God should allow. "Not particularly."

"So, why are you praying?"

"Sophia." Javier's voice had dropped a dozen octaves and gone straight between her legs. Her heart managed to beat, but breathing seemed to stop. "You're gorgeous. You're sexy. You're… asking me to *cut* that dress off you? I'm *praying* for strength."

Her head went light. Knees like noodles. Oh God. Did he really say all that? "I…"

"Turn around, Sophia." His large, warm hands braced on her shoulder, pivoting her, then they slipped down her back, skimming across her lace-covered skin.

Snip, snip, and she could breathe. Every sensation and indecent thought evaporated as the way-too-tight dress loosened. Better than sex. Almost. Or at least, sex with Dr. Josh, though maybe not with Delta Javier. God, she shouldn't be thinking like that. But seriously... "God, that felt good."

"Not normally how I get that reaction, but I'll take it." His fingertips drifted along the hollow of her neck, skimming to her shoulder. It wasn't an innocent touch. It wasn't provocative. They were safely in the land of questionable and erotic, where her skin was prickling and her body was on fire and growing wet for his touch.

Semicapable of stifling a hitched breath, she turned to face him, memorizing the fact that he was flushed too. "Thank you."

"*Não faz mal.*" Javier tugged his bottom lip into his mouth before letting go. "No problem."

"Okay, so..." She loosened the ribbon that had run the length of her spine, and his eyes became darker, more intense. That honey-warm, tingling-all-over feeling had amplified, and she was almost too turned on to be aware of how awkward she must look in the loose dress. "Thanks."

"Welcome." His voice was just as quiet as hers.

Spellbound, Sophia forced herself away to tame her easily broadcast thoughts. She crawled onto the bed and grabbed her cake—ignoring him, her shaky breaths, and disappointed hormones—and focused on the next best thing: sugar. Cake. Calories. Fondant. Her original grand plan. Anything but the six-foot-tall daydream of a man watching her. But when she looked up, Javier hadn't moved.

"What's a matter?" she asked, not touching the cake.

He took a step closer, away from the door, his exit. The pink tip of his tongue darted out and licked his bottom lip. "You're just going to eat cake and get drunk by yourself?"

She shrugged with fake nonchalance while imprinting the vision of him licking his lips in her memory. "Not everyone's ideal wedding night. But turns out it's a good thing for me."

What could've been a perfect predatory gleam in his eyes froze. Yeah, she'd mentioned the wedding. Hell, she was *partially* wearing her wedding dress. That had to be enough cold water for anyone. Anyone except her.

He shifted as though he wanted to retreat yet needed to join her on the bed. "Do you want me to find, I don't know, a girlfriend of yours?"

"Not really." She wanted *him* to stay. To touch her. Take her. Hell, feed her cake again. Just stay in the room with her. But it'd be great if he chose a lot more.

"Why?"

Javier wanted to have a conversation, and she was feeding him cake, naked, in bed. Sophia tossed her head back.

"What's funny?" Javier asked.

"Nothing. God. Everyone wants to powwow over the good doctor Josh, and I'm done."

Javier smirked. "The good doctor Josh?"

"Think that's what my mother calls him. He's a pediatrician. Apparently, the job of saints."

"And you're done. Just like that?"

She nodded. "Decision made. Actions have consequences. I should've seen it but didn't. It's time to move forward." She pointed. "With calories and alcohol." And happy thoughts about a Latin Delta man.

He pinched his eyes closed. "You are not what you seem, Sophia Cole."

God, he had no idea. "I'm going to take that as a compliment."

"You should."

"You're not what you seem either, Javier don't-know-your-last-name."

Then he leveled her with a stare that made the Cole house twist sideways. "Almeida."

"Javier Almeida," she repeated as though it needed reverence. "That's..." Perfect. Exactly suited for him. "Beautiful."

"Glad you think so."

He was tall, dark, and exotic. His muscles bulged. He could wear the hell out of formal wear, but she'd seen him in jeans and a T-shirt yesterday before the rehearsal dinner and thought he'd make one heck of an action-movie star. Cut body and chiseled face. Not that she was checking out the scenery the night before the big day, but when a man that looked like this guy walked into a room, it was impossible not to notice.

She hadn't interacted with him much, hadn't even stared directly at him, but here she was, sinking into the bottomless abyss of his soulful brown-black eyes.

Her eyes dropped to the Berber carpet. "The champagne's made me lose my mind. Apparently."

Her fingers knit into the silk skirt, and she concentrated on avoiding him, suddenly aware of how much of a goof her normal self was, when this guy had smooth charm. Her peripheral vision caught him moving, stopping next to the bed. He extended his hand, two fingers touching under her chin to raise her face. Every cell in her body reacted as his touch fell away. Heart thudding, Sophia locked eyes with him. "Nice to chat with you, Javier. I'm sorry that I'm blathering."

He shook his head. "Not nice, *gatinha*. You're here for a fucked-up reason. Because an asshole didn't appreciate you, and a best friend didn't stay loyal. Blather if you want."

Sweet too? A breath lodged in her throat. Everyone had been overly nice and too accommodating as she said her hellos. They'd said everything except what Javier had said. All their words sounded like blah, blah, blah, blah. But he'd cut through the BS. "Dang."

His lips quirked. "Dang, what?"

"*You.* No one said anything like that all night."

His face warmed and gentled. There was an indescribable, almost imperceptible change in his demeanor, but it was there. "Most people are selfish. They comfort others to comfort themselves, and it is complete bullshit. Know that, and you'll do fine in life."

How she needed to hear that. "Javier... I don't want to eat cake alone."

"I..."

"Please stay."

He tilted his head toward the headboard as though it was an invitation to sit back there. She expected a rush of excitement at his agreement, but the flood was more appreciation than arousal, warm and fuzzy. Like a hug.

"Thanks."

Together, they moved across the fancy comforter to the carved-wood headboard. It would've been awkward, but nothing about their odd conversation and crossed personal boundaries felt that way.

Sophia took a deep breath and let her gaze shift over the bedroom. This house was so not her. There were fine china and crown molding that had been designed especially for the place, which was absurd, since the accent pieces looked identical to stuff found in any hardware store. The formality was strangling her. Just like the dress—and just like the idea of marrying Josh when she'd stood at the top of the altar.

She kicked her high heels across the room, flinging them with more effort than she meant to use, then wiggled her free toes. "I hated those things."

He laughed, making himself more comfortable with a pillow behind him. "Are you drunk?"

"Probably buzzed. Pass the cake."

He reached to the nightstand, and they shared a fork back and forth, alternating bites.

Licking icing off her lips, she smiled. "Can you imagine what the pearl clutchers would say?"

"To what?"

"To hiding away. To not wearing pantyhose on my wedding day. To me not playing the role of hostess in a house that was built to entertain. To eating cake in my loose dress while my dad and brother are likely torturing Josh."

His silent laugh shook his chest. "Fuck Josh."

"Fuck Josh," she repeated, turning to see his head in his hand. "I'm sorry you had bad news earlier."

His heavy sigh hurt her insides, and she turned, tucking her legs under her and accidentally touching her knee to his thigh. Even through her dress, electricity zipped through her.

His eyes jumped to their knee touch, and she didn't pull away. After a quiet moment, he leaned back, stretching. "Life continues. I try to also."

A lot was loaded in those few words, and she didn't know what to make of it. "Where are you from?"

"Brazil."

"What did you do? Military, police?" *Gladiator.* He had that hulking, dangerous look.

"No, I wasn't military like Colin. Delta recruited me, trained me."

Interesting. She reached over him and took a long, unladylike sip of her champagne. "Why?"

His powerful shoulders lifted as if to play down whatever he would say. "Because I'm good."

"Good at...?"

But he didn't reply, so she pressed for an answer as she replaced the bottle. That close to him, he was warm and smelled faintly like cologne, making her mouth water. Ignoring that reaction, she sat back and hoped not to forget his scent. "They went to another country and found you?"

Again, he lifted both his shoulders in reply, making his shirt curve over his muscles. "I have a working knowledge of something they've honed in on." He swigged from his bottle of champagne, offering it to her. "They asked if I wanted in, and I said yeah."

There was something carnal about sharing the bottle. As if he knew hers was inches away, but he wanted her lips and his to have a shared bond. "That simple?"

The truth played on his features before he shook his head. "Not at all."

She took a sip, curiosity piqued, and she let the bubbles slide down her throat. "What's your working knowledge?"

"My working knowledge..." He took the bottle back, his sure fingers grazing her paler ones, then he took his turn with a drink. Javier's dark eyes closed, and he held the expensive bottle in his large hands, toying with it as though he needed a distraction. "It's nothing pretty. The world's ugly. Nothing you need to worry about."

If he only knew. "You're the protective type?"

Javier chuckled as though she were asking something as obvious as whether he'd ever seen a street fight.

"Okay, you're the protective type." She was, too, in her own way, but explaining that was hard—or classified—so Sophia leaned into him, wanting to experience his strength but also to explain as best she could without spilling a secret. "I know you see what you see."

"What's that?"

She pointed to the lace. "Fancy dress." Then drew a finger in the air, encircling the bedroom. "Fancy house. Whatever you think you see, it isn't me."

"Same." His gaze didn't fall on her but past her shoulders and out to nowhere, where the wallpaper melted into another world. The warmth in his cheeks, the smile on his lips—they were gone, and a deeper pain that she knew he wouldn't admit to appeared on his face.

She hugged him without thinking, needing to feel their connection again, that warmth from his touch, that salve to the wound. She needed the distraction, the reminder that something could feel good, not just this gray cake-and-champagne haze.

Javier stiffened, hands dropping to his sides, apparently *not* needing a connection. But even for the moment, their hug made the rest of the world melt away. With a happy little sigh, she inched away, not apologizing but not willing to make a fool out of herself for an extended period of time. "Just needed that. Thanks."

His hand jumped and wrapped her back, holding her in place, halting her slow retreat.

"Oh."

He bent, his forehead touching hers, and the light scent of his peppery cologne was better than cake and champagne. It was better than getting married, just to be that close, to smell someone who made goose bumps jump on her skin and her mouth water for a kiss.

Forcing herself to look him in the eye, she tilted her chin up and whispered against his lips. "You needed that too. A hug."

Seconds slid by without a sound.

"Yes." His warm breath tickled her skin. "Bad news sucks, whether it comes from the phone or at the altar."

Sophia nodded, dropping her head against the crook of his shoulder as his other arm came up to her spine. Two powerful arms held her to his impossibly broad chest. Javier felt like a man should, powerful and sexual. Her face pressed into his collared neck, and she inhaled loudly enough that he had to have heard.

He gave her a squeeze and then leaned back. They were against the headboard again, but this time, their bodies were aligned, with shoulders, sides, and legs touching. She rested her head on his shoulder. A tension swirled around them, inside her, reaching deep. Her mind raced as fast as her pulse, and she leaned her weight against him, needing to be closer. Snuggling him.

"Sophia." His low voice hit her hard. "You don't want to do that, *paixão*."

Paixão? If he'd say that word again, she'd do that and so much more. "It's one of the only good things I felt today—leaning up against you."

He nodded, his stubbled cheek brushing against her forehead. "I know what you mean, but still."

She twisted to rest her chin on his shoulder, her chest feeling full and her mind fuzzy. "Still what?"

"Still…" He took a deep breath, turning his head so that their cheeks touched. His dark stubble scratched her skin, forcing a wave of goose bumps down her back. His lips and breath were dangerously close to her ear, each breath nearly silent and absurdly erotic. "This… isn't a good idea."

She leaned into him. "Yes it is. It's the only thing that feels good right now."

He mumbled what could've been a curse, but his hand sifted into her hair. "Softer than I thought."

His other palm went to her waist, sliding over the loose gown up her stomach to the curve of her breast.

"That's nice."

Fingers flexing, his hand didn't waver. "Yeah?"

"Yes." Her mind stuttered to keep her mouth from begging him to touch her, take her.

"I shouldn't." His full lips brushed her neck. Excitement prickled across her skin with the simplest of his touch.

"Javier, yes." Her breathy command begged as his absurdly defined body pressed to her. The entire world washed away as he moved closer. "You totally, *totally* should."

The idea of him undressing her, running his tongue along her lips, and drifting his palm over her bare skin made the sensitive flesh between her legs awaken. With short breaths and a needy core, Sophia cupped his cheeks, loving the way her palms scratched against his shadow, and ran her fingers into his thick, dark hair.

"Paixão." The weight of his head shifted in her hands, urging her fingers to delve deeper into his locks. "*Eu queria que você me fizesse um cafuné.*"

She had no idea the meaning, but his sinful mouth touched hers. The velvet slice of his tongue urged her to kiss him back, and it wasn't a request she could deny. She hadn't kissed anyone but Josh in years, and the anticipation of what might come flooded her. Her tongue touched his, and he tasted sweet. Within seconds, there was no question. This was the best kiss. *Of. Her. Life.* Intense and passionate. Deep and seductive.

Javier groaned, grabbing her possessively.

Sophia opened for him, letting him delve as she hungrily matched him. He tasted like sweetness and strength, like champagne and cake. Her head swam as she dropped her hand to explore his hard chest. The buttons caught under her manicured nails, and she toyed with the one under his chin and the two farther down his chest. A primal need urged her to rip it open, but instead, she concentrated on the delicious idea of undressing him. With care, and with far more attention than was needed, she unbuttoned his dress shirt. One button at a time. Slowly. Seductively. She let her fingers tease inside his shirt even though she was a woman on a mission to bare his chest.

Catching his eyes, feeling his soul down to her stomach, she explored his warm flesh, raking her fingers through the smattering of dark chest hair and up to his broad shoulders, then she pushed his dress shirt down his biceps.

There was no *oh my God, what are we doing*. Breaths slamming, they were kissing, trembling, rabidly out of control. Panting, she pulled back to savor Javier's well-defined, corded, *inked* chest. "You are…"

He hushed her to let her know she shouldn't gawk.

"*Handsome.*" Not all his skin was tattooed. But the parts that were inked were simply magnificent.

He ran his fingertips along her neckline, tracing down the side of her dress, giving it a light tug. "You're sure, Sophia?"

"Yes." She was surer than she'd been about walking up the aisle to marry Josh.

"Good." Javier slid her dress down her arms so it piled around her waist then swept her into his arms as though she and the fabric weighed the same, which they didn't. That dress was heavy, and she was no feather.

His starving stare worked up her legs and over her lingerie. It was about the only thing that she'd chosen without comment from others— not Liz or Josh or her mother. It was the only thing that, *truthfully*, she hadn't thought of for anyone but herself. Josh wouldn't have noticed it anyway, but she did. She loved the silk, and the cut was sexy and feminine while still making her feel like a princess.

"This is…" Javier graveled so low it rumbled. "Gorgeous."

Her fingers touched his chin, and her thumbs swept across his cheeks, brushing his dark eyelashes and stilling over his cheek. Javier didn't just notice what she wore but appreciated it. Ironic.

"I've never…" He didn't finish.

"You never, what?"

"Wanted to savor a moment before." Javier stretched her across the bed. His tongue licked above her ankle, bending her knee as he slowly kissed up her leg.

Kiss wasn't the right word. He made love to her with his mouth, touching her with such concentration that she mentally surrendered. Defying all she expected from a military man, he worked his way up to her thighs, sensually kissing the white silk lingerie that all but bared her. "Please."

A hot, lashing lick pressed over her fabric-covered clit, and Sophia cursed. Her hips writhed. Javier ignored her pleas and prayers, instead trailing up her stomach to torture her breasts. Heat enveloped her nipple through the bra she thought would always be ignored. "Oh, so good."

"I'm going for better than good." He pulled down the cup, taking the tight bud into his mouth as his hand slid under the thin silk of her panties, delving into the hungry slickness between her legs.

Her head pressed into the pillows, and her eyes rolled into heaven. Sensations she'd only dreamed of swam through her head as Javier teased her pussy folds open, stroking slowly, steadily, creating a rhythm that matched the pounding of her heartbeat. "God. Javier."

"Better, gatinha." His fingers encircled her sweet spot at the same rhythm as his tongue trailed kisses to her other breast, sucking and toying with her nipple. His teeth tugged. Hard. Harder. She felt pain and ecstasy both at her breast and deep inside her body, where he slipped two thick fingers inside. And...*oh...* the flicks of his tongue, the heat and the suctions. There was no other way to think of him: Javier was a *master.*

"Open for me."

"Yes, sir." Her breath stuttered, trembling her legs wider. "Javier."

He steadily pumped his hand into her tightness while his thumb worked her clitoris. His mouth *never* stopped flicking and sucking her nipple. God. *Never!*

"I'm—" Gasping, she couldn't find the words to explain the building wave of climax. He knew her body, knew what she needed. The pressure, the thrust, the bites of pain and pleasure, the *everything* increased, and Sophia moaned. Quaking against him, clawing her hold to his massive hulk, she hurt for how good she felt.

"Come for me, Sophia." The accent had nothing on his honed attention.

"Yes." She arched, letting her most intimate muscles clench his fingers, and she scratched down his back. The room went warm as the lights swirled and twirled. An addictive wave of euphoria hit, and all was amazingly perfect.

Javier took his hand from her, cupping her face and kissing her lips. The gesture was sweet but packed with intent. He ran a palm down her back, unhooking her bra, and she shrugged it off, letting her hands slide down his inked chest.

His ripped abdominal muscles were defined in a way Sophia had never touched before, the tan skin covering them warm with a short, tight teasing of dark chest hair. Her hands rested on his belt, and she noticed his dress pants hid nothing. An impressive bulge waited for her—intimidated her. He made her mouth water as much as he made her anticipate the sleek gorgeousness of his Latin body.

She tugged on his leather belt when his strong hand clamped over hers. "Tell me to go, Sophia. Throw me out of your bed. You got what you needed. I did, too, in my own way." His grip squeezed her hand tighter, punctuating his absurd request. "Tell me to leave."

"No," she whispered then kissed his chest with tongue and teeth, letting her hands unbuckle his belt as he growled in approval, his hips flexing. "You've given me just a start of what I need."

She bit the flat disk of his nipple, and his breath caught.

Under her control, the zipper gave way, and she tugged at his pants. Massive, powerful thighs and a thick erection were her reward. He moved from her, kicking his shoes and socks off then grabbing a condom from his wallet and holding it up as if asking for silent, final permission to make love to her on her wedding night.

"Please." She nodded intently, both begging and promising what they both wanted.

His eyes glimmered, locking on to hers, staring at her as though he were starved—for her. God. He tore the packet open without breaking their visual hold. Javier stroked his length, covering his shaft, and eased back onto the bed. He held his hands out, waiting for her to take them.

Carefully, she placed hers in his, her dainty and pale ones contrasting with his tough and bronzed. He squeezed, and Sophia crawled over the sculpted muscle of this sexy man, memorizing the carnal flush in her veins.

It was too much: the intense desire, the wicked want, curiosity and cravings that came with straddling Javier's thighs. "I had the shittiest day until I walked in here and saw you." Then she moved over him, using her hand to press his sheathed crown to her ready entrance, parting her flesh as the tip of his erection pressed into her body. "God…"

With his hands on her hips, Javier's mouth took hers, and with every deep, sweeping kiss, the man inched his thick cock inside her ravenous core, the push deliciously mind erasing.

"Soph…" He breathed as he kissed her. "Incredible, paixão."

The sweet sound of that perfect word. Her eyes shut. The stretch and fullness were more than she expected. Deep and thick, he invaded her, each thrust making her jaw drop. "Amazing."

Javier set a deep, slow rhythm that could make a girl cry. He speared his length, making love to her as she rode his cock. His heavy arms gathered around her, enfolding against his tattooed pecs. The crisp scratch of his chest hair drove her sensitive nipples mad, and that, coupled with the safe possession of her within his solid muscles, made her lose herself. Every thrust and every powerful slide away from her drove her to the point of screaming.

"Give me you." He growled, making his words rumble. "More."

Sophia buried her head against his throat. She'd never moved like this before, never felt as though she could flow and come alive with sex so forceful and still somehow passionate. She moaned, not breathing, not gasping but just living for every second Javier took her.

He held her tighter, and she bit his shoulder. A building onslaught of orgasm-induced madness got ready to hit her again. A fire burned between their bodies, and he owned her every thrash.

"Javier," she cried into his neck, bucking against him, feeling consumed by his strength.

An insane eternity passed as she climaxed. Lovely. Like floating… until she lulled, and Javier turned her over. That was still lovely, but definitely back to reality. His hand curled around the back of her neck. Sophia scraped her fingernails down his muscular back as his gorgeous torso towered, and she wrapped her legs around his powerful thighs.

"Like heaven." He moved like a piston in her in a way she'd never dreamed possible, constant and capturing her, concentrating his slanted kisses and rhythmic attack on her, bringing her to the brink of implosion.

"I could take you forever," he growled against her lips.

"*Yes.*" Please. Never let this stop.

His weight pinned her, and with their hips connected, he ignited the start of her next orgasm. Building. Building. Javier thrust with deliberate, perfect precision, and Sophia pulsed and panted, clinging to him as though he were the savior of her most miserable day.

Somehow he *knew* exactly what she needed, and how she needed it, and when. Javier called the shots about what her soul needed.

"Sweet Sophia," he whispered, breathless, slowing his roll into her still-quaking muscles. "You did so good for me."

Tears pricked her eyes; she had no idea why. The tone of his voice coaxed them out, and the caring in his arms made her dizzy with a fulfillment she'd never experienced before. "Yes."

He abandoned her mouth, dragging his tongue to her neck, making his stubble-covered cheeks scratch her skin. He palmed her breasts and took his time, *savoring*.

His forehead touched hers. "Yes."

She nodded.

"I want to wear you out." Gently, he kissed her lips. "If you think of this day, you think of me."

"Please."

"Good girl."

Panting and building all over again, she hugged into him, emotion choking her throat, stinging her senses. "More. All of you. Make. Me. Forget."

Javier thrust. He *drove*. Her hands clasped his ass, and his hips slammed against hers. She'd feel this for days—the soreness, the claim he'd made to her mind and body. Minutes, hours, days could've passed. This was a dream.

Every part of her loved how alive she was, and she fell over the edge again as he ground into her and grunted and groaned, harshly whispering, "Paixão."

Javier's tight body plunged into hers until he went lax. She melted into the mattress under his caring weight. This man… he was terrific. Absolutely, out-of-this-world amazing.

They lay tangled together, in total silence with the exception of their pounding heartbeats, which even the neighbors should have been able to hear. "That was…" she said.

"So…" He breathed.

"… needed."

He nodded, their cheeks touching. "Needed."

Who knew how long they lay there or if anyone had heard them. She didn't care. Sometime during the night, he got up and went to the bedroom's adjoining bathroom. As he walked back, he went to the door, locked it, and slid into the bed, tossing her dress to the floor and pulling the covers down. Javier pulled her into his arms and against his gorgeous body and rubbed her back as she drifted off to sleep.

CHAPTER FOUR

THE FAMILIAR BUZZ of his phone on an unfamiliar surface woke Javier. He froze at the soft sounds of Sophia sleeping in his arms. What had he done? Stupid. But for the moments when she was with him, he'd let go of the disappointment from earlier. Kissing Sophia, taking her in a way that had saved them both from bad thoughts, had been a reprieve.

He reached for his phone and scrolled through the missed calls and text messages.

J—you leave?

Hey Brazil. Looking for you.

Where the fuck are you?

Report in. Job came up. We're out asap.

Shit. No, wait—an assignment. That was good even if the boss would tear him a new asshole for going MIA for a couple hours. He needed back out in the field. Being in some WASP mansion in the United States wouldn't help with revenge, his only focus in life.

Sophia stirred, and his eyes dropped to her. What was he supposed to do? Say good-bye? Slip out? He had no idea. He'd never slept with a woman before. Never stuck around past the moment that everyone had a good time. But the circumstances tonight had been different. That was sex for a reason. So even if he'd fallen asleep, it had been for a good cause.

Colin's voice played in Javier's head. *Don't touch her* had been the only warning. Yeah, well, that hadn't gone as planned. His phone buzzed again, and he silenced it. "Sophia?"

She slipped sideways against him, hugging her arm around his naked torso.

"Soph?" Brushing her soft hair off her shoulder, he took more time than he needed to and slid his hand down her smooth back, trying to rouse her but wishing he didn't have to. No one should have a day like she'd had. Waking her might start the headache all over again. But it'd be a huge dick move to leave without a word. Javier bent and kissed her neck.

"Hmm… hey," she whispered as she woke.

"Sorry, paixão. Work calls."

She sighed as though remembering everything they'd been hiding from. "How long have I been asleep?"

"We've both been out, um, about an hour."

" 'Kay. So…" She sat up, tucking the covers around her. "Thanks, I guess."

God, he didn't want to hear that embarrassed sound in her voice. A dim light was still on, and he turned her face to see her pink cheeks and avoiding eyes. "Look at me, gatinha."

She flicked a look up that didn't stick and then burrowed her face into a pillow. "I've never had a one-night stand before, so don't think I'm the gutter-slut type. Okay? I just kinda needed that. Sometimes I get nightmares. I can't even wake from them. Tonight, not even a shadowy dream. So, bonus points."

She was beautiful in a way that he'd never experienced before—soft and vulnerable. Everything that fell from her lips was unguarded. He didn't know what she did for a living, didn't know who her friends were or what she was passionate about. All he knew was that she was more honest with him than anyone he'd met.

"Don't play tonight down. It was good for both of us."

She gave him a sleepy grin. "Trying."

"One truth for another," he mumbled. "You've never had a one-night stand, and I've never fallen asleep with a woman. Two firsts in a night that would otherwise have been really shitty."

"Really? You've never slept next to a woman? Ever?"

"Yeah." Laughing self-consciously, he didn't want to get out of the warm confines of the bedding. The sheets alone had to be worth more than the housing where he'd grown up. "Are you okay? I don't mean *this*. I mean, are *you* okay?"

Her delicate chin jutted in a show of strength. "I'm okay."

"And this?" He bounced a finger between them. "Okay?"

"Yes." She smiled, blushing—again such a giver of truth, even if it was unintentional. "Thank you. For tonight."

"Alright." He bent over and kissed her cheek then unhappily left the bed, ignoring the uncomfortable desire to stay and appreciate their two firsts.

CHAPTER FIVE

HOLY. CRAPOLA. SOPHIA'S head pounded—like, *pounded*. As did the rest of her body. She pried her eyes open, the feeling of unremoved makeup making her skin feel oily, and she had cotton mouth that killed.

God. What had happened—thoughts came to a screaming halt. *Holy shit* was right. She was semihungover and very well screwed the day after her wedding. She was single—in a major way. *That* felt great, almost enough to minimize the pounding headache. But it did *not* take away the sore, almost throbbing deliciousness of her well-used body.

God. Javier. She'd slept with her crush; she'd had a one-night stand the night of her wedding. What was she—a hussy? But it had felt like magic. No one had ever touched her like that before. It was amazing, and if she hadn't believed in miracles, last night was a case to start. Because who did that ever happen to? She'd been whisked away in the arms of tatted-up, muscled perfection, a man who whispered foreign-tongued words that made a wave of warmth roll through her again.

Sophia clung to the comforter and smiled. A new era had arrived—sans Dr. Josh. Nothing would compare to what her body had experienced last night, so screw looking for a rebound man. What to do... what to do? Eventually, she'd have to get out of bed and face the world, maybe talk to *Lizzie* and probably spend more time with Tabby. She'd definitely try to online stalk Javier and see what the world of social media could tell her. Oh, and Colin's brain would be picked. It would be very much on the down-low, but nonetheless, her brother would share what she needed.

Which was what?

It wasn't as if Javier had said a word about seeing her again.

It wasn't as if she'd suggest they should. Hell, he'd undressed her out of *her wedding dress.* The guy likely thought she was crazy. Or a slut. Though nothing he'd said or done the night before would make her believe that was true—

Knock.

Hope crawled out from her hangover and jumped in Sophia's chest. A knock like that? Hard and harsh and to the point. God, would it be Javier? She sat up, smoothed down her wild hair, and ran her fingers under her eyes to ward away mascara smudges. "Hello?"

"Sophia?" It was her father. Okay. He wasn't stupid. How bad was her just-had-sex hair? And the champagne bottles! At least there was only one fork...

"Soph?" Dad cracked the door. "Morning."

She tugged the comforter up to her bare shoulders, burrowing against the pillow, trying for that casual, morning-after-wedding-disaster look without looking as though she'd had sex. "Hey, Dad. I didn't think you guys would be here this morning."

"Your mother and I were worried, honey." His eyes dropped to the wedding dress that had spent the night on the floor. "Why don't you get up and get dressed, and breakfast will be ready downstairs."

Her lips parted, surprised. "Mom's here?"

Dad tilted his head. "Yes."

"*Why?*" Didn't she have an event to run off to, press to spin the wedding debacle turned fundraising success to? Sophia groaned.

"Eggs Benedict. Downstairs. Now."

She nodded, feeling the reproach in his tone. He gave no shits about her having had way too much to drink, and he hadn't yet had the fatherly talk with her about how he didn't like Josh that much anyway. But Dad would not let her and her mother's snippiness go without a discussion.

He shut the door, and Sophia pulled the blanket over her head. Drawing in a deep breath, she—*whoa*—her insides turned to mush as her sluggish brain realized that sinful scent on the pillow and blankets was a very faint reminder of Javier. Sex and cologne. The combination was intoxicating. Staying a few deep breaths too long, she embraced the shivers that rocketed through her at the memory of all that had occurred. Each kiss. Each thrust. The way he'd murmured into her ear and opened her eyes. That was *a lot* to get from a few breaths, but wow, did it bring her back to last night.

With too much interest in keeping the comforter, she pulled it off the bed, wrapped it around her nakedness, and did a walk of shame to her bedroom.

The room looked almost identical to the room she'd spent the night in. Everything was perfectly designed. The drawers were filled with a few things she'd kept at her parents' house so she didn't have to pack a bag if she spent the night. In the corner was a pile of clothes and the remnants from getting ready for her wedding the day before. But it was all so foreign.

With a wayward sigh, she dropped the comforter, found appropriate clothing, and quickly ran into her bathroom to wash her face and brush her hair. They were such simple tasks, but they made her feel a thousand times better. Sophia popped a couple of headache pills then folded the comforter and placed it on her overnight bag. The overstuffed queen-size blanket was going home with her no matter who raised an eyebrow over it.

She let her fingers drift over the cotton. Funny, she cared more about that blanket that moment than she did the wedding dress that was left abandoned on the guest-room floor. So very telling.

Shaking her head, Sophia headed to breakfast. Her parents remaining home came as a surprise. The fact that someone had made breakfast was not. Half expecting to see Colin, and hoping maybe a certain friend of his was wolfing down eggs, Sophia pushed her shoulders back and entered the kitchen. No Colin or friends. Just her parents—and whoever that was making eggs at the stove.

"Hey." She smiled, slipping into the chair across from her dad and next to her mom. "Thanks for last night."

Dad nodded. Mom pressed her lipsticked smile closed.

The woman Sophia didn't know placed a beautifully arranged plate of food in front of Sophia.

"Thanks."

Then she disappeared as though the scene had been scripted. "So, yeah, thanks. For making last night as nice as it could have been."

Mom speared a strawberry from a fruit bowl and focused on that instead of responding. Dad took a sip of coffee from his mug.

"Are you guys mad at me?"

"No, honey." Dad placed his black coffee down. "Your mother and I had an idea she—*we*—wanted to run by you."

"To get your mind off Josh." Those were the first words her mom had said, and they bugged the crap out of Sophia.

"I don't need my mind to get off him," Sophia snapped.

Dad cleared his throat. "There was an opportunity that your mother mentioned, and…" He worked his jaw. "I tend to agree."

Great. Reform school for wayward brides? A class on how to land a husband and keep him faithful? "I think I'm okay—"

"There's a young woman in Honduras," her mom started, stealing Sophia's snarky thoughts. "She has a great deal of influence and is helping us already in Bolivia with a cartel intelligence project."

"Wait, what?" Had Mom just said *help with cartel intelligence*?

Mom speared another strawberry, remaining silent as though the shock of her talking about something other than society culture had shocked them both.

Dad took a bite of his breakfast, watching Sophia try to hammer through the dynamics of what was being said while her hangover was screwing with her.

"I don't understand," she said.

"Your mother's idea." Dad swallowed another forkful. "There's an opportunity for you to expand on a relationship we've been cultivating."

"In Honduras?" Her eyes swung to Mom.

"Yes," she said primly.

"Doing?"

"Do you want to go to Honduras?"

Hell yeah, she did. "Probably."

Mom smiled. *Smiled.* What was going on? Was there a society bigwig or a press op Sophia couldn't pinpoint?

"You would do a good job," Mom said.

Sophia's heart jumped through a fiery ring of disbelief. Her mom had not only suggested but encouraged her going to Honduras. "What's the catch?"

"None," Dad answered.

Sophia narrowed her gaze on the society queen in front of her. Some people relaxed and let their hair down, but never her mother. Never were Sophia's grades high enough, friends good enough, or fiancés—well, cut that. Mom loved Dr. Josh. It was *Sophia* she didn't think her mom liked. Mom loved her. Sophia loved Mom. They had a good relationship, mostly, though it was formal more often than not, and there was always something missing.

"Go to Honduras, Sophia Marie. Take the job." Mom delicately took another bite of strawberry as Dad nodded. He never played second fiddle to her mom. They acted as equals, which Sophia respected even if she didn't understand how her father could put up with all the PR-focused crap her mother lived for. But had there ever been an order like this from Mom?

No. Never. So there was one answer, even if Honduras didn't already sound like Sophia's kind of gig. "Yes, ma'am."

And that was that.

Sophia didn't need twenty-four hours to consider the travel and work that Josh had seen as a weakness—and that he'd used as an opportunity to cheat. She was always ready to leave for a job, and each one grew in intensity. They were the adrenaline-filled, never-sure-what-was-next missions that her parents—mostly her *dad*—had helped organize her for.

Mom smiled. Dad nodded. And Sophia dug into her eggs Benedict, ready for the distraction a job could give her. Two out-of-country surprises in one day. Not bad.

CHAPTER SIX

Six Months Later
Honduras. US Embassy.

THE WORST PART of the addition of armed "company" at the Honduras embassy was that it meant they were sequestered. Sophia chewed on her bottom lip. They already lived in a concrete bunker surrounded by armed troops. The last few months had seen highs and lows in regard to safety and threat levels.

Only twice in her time there had they required the assistance of off-the-books teams. Hiring out a military endeavor meant the US government had deniability and their allies could turn a blind eye—much as they were doing with her in the middle of this hellhole. Sophia was the face of American compassion. She was the aid worker willing to walk the streets of the "murder capital of the world," where women were seen as the lesser sex. Sophia did so to foster a health program with a local senator, Marco Ferrera, led by his wife, Hana.

What that local politician did not know was that his wife wanted out of the marriage, out of Honduras, and away from the horrors she'd seen perpetrated. She was willing to trade information on his position of leadership in the Primeiro Comando in exchange for an eventual free pass to the US.

The health program was the perfect cover for Hana Ferrera. But when the hired mercenaries showed up, Sophia couldn't do anything that an aid worker wouldn't do. She was stuck inside until it was safe.

The newest round of super-alpha soldier-protector men clattered through the stately front door with their dust and noise. They carried a harshness that tinged the air with a violent breeze as Sophia peeked over the edge of the second-floor railing. Guns were strapped to their bodies and in their hands. Their faces were covered in dirt despite the urban location. *Wonder where they've been?* They looked as though their day had been jam-packed with saving the world, or whatever they did on their always-classified projects.

At least there were new faces to chat with over a couple of meals before they swooped out as loudly and brashly as they'd come in.

Booming laugher and the baritone voices of men at the peak of an adrenaline high echoed through the embassy's expansive foyer. It was a grand fortress of US territory in a dangerous, deadly part of the world. Honduras was a land of living pain, her home away from home until this assignment had run its course.

Operation Whispering Willow had been Hana's brainchild. She fought for women's rights in Honduras, for women to exist as more than second-class citizens. Hana knew her husband was a dirty politician who likely did more than turn a blind eye to the Primeiro Comando's activity in Tegucigalpa. She was in secret conversations with the Americans. All Sophia had to do was publicly play the role of an aid worker and privately act as a conduit of information.

"Sophia?"

She jumped, caught staring by Janella, the embassy's housekeeper-cook-laundress. *Or house mom.* Janny made sure everything ran smoothly for those who lived there. She was also the only other woman on the premises and, therefore, Sophia's closest friend at the moment and a giver of opinion cloaked as advice whether it was asked for or not.

"Hey, Janny." Sophia pushed away from the railing. "The cavalry has arrived."

She tossed her hand. "More mouths to feed. Maybe this bunch brings a couple funny stories to liven up the dinner conversation." The start of wrinkles at the corners of her eyes crinkled. "I wish this place was back to the bustling building it used to be. Not this empty cavern it is now."

"I know, I know." Not for the first time, Janny made it clear she was bored with the skeleton staff currently residing at the embassy. The post had been shut down previously, the risks making it not worth maintaining a full staff. Earlier that year, they'd reopened with two on-site political advisors, Ambassador Jensen and Mr. Brackster, who couldn't survive without Janny. She came back.

Both advisors were interesting in a reserved way—the complete and total opposite of Janny. Where they were skinny, old white men, she was a heavyset black woman who didn't give a fuck and supplied no BS-enhanced answers. But Sophia had to give both men credit. They were tough in their own ways, and they had to be in order to work in Honduras.

Ambassador Jensen had known Sophia since she first went overseas with her parents. He understood her, maybe because he knew *both* of her parents. She was tough as her father and as assertive as her mom. Jensen respected Sophia, as well as her assignment, when there were many people who wouldn't give two thoughts to what she was risking her life for. The PC didn't affect most Americans directly.

But that was all relative. At any given point in time, different terrorist groups, dictators, and cartels could shift power, and the worst of the worst would be a different list of bad guys. The truth was they were all awful, but there was only so much evil and doom a person could focus on at a time.

"Let's meet our guests." Janny put a heavy hand on Sophia's shoulder. "Maybe there's eye candy in addition to dinner conversation."

"Right." Yes, let's. There was nothing quite like men who looked as though they bench-pressed locomotives for fun. But really, Sophia was stuck in her head. She'd been uninterested in anyone since—

"You coming?" Janny led the charge down the stairs, and they took the last step in stride, her house-mom act coming out in full force as Jensen and Brackster arrived from their downstairs offices.

Sophia's gaze danced from the casual dress of embassy advisors to the camouflaged and well-armed gaggle milling through their introductions. They looked like giants. Their equipment carried the edge of danger and their weapons the promise of safety.

She tried for a deep breath, but when guys like this showed up, they generally sucked the oxygen out of the room. It was just their presence—the foreboding, dangerous nature of their very existence. Yes, the embassy had RSOs—regional security officers, the normal armed guards—but the off-the-books military guns for hire were different. They were on-site because of specific threats. Honduras was hostile, a black hole of death. No matter how easily the local villagers welcomed Sophia, their local leaders did not often appreciate US intrusion.

So many people. So many opinions.

As introductions were made, she kept a smile in place. One by one, names were given that were... *familiar*. "Brock Gamble. Grayson Ford. Ryder—"

Her eyes rounded. They were not just familiar names, but their faces rang a bell, too. With only a smidge of doubt, Sophia knew they were friends of her brother. Maybe even Colin was here. Her excitement grew...

"And Javier Almeida."

Oh. Shit.

There was no Colin in sight, but it was definitely Titan's Delta and definitely *her* Javier. Heat rocketed up her spine, tingling her cheeks and making the world swim sideways for the moment as she thought about her defunct wedding night and the one-night stand that she couldn't forget.

Oh God... what if he didn't remember her? What if introductions of embassy staff were made, and his face didn't show a glimmer of remembrance? How embarrassing.

Surely, someone on Delta would remember her. They knew her family; some had come to her almost wedding. Javier should have to remember Colin's little sister. Right? The speed at which her confusion and hope slammed together was nothing short of supersonic.

Which would be more awkward—if Javier recognized her or if he didn't? God, she was about to spiral into an uncertain-girl-sees-super-hot-guy mess.

"And this is Sophia Cole and Janella Winkler."

Brock nodded to Janny and tilted his head at her. "Colin's sister."

"Hi—"

A low, near growl pushed from behind Brock and Ryder. Then Javier sidestepped in front of his team. His eyes swept up and down, confirming that he not only *knew* her but that he wasn't happy. "What are you doing here?"

All eyes went to her as the sting of his words hit. Sophia's mouth dropped open as the daydreamed-about, super-hot guy stood in front of her like an imposing, *angry* asshole. A tingle of apprehension skirted up her neck, and stumbling thoughts killed off her nervous excitement. "Uh—"

"Excuse me." Ambassador Jensen stepped forward, protective of both her and his post. "Miss Cole is with the State Department."

"Bull."

Jensen's posture tightened. He might've been a bureaucrat, but it took a no-BS reputation and the heart of a badass to live day in, day out in Honduras. "Speak to my aid worker like that again, and you're gone." He turned to Javier's team leader. "Read me?"

Brock nodded. "Step aside, Brazil."

Javier's eyes locked onto hers, severe displeasure marring a face that she had wondered if she'd ever see again. The flutter in her stomach that happened every time she thought of him was replaced by a dark, hurting feeling as though all the butterflies that he'd made her feel had just died.

"Hey all." She gave a small wave to disperse the tension. It didn't work. Janny's stare was the strongest, a look that said *Oh boy, do we have gossip to share.*

"Hey, sweetheart," Ryder said, stepping in front of Javier and saving her from the uncomfortable gawks. "Nice seeing you again."

"You guys too." Yay for Ryder trying to break the tension, but her gaze went back to Javier. His brows pinched tight, and his dirt-smeared, bearded face scowled. There wasn't a flicker of interest or heat coloring his skin. Nothing except annoyance. Or anger.

Alright, so Colin hadn't lied. Javier wasn't the playboy who went back for seconds. Duly noted. What her brother hadn't mentioned was that the sweet guy she knew as Javier would be a jerk at their next run-in—though Colin didn't actually *know* about her and Javier and would *never* know. She'd gleaned that intel by asking about his Delta team.

"Okay, then." Janny clapped, breaking the room's focus on her and Javier. "Let's get everyone settled. Dinner's in an hour. Hope you boys like beef and potatoes."

Murmurs about hunger and the need for showers filled the hall, and

Sophia used that break to dash back up the stairs. Instead of finding solitude, she heard a thump of equipment hitting the ground and heavy-booted steps chasing her.

"Aw, shit." Ryder's Australian accent and laughter trailed behind her, and the boot steps were hot on her tail.

Dang it. Eyes locked straight ahead, she was 100 percent certain Javier was making a scene—and she had no clue why he'd do that after their uncomfortable hello.

At the top of the stairs, Javier's strong fingers hooked her shoulder, slowing her down, pulling her to his flak-jacket-covered chest. The smell of outdoors and exertion made her painfully aware of the warrior behind her, and with one smooth move, as only Javier could pull off, he had her spun around and backed to the wall.

"Sophia." It was her name—not a question. Not even a confirmation. His hard voice was upset and protective. Actually, it had a million qualities, but none were nice.

Her heart slammed, and her cheeks burned. Only inches separated their faces, and the last time they'd been that close, he'd been doing things to her body that could only be classified as wicked. Delightfully, danger-ously devious. She'd dreamed about them so many times that having him this close, even as upset as he was for whatever inane reason, made her feel weightless.

"What are you doing here?" The sexy musk of dirt, gunpowder, and outdoors came closer as his deep voice hinted a growl. Near-black eyes—matching his almost-black hair—and deep-tan skin covered with flecks of mud invaded her space. But for that flash of a moment, all she could think about was the past, when she had bitten into his shoulder as he made her come the first of many, many times.

"Answer me," he snapped, inching close enough that his breath was hot on her skin.

The uneven cadence of her breathing was embarrassingly evident. "I'm working."

"You're in *Honduras.*"

She blinked, incredulous. "You are too."

"*This* is my job."

"What do you think I just said?"

"You don't get to play crusader—"

Crusader! "*You* don't get to embarrass me at work."

Javier licked his bottom lip, taking a step back as though he realized that he had her pinned in the US embassy and they were *both* at work. "You shouldn't be here."

She'd had that thought on occasion in every job she'd had in a dangerous area. But Javier didn't know the first thing about her, her background, or what her goal was. She saved lives. He might do it his way, but she most certainly had her own style, and she made a difference. Instead of letting Javier in on that secret, she turned away from him and forced her feet to retreat to her bedroom. "*Nice seeing you again.* Good night."

"Fine. Whatever." The cold sound of his steps turning and heading down the stairs stabbed her heart.

What did she think he was going to do—sweep her off her feet and tell her that night had stayed with him for months as well? Not a guy like Javier. He was a legend. Apparently. Well, *apparently* because all it had taken was for him to look at her sweetly, and they'd fallen into bed. Best sex of her life on one of her most embarrassing days. Her only defense against him now was sarcasm and separate rooms.

Reaching her utilitarian bedroom suite, she slipped inside and collapsed on the bed. Tears burned into her eyes, slipping down. God, she wished Javier would just... have held her instead of yelling at her. Instead of ruining her favorite memory.

CHAPTER SEVEN

RUNNING HIS HANDS over his grit-covered face, Javier needed to expend energy. Something—anything—to get Sophia Cole out of his mind. But they were trapped inside with strict orders not to engage. He couldn't start shit with hostiles just to blow off steam, couldn't seek comfort from the bite of a new tattoo, and couldn't find a brawl where he'd let the punches land just to feel the pain. Those were the distractions he knew, his drug of choice: adrenaline. Endorphins would clear his mind of the beauty he'd just snarled at. But none of his regular options were available. Nor sex. He couldn't fuck her again until they both came, screaming in exhaustion.

Fucking hell. If he'd had any idea she was here, he could've prepared. Why wasn't Colin on this job?

Or maybe thank God Colin wasn't on this job. Javier's actions had been glaringly obvious. Concern like he'd not felt in years crushed his throat. He wondered how he hadn't known that she would be here—where Delta was brought in because shit was too dangerous even for *Honduras*.

Damn it. He pushed down a hall with no idea where he was going. The faint rumble of his teammates' voices acted as his compass, and after one wrong try, Javier found the room they were bedding down in. The conversation died. Shit. He rubbed his forehead and then, taking his hands away from his face, met Grayson and Ryder's curious looks and the pointed stare from their team leader.

Crap.

"Brazil." Brock crossed his arms, face stern and eyes narrow. He stepped forward, the sound echoing in the basic room. "What was that shit?"

"I have a headache." He went back to massaging his temples. *She* was a headache—a perpetual one, seeing as he'd never quite forgotten their night. And she was a responsibility. He'd already done her wrong. Colin said not to touch her, and what did Javier do? Screw her *then sleep next to her* on her wedding night. What an asshole move. "It's personal."

"I got that. Don't create problems on this team. You read me?"

"Loud and clear, boss man," he mumbled. "But it's nothing like that."

Grayson coughed a laugh, shaking his head, and Ryder didn't try to hold back.

Javier's muscles bunched. "Thanks, assholes."

Ryder only laughed harder, and now Grayson didn't try to hide it.

"Shut it, pretty boy." Javier glared at Grayson, which made Gray go back to shaking his head.

"If she's feeling lonely, I'll…" Ryder smiled his megawatt grin, drawing out that Aussie accent of his.

A jolt of protective possessiveness blasted through Javier. The only accent that was going to help that woman would be his. Or not. "She's Colin's sister. Back off."

"Know who she is, mate."

Javier kneaded his fists in the hollows of his eyes, cursing away thoughts of anything soft and sweet like the woman who'd told him good night with all the warmth of a fuck you. "Stay away from her."

"Easy, man." Grayson chuckled. "If you like the girl, you like the girl. No commentary from me. Marlena, maybe. Ryder, yeah. But I'm just gonna watch the show."

Javier kicked off his boots, undressed to just his pants, and ignored the trailing comments as he headed for the showers with a change of clothes in hand. The bathroom was set up like a locker room. This location was used for teams coming in and bedding down. There was a row of sinks and mirrors and, around the L-bend, a row of partitioned showerheads. Stacks of towels, cloths, and soap sat on a ledge. He needed to get under a stream of hot water, to wash away the hours they'd spent trudging through the elements and forget about the last thirty minutes.

Grabbing a towel from a shelf, Javier twisted a knob, and hot water poured down. He finished stripping down and stepped into the cascade of hot water, breathing in and trying to focus.

Delta was on the trail of the Primeiro Comando traffickers. His driving force in life was revenge. Take out the PC, avenge his sister, then one day he might have time for other… thoughts. But until then, distractions like Sophia Cole were just that: distractions. They had to be filed away as a good time. He had no room in his heart for another person to be concerned about.

Adélia. The idea that his sister could've been sold by the PC from one side of the globe to another, passed through Brazil to Honduras, was sickening. She would've been scared. Terrified. Brutalized. And every time he thought of that, his heart hardened because there was nothing he could do except dismantle the buying-and-selling network.

The Delta gig was perfect. Sex trafficking funded terrorists. Titan Group did the right thing no matter the cost, focusing their talent on the bad guys who helped other bad guys. Delta had a contract to dry up terrorist money sources. If there were no girls to sell on the human market, there'd be no money for jihadists on a misguided path to kill innocent civilians.

"Fucking cartels. Fucking terrorists," he murmured into the stream of hot water then unwrapped the soap and lathered. He scrubbed his skin until it was nearly raw, but still, he worried about why Sophia was in Honduras.

He needed to stop thinking about her. Distractions could make him off guard when he needed to only concentrate on the global networks and partnerships that these organizations weaved like spiderwebs. The drug cartels partnering with the human traffickers who were making deals with the oil-and-petroleum billionaires—it would astound even the most jaded person.

Hell, he *had been* the most jaded. And even he was surprised at the labyrinth of criminal networks these monsters had. He tossed the washcloth over the shower knob, used the dispenser labeled "shampoo," and ran his hands through his hair.

Sophia Cole. He couldn't keep his mind away, and that twinge of awareness traveled all the way to his dick.

She was beautiful. Sexy. Honey-brown hair and matching eyes that mapped a passage to her soul. His muscles relaxed under the water even as blood pumped to his cock. Javier breathed in a steamy breath, letting his head drop back. Those truthful eyes of hers were in his mind.

Screw it. He grabbed the soap, lathered his hand, and pictured her full lips and sweet tongue. He grasped his cock, and the pleasure made his chest shudder. With slick, strong strokes, Javier pumped his hand over the rigid flesh. Sophia on her knees. Sophia with her mouth open, her tongue reaching for a lick, for just a taste.

God. Damn.

He put a hand on the wall, breath coming faster as the shower rained overhead. Her small hands would grip his shaft, tug on his sac. But as much as he wanted to come, he wanted inside her again. Just to press her to the wall, to sink himself deep into her pussy and feel that searing tightness grip him with every. Single. Stroke.

Straining, his fingers bit into the tile as he remembered the sound of her moans as she gripped his body, her pulsing muscles milking his throbbing cock. *Paixão*. His shoulders tightened, and his thighs flexed as he palmed himself to the brink, thinking one last time about how she sounded. Javier came hard, spurting his release into the shower and heaving a gasp, wishing to God he'd been inside her.

His head dropped back as he released his cock, but the hand he'd used to hold himself against the wall bunched into a fist. Not for a punch—just one solid slam against the wall. He'd just come, but it wasn't anything like he wanted. Like *he needed*. It wasn't Sophia.

Washing off one last time, he turned off the shower and towel dried, wrapping it around his waist and heading to a sink. What he needed to do was brush his teeth and crash. But instead, he wiped the steam from the mirror and focused on the tattoo of the abstract eye over his heart. It wasn't large, and it played into the others across his chest. It was supposed to stand as a reminder of all seeing, all knowing when it came to the matter of his heart—his sister.

Javier had that eye there to sharpen his focus, to remind him to be prudent in the path he took, so long as it helped him meet his goal. With it, maybe he would have foresight to finish the job expediently.

Why hadn't he had the foresight to see how Sophia would affect him? He'd been jerking off to her for months, and then when she was in the room so close... Sophia could be more than a dream if he had the opportunity for that—for a girl and a relationship.

Which he didn't. Not until his demons rested. And they probably never would.

He breathed in the steamy air, feeling bitter anger more than arousal. That was better, what he was more comfortable with. His eyes narrowed on the reflection in the mirror. There was the machine, the heartless bastard that would care about nothing except Adélia until the last PC cartel men bled for her pain.

That was enough to make him forget about sleeping under the same roof as Sophia Cole. But as he turned away to dress, the last glimpse of his reflection laughed at the lie.

CHAPTER EIGHT

O N HER THIRD outfit and second mini you-can-do-this speech, Sophia opened her bedroom door to head for breakfast. The muffled voices made anxiety spike in her veins. Delta team was louder than the small contingent of staff at the embassy, and while it was nice to have new faces, she wished her first and only one-night stand didn't need to be there.

He's just a guy. We're two adults. It was months ago. The three sentences were on constant mental repeat. She squared her shoulders and ignored the awkward feeling that her arms were hanging heavy like an orangutan's. She didn't know what to do with her hands, which was one of the reasons she brought a notebook to breakfast—at least she had something to hold onto. If she wanted to fidget, she'd twirl the pen. If she needed to think, she could outline her thoughts on the upcoming meeting with Hana. If she looked up, and Javier did the same, she could quickly bury herself back in the notebook.

Brilliant plan.

The sugary scent of sweet dough and coffee hung in the air. Janny's sticky buns were legendary, and she made a mean brew. Coffee kept Sophia sane. Caffeine kept her going. All would be fine.

"Morning." Sophia beelined for the coffee carafe and went about making a large cup with a smidge of sugar before finding a seat at the table.

Ambassador Jensen had the newspaper spread out, and Mr. Brackster clacked away on his phone. Brock Gamble slugged back coffee as he nodded hello to her. Grayson and Ryder were both handsome and blond. Their golden-boy looks showed more now that they were showered and out of gear.

Then there was Javier. His hair was no longer matted down after hours trudging in from God-knew-where the previous day. His face was wiped clean of the dirt splatters, but his expression was a mask of anger and indifference, rolled into one. Whereas everyone else was polite enough to say hello in their own way, he simply stabbed a fork into a piece of fruit and ignored her.

Not awkward at all…

The part of her that no one could see, her internal strength that was trying so hard to keep it together, sighed sadly and slouched while she sipped her coffee as though it was any regular day at the embassy.

"Sophia?"

Her head shot up, and it was evident from the annoyance on the ambassador's face that he'd been speaking to her. "Sorry, sir?"

"The embassy lockdown will continue, and we will remain inside for now."

She could have guessed that, with Delta making themselves comfortable. "How long should that take?"

Brock leaned his elbows onto the table. "A day or a week. Depends on how quickly we come to an agreement."

She wanted to ask what they were willing to kill each other over this time but kept that to herself. Her concern went to Hana, whom she hadn't been able to reach on the phone for almost two days. While Hana was an asset, she had also become a friend. Jensen would give Sophia an update, privately, as to how the lockdown would affect Whispering Willow, which in turn would ease concerns about Hana.

"So, Sophia?" Grayson asked. "When you go out there, who goes with you?"

"Well, until about two weeks ago, there was another aid worker here." *One who was* actually *an aid worker, who gave me street cred and made introductions.*

"Female?"

"No, a guy."

Their heads nodded as though that made sense. And it had made sense to her, too, at first. In the area, it wasn't normal for a woman to be unaccompanied. When Sophia left the safety of the embassy grounds, she was *properly* dressed and clearly known as someone there to help. It wasn't anywhere near foolproof, but it was the best thing she had going.

"But," she continued, "he left, and I had a job to do. So…" She shrugged. "I did it."

"Alone?" That one word growled in Javier's accent. She remembered how he'd sounded against the shell of her ear. She remembered how his lips tasted.

Though her heartbeat picked up speed, she focused her faked indifference at him. "Alone."

Ambassador Jensen gave that bureaucratic chuckle that he used when defusing heated conversations. "Sophia's been perfectly safe. It's been quiet around here."

"Until it wasn't," Javier replied. "And it's never really."

"Agreed." Ambassador Jensen didn't pale in the face of angry soldiers—one of the reasons he'd done well in this post. "There's been unrest; you're here to deal with what I won't. Sophia's been smart and safe about her work."

She smiled at the compliment, but it didn't lessen the freeze in the room. "I'm fine."

Javier leaned into the table. "You're—"

"Stand down," Brock interrupted, focusing on his coffee as though he wasn't monitoring their back-and-forth.

With concentrated effort, she flipped open her notebook and jotted a few pointless notes. Still, all the note-writing in the world wouldn't take away the questioning glances of every man in the room.

"Who's up for a refill?" Janny bound into the room, breaking the tension with her fresh pot of coffee.

With that as the distraction, Sophia grabbed her refill and a sticky bun to go, made a pleasant good-bye to almost everyone at the table, then hurried to her bedroom, where she could sulk and stew, wondering why Javier was as devastatingly handsome as he was—even when angry.

As her door softly clicked shut behind her, she dropped the notebook and placed the plate and coffee on the desk then picked up her binoculars to stare out her window. It was tiny and the only source of natural light in the room. She'd been told to stay away from it, and for the most part, she did, except when she was bored, irate, or worried. At the moment, she was two out of three of those. The binoculars allowed her to see the main street.

From her vantage point, she knew things locals didn't expect, which made them think twice about acting a certain way. Her opinion mattered, especially to Hana, and for that, she was grateful, maybe even hopeful, that she would have a long-lasting effect—

Knock! The knob twisted the door open.

"Hey!" She jumped, not unsurprised to see Javier. "You can't just walk in here!"

Shrugging, he seemed indifferent to her reaction. "Just did."

"Well, you shouldn't. Knock and wait. Like normal people. Or don't, and go back to being a jerk to me in front of everyone. That's really nice of you, by the way."

He smiled, and God, it wasn't fair how great his smile was, nor was it fair that he'd been there since yesterday and was just now smiling. Someone with a grin like that shouldn't hide it.

"Knock next time, Javier."

His dark eyes twinkled at the mention of next time. What was it with him? She couldn't get a read on his mood swings, but something had shifted between the dining room and her bedroom.

"You should go." *Before I stick my foot farther into my mouth.* She pressed her lips together in an I'm-done-with-you smile and twisted to her desk.

"What were you doing?" He sidestepped her as she placed the binoculars down.

"Nothing."

"You're not hanging in that window." He clucked. "Right?"

"Right," she said even though hanging out the window was something she did regularly. Not that that was any of his business. "Did you come here to lecture me? Tell me to go home a few more times? What?"

"Maybe."

"Then get on with it. I have things to do."

"You can't leave the grounds. What do you have to do?"

"You have no idea why I'm here. So back off, and get out."

"Then tell me."

"Ha. Not a stinking chance." Sophia grumbled, trying to figure out how to place more room between them. Her feelings were evident and his for the taking, so she needed to protect herself. Not that she even liked him, but he'd been there for her when she hurt, and he made that dull ache go away and made her feel something. God, she was mentally rambling. He made her blather even in silence. Overthinking to the max.

"You shouldn't be here, Soph." Javier stepped closer, his hand drifting up to tuck a wayward lock of her hair behind her ear. "I don't care what it is you're doing."

"I'm doing something important to me." But it came out less forcefully than she wanted it to. "You don't have to get it, but respect it or leave."

He rolled his lips together, ignoring her suggestion, and let his fingers glide over her cheek before he dropped his hand. The touch was too intimate, making a tingle of excitement burn where his fingers brushed.

"Paixão."

God. That word. Whatever it meant. It sounded like sex. Which was likely all he wanted. That hurt. "I'm not here to be your piece of ass." Her throat ached. Sophia didn't want him to see her as a grab-and-go screw.

His beautiful, near-black eyes widened at the accusation. "No kidding, gatinha."

"*Paixão. Gatinha.* You were rude to me downstairs, and now you're all suave and—"

"Suave?" Amusement tickled in his question.

Awesome. She was inspiring him to run the gamut of emotions, from anger to amusement. "Yes, suave. Do you have anything to say except to mock me?"

"I'm not trying to. I just want you to go home."

"Why?"

"Because Colin wouldn't want you here."

That sentence was proof that Javier had never breathed a word of their encounter. "Colin doesn't care. He probably knows exactly why I'm here."

But that also meant Javier hadn't asked about her. That hurt more than she wanted to admit because she'd grilled her brother on all his teammates to learn more specifically about Javier.

Slowly, he shook his head. "Then *I* want you home, safe."

"This is what I do. Like what you guys do, but different."

"Not different enough." His head dropped, shaking slowly, and he balled his fists, rubbing his eyes, and then threaded his hands into his hair. Without looking up, he said, "We all start for a reason." He paused. "Delta team—war on terror, drugs, traffickers, militants. Protecting the homeland, your home country." Javier tilted his chin up and let his arms drop.

She swallowed, remembering the day her brother had enlisted and then later when he'd left the military and joined a private security firm called Titan and referred to the men on his team as his brothers. She remembered the day her father had asked her to work small assignments as he built her up to taking on Operation Whispering Willow.

Sophia was more worried about Colin than she was about herself, and she wanted to prove that she could do something just as powerful as he and Javier did. There was also a part of her that wanted to prove to her mom she wasn't a lady who lunched as a social activity.

"Somewhere along the line, things change." Javier's voice dropped. "It's less about the greater good and more about making sure the men on either side of you make it home."

Her defensiveness dropped a notch. "I'm going to make it home. I always do."

Javier's jaw twitched, and his eyes hardened, conveying more before he blinked than he'd said any other time they'd been together. He was worried, protective, accepting that he was acting like a jerk but needing her to understand. His unsaid words were more intimate than sex, more promising than a kiss. They were antagonistic and well-meaning.

"I'm being careful," she whispered. "I stay in when it's not safe. And when it is safe, I go out and do my job."

"It is *never* safe enough for you."

"It is. I follow the rules. I watch my back."

"You have a window perch and binoculars. What rules are you ignoring or which do you not know?"

Busted. She bit her lip. "I'm not leaving Honduras or any job because you have a problem with it."

"Go home, Sophia." He leaned over to kiss her cheek. It was careful yet cold, and then he left. The door quietly clicked shut, separating her from the man who could make her cry for the first time since her pity-party wedding night.

"You're such a jerk." Wiping away a rogue tear, she grabbed her binoculars in spite of him and went back to staring outside for no other reason than she needed to focus on anything but how he made her feel: special.

CHAPTER NINE

BROCK'S ARMS WERE crossed over his chest. As he leaned against the wall, tense and terse, his posture spoke before Javier's team leader took the opportunity to growl in displeasure. "Brazil."

"Yes, sir."

"Get your shit together." Brock's jaw cracked, whether from the grinding of molars or just holding back his sheer force of nature under the excuse of acting like a boss.

"It's together," Javier lied and took a seat next to Grayson. The makeshift war-room table should focus him on the business at hand. He took a deep breath, letting the world apart from his Delta brothers slip away.

"Then don't be late to my meetings, Brazil."

At least, Javier was *trying* to let it go. He grunted an agreement and wished that Luke had been part of this job. That guy would get where his head was at. They were made of the same fabric, expending energy and adrenaline the same way: women, ink, and street fights. All of those extracurricular activities drove their team leader to the edge of sanity—which was maybe why Brock was acting like king of the pricks today—but they worked for Javier and Luke, and Brock let them have their escape.

Javier cracked his knuckles, swallowing the tinge of adrenaline-laden saliva that came with thinking about a fight. His pulse picked up, and he took a breath and popped another knuckle, trying to forget about everything—*everything*. Had he really left Sophia crying upstairs? What kind of man—

"Javier?" Brock's attention bore into him. "Do we need to speak in private?"

He should be in this room, listening to his team leader, not worrying over a few crushed feelings when a girl needed to hear the truth. "No."

Brock held his gaze, assessing the lack of truth of Javier's answer, then shook his head and turned back to the whiteboard. They'd arrived the day before with two mission objectives: make their presence known—which they'd done in a big way on the outskirts of Tegucigalpa—and help the local government maintain the semiregular peace that they seemed to enjoy with their number-one trade partner, the United States. All while collecting intel.

The mission was half peacekeeping and half intelligence seeking. One hundred percent, nothing was ever as it seemed. The local police lacked a unified, dependable structure. There was a clear concern about cartel infiltration in the ranks of law enforcement. Delta did a few training sessions, a couple upgrades of local law-enforcement weaponry. They also kept their ears to the ground about PC traffickers who were moving people and product.

That was the high point of this job: PC intel. Not Sophia. But could it be both?

That was not an option. He shook his head, slowing it into a stretch when Brock turned around to ask Grayson about an ammo count. Javier forced his body to relax, focusing on Grayson's report, Brock's whiteboard mapped with arrows that pointed to thermal imaging. This wasn't a danger zone like one of the ones they'd worked a thousand times before. It wasn't great, but really...

"Javier?" Brock's brow was up. "Got your head in the game?"

Shit. Grayson and Ryder had eyes on him too.

"Absolutely." *Not.* He was distracted and needing to clear Sophia from his concerns. But even as he stared at the whiteboard, his mind was still upstairs with the sweet girl he'd hurt on purpose to try to scare home.

SO WHAT IF she had a perch and binoculars? They were perfect for peering at four armed men who were heading out of the embassy's secure gate and for watching Javier leave after they'd had a fight. She wondered if he'd be back. Wasn't there a rule—never fight with a military man and then let him go off to work? And *he* was worried about *her* in her safe suite surrounded by twelve-inch-thick walls, sirens, a protective guard, practice drills, panic rooms, and first-aid kits that rivaled some hospitals. The place was impenetrable.

God, her stomach turned, though—*for them*—despite the fact that she went out that very same gate without so much as a gun. They had high assault power attached to every limb. Maybe Javier had a point.

She put the binoculars down, and her mind went to Whispering Willow. What was Hana working on that day? Did Delta's arrival have an impact on her?

Sophia slid to her desk and opened her notebook. The area was controlled by gangs and cartels, by criminals and the corrupt. The country had more kidnappings and ransom extortions than anywhere else in South America. Sophia was a prize, an ambassador's daughter worth a hefty ransom. The identity of her parents was kept quiet enough that some of her security was even unaware of it. They could never be too trusting. But despite those concerns, along with the rampant highway assaults and carjackings, she felt safe.

Hana's husband commanded respect. He gave orders and monopolized law enforcement and other local politicos, never suspecting that his obedient wife was smart enough and evolved enough to think not just in terms of her community but on a global scale. Hana knew her husband's criminal efforts in connection with the PC cartel and knew that women and children were in danger because of the *work* the cartel did.

Hana was a martyr without having died—yet. And Sophia would do everything she could to make sure Hana stayed alive while relaying back to the US any information that would slow the trafficking of women and children.

This was the type of work she needed to do. It was her calling.

The cell phone buzzed on her desk. *Hana.* A surge of excitement pulsed in her blood. "Hello?"

"Sophia."

Thankfulness that her friend was okay surged through her. "Can you meet today? We have activity here. I didn't know if maybe you—"

"Your presence was very much known."

Yeah, I bet. Delta had clamored into the embassy with the purpose of announcing their presence. "Meet you at the cafe? On the corner of Av. República de Mexico and Calle República de Ecuador?"

"Perfect."

Hana wasn't what Sophia had expected. They were the same age. Both were city girls, and though most Americans would consider Honduras a third-world country, Tegucigalpa was a thriving capital city. Hana was also wealthy. With her family and marriage, she had access to money and power.

Time spent with Hana actually meant enjoying sake at sushi bars, pizza from American takeout places, upscale cuisine, and the Honduran nightlife.

The most important part of all the socializing was Hana's husband, Marco. He believed that his wife's relationship was a status symbol for *himself.* Everything about Marco Ferrera was about him. Never in a million years could he fathom she wanted to leave or that Hana would pass along secrets.

Actually, he expected the *reverse* to be true. Marco bragged about Hana's relationship to Sophia and, in some of his more illicit circles, used it as bait and currency. Their friendship meant access to power and prestige for him. It was his connection to America, Honduras's largest legal trading partner.

"And Sophia?"

"Yes?"

"The cables? Those, you're sure, are okay?"

"Completely classified." Sophia used the cable system to forward every bit of information she obtained to the Pentagon. They'd given Hana a port access, also, where she could snap and scan documents—even if she had no idea what they were for—and her cables would be reviewed and action taken if that was appropriate. There were many things Hana didn't have to converse about. That made her covert activities safer.

But Sophia didn't always know what had been relayed back to the US, and maybe that was why Delta had arrived. Pressing the phone to her ear and picking the binoculars up from the corner of her desk, Sophia went to her window perch, wondering where Delta had gone, what Hana had known, and where the invisible lines of information crossed.

CHAPTER TEN

CONGESTION MARRED WHAT would otherwise have been a relaxing stroll down Calle República de Ecuador. Sophia could only relax so much, never knowing where danger lurked. More often than not, she had a security detail with her, but not on her Hana meets. Discretion was best and made her more comfortable. The lack of safety protocols probably gave Marco a better feeling about what he thought his wife and the US aid worker might discuss.

The pizza place on the corner called to her. It wasn't quite American or Italian, but it worked for her cheesy-calorie fix. Hana's chauffeured sedan appeared across the street and pulled in front of where Sophia had her heart set. Thank God for pizza.

Not stopping to greet Hana on the street, Sophia pushed through the red door and let the warm scent of dough and cheese wash over her. The hostess smiled and escorted her to the table that was now known as her favorite. It had a view of the front door and the hallway leading to the kitchen and bathrooms. One sweeping glance could cast a visual gaze over every occupant of the restaurant.

"*Hola.*" Hana smiled as Sophia stood, exchanging a kiss on the cheek, before they both fell back into their chairs. Just a couple of girls ready to gossip and eat, who wanted to talk about fashion and whatever else well-off young criminal wives discussed with their inner circle.

After colas and pizza were ordered, Sophia relaxed but noticed Hana's posture was upright, her lips pressed into an uncomfortable smile. Something was off. "What's up?"

"I'm worried," Hana said.

"I could tell."

"We should go on a vacation together. Have girl time."

"I'll never get cleared for that."

Hana bit her lip. "I know."

"So, tell me something fun."

"Like?" Hana asked.

Like Javier was the one-night stand who wouldn't quit, and Sophia couldn't help but think about him. And she was worried that Delta's arrival had something to do with Marco's connections. Though none of that was fun. Just the Javier part.

Their colas arrived.

"I need a distraction, and you have a twinkle in your eye, *mi amiga*."

Sophia grumbled in good fun. "Or I have a headache."

"Handsome, burly American patriots have taken residence at your embassy, and you're primed for interesting nights in the near future."

Gah. "I could only wish."

"So there *is* someone."

Janny would say yes. "Perhaps."

"Part of this armed contingent that is making the streets buzz?"

"Eh." Sophia pulled her lip back, waffling her head. "Maybe."

Hana's beam broadened. "Please. Do tell."

"Nothing to say."

"I'm a sad, old married lady. Give me something to live vicariously through."

"Oh, BS!" Sophia laughed. Hana wasn't old and was nowhere near sad. Maybe one could say she was trapped, or put in a position where the world she knew and the one she wanted were at odds. "A friend of my brother's is in town."

"Oh, nice. And?"

"We… *spent time* before." She studied her soda glass as though it were more interesting than the South American in her mind and tried to think of the best way to explain the one-night stand on her wedding night without sounding like the queen of the slut puppies. "I was in a vulnerable place. Think he was too. So we leaned on each other—"

"Figuratively? Literally?" Hana laughed as the pizza arrived. "All of the above?"

They doled out slices while Sophia's cheeks flamed. "Maybe."

"*Nice.*"

Trying and failing to hide her blush and silly-girl grin behind a large piece of cheese pizza, Sophia shrugged and chewed, content to plead the fifth.

"If I ever get to"—she mouthed *America*—"we could go on a double date."

"Okay." Sophia put the pizza down. "First, we're going to make that happen." Because for the amount of danger Hana had put herself in, she'd earned a setup and new identity in the States. "And second, ready to date so soon?"

Hana held her hand out. To anyone taking a glance, they were both admiring the rock on her hand. "I was promised to Marco before I could walk. I was part of a business negotiation. Now, I won't say he's hard on the eyes."

Which was true.

"But he's evil."

Very true.

"Not a sadist. Never hurt me. But the marriage, that is all a formality, like a business transaction. I want to go on a date. A real, hearts-and-flowers date."

"Men are headaches," Sophia said, but there was merit in being... wooed. If Javier did something to make her swoon, other than his ordinary actions, she would be ruined for all other men. But it'd be a hell of a memory to have.

"I want the opportunity for that kind of a headache." Hana bounced her eyebrows, giggling, before she sobered. "I want a choice."

How could it be that someone as good and beautiful as Hana had never had that? In a way, Sophia was lucky to be born into a life that was relatively easy compared to what it could be in Honduras. But she'd never *lived*.

She swallowed more pizza as Hana did the same. They were both lost in thought, probably about the same thing but with very different outlooks. "Alright, when you come up north, we'll go on a double date."

Hana beamed, her smiling glowing as bright as her dark eyes. "You with your crush, and... me with your brother!"

"What?" Sophia squeaked. Other than the obvious facts of living in another hemisphere at the moment and Hana's pseudo-involvement in the underground world of Honduran hell, Colin and Hana would make a nice-looking couple. "Oh, wow. That would be... cool."

"Very."

"Ha."

"Thank you. For everything you're giving me—*a date with your brother*"—they both laughed—"and a chance to leave one day."

Sophia watched the lunch crowd. "Promise me you won't run back to Central America after you actually meet Colin."

Hana smiled. "Let me take care of what I need to here so that one day I might actually be able to date."

Sophia felt as though maybe Hana was more like a sister or best friend than she'd had before. More so than Liz. Different than Janny. They had a bond that they'd both risk their lives for. "Sounds like a plan."

CHAPTER ELEVEN

SOPHIA LET HER legs swing from her perch on the kitchen counter. Janny's large frame and extra curves worked around the room as though this was her dance in her domain. There, she ruled the roost, knowing where everything was and how to do each task with flawless elegance. No, Janny wasn't a lithe, little wisp of a woman, but her dance in the kitchen was as mesmerizing a ballet.

"Lawdy, child. Are you daydreaming about the hunk of burning love?"

"*Actually*, no. I was thinking about *you*." Sophia laughed and popped a granola cluster into her mouth. "Though he would actually be nicer to think about."

Janny hummed and snapped a hand towel. "Alright. I'll buy that one time, only because you got your girly-girl convo fix earlier today. But if you think I don't want to hear about that fine, strappin' young man, you are wrong."

"Not that much to say."

"He buy you that necklace you keep touching?"

"No. Hana."

"A case of *keep your friends close, your enemies closer*?"

Sophia shrugged. "I legitimately like her."

Janella coughed out a sarcastic laugh. "So does the Primeiro Comando. Careful."

"I'm fine."

"Just like you're fine to walk down Av. República de Mexico?"

"If there was a problem with it, Jansen wouldn't let that happen."

Janny shook her head and turned to the fridge, pulling out spinach and tomatoes for a salad. "If you say so."

"Since when have you started beating around the bush?"

"I'm not." Janny put the spinach on the counter, emphasizing how *not* she was.

"You *are*."

"I get that you lost your best girlfriend to your scum-bucket ex."

Sophia's jaw dropped at the comment that had come out of left field. "Wh-what?"

"But you don't need to replace her with someone you can't trust."

"Janny!" Her eyes bugged. Trusting Hana was easy. Janny hadn't met Hana, and while on paper there was a trust concern, in real life, where they walked and talked and dined and traded secrets, Sophia had found a counterpart whom she relied on.

"Take what I've said as a woman who loves you, who has twenty years or more of experience on her side."

Sophia ignored the uncomfortable overprotectiveness that she could appreciate from Jensen or Brackster but not from loud-mouthed Janny. "You haven't been in Honduras for twenty years."

"And you are intentionally missing my point. Gossip with your girl; work your contact. I've cooked and laundered in places like this long enough to know it's nice to have an asset who is friendly and fun. *But* remember why you're here and *who* she is."

"My friend and my partner."

"Hana Ferrera is first and foremost a friend of the PC, whether for show or for real. She's *their* friend."

"But she's my informant," Sophia countered.

Janny blew out an exasperated sigh so large and long that Sophia half expected the woman to deflate. "I know you've been around long enough to know the flaw in that logic."

Blurg. Sophia did know what Janny meant, no matter how much she wanted to ignore it. Loyalty could be won, bought, or sold. Hana was only as good as the last piece of information she passed to Sophia or protected her with. And why had she chosen to ignore that anyway? Her father— heck, *her mother*—had taught her better than that, expected more from her than that. Sophia's chin dipped as the tickle of guilt burdened her chest, weighing down her shoulders.

"Anyway." Janny cleared the air with all the subtlety of a grenade launcher at a golf range. "Subject change. Tell me about that fine Delta boy that likes to pin you against the wall."

"Janny!" The heaviness that squeezed her lungs dissolved with a deep, surprised breath. "How…?"

"I know all." Smiling as though she could feel how hard Sophia's pulse pounded, Janny shook her knowing head. "I see all. And I hear all."

Sophia ignored the thump of blood at the base of her neck that was a constant, drumming reminder that Janny had nailed what Sophia had on her mind already. "Alright."

"I'm not kidding. For as stout as this building is, just know some of the walls are paper-thin, and I *do not* want to hear how close you and Sexy McHotterson are getting. And don't even play that we aren't going to delve deep into the gossip on this one. I want all the deets on McHotterson. You two will be better than the soaps, I can tell already."

Sophia laughed, letting the surprised embarrassment make way for the flutters of a crush that had lust-drunk butterflies circling her stomach. "He's *Mc*-nothing. Pure-blooded South American, and I melt when he talks."

"Sexy El Hotto." Janny grabbed the knife off a chopping block and sliced a tomato. "I like *El Hotto*. I bet he could make you La Screama. I think I read something in Cosmo once that our South American *hombre* friends are *packing* south of the border."

"Janny!"

"They invented Brazilian waxes and tangoes. I'd say as a whole, you can't go wrong with a Latin lover."

"I can't believe we're having this conversation."

Janny pointed the chopping knife at her. "*He's* the one who should give you jewelry, amongst other things, so long as I don't know about it firsthand."

Cheeks back on fire, Sophia grabbed a handful of granola to redirect her attention, but thought that really, if Javier gave her a necklace and said not to take it off, she might die with the thing around her neck.

CHAPTER TWELVE

EYELASHES FLUTTERING, A noise had her attention. But what was going on? She'd been asleep? Yes, yeah. Asleep. Okay. Sophia blinked in the dark on her bed when a soft knock pulled her further awake. Her e-reader was in one hand, her daytime clothes were still on, and it took several seconds to register the knock as coming from her door as if someone was asking for her attention and she needed to snap out of her dreamless dream world.

Javier. Snapping commenced. She ran a hand through her hair. Janny wouldn't knock like that, or in the middle of the night—unless there was a problem, in which case it would be a slap to the wall and a "Get-up-and-hustle." Janny's very distinctive mama-bear knock was always more *Open up* than anything else.

Sophia pushed out of bed, eager and nervous, checking there wasn't dried drool on her chin or something embarrassing, then cracked the door. There he was. Dark, soulful eyes that made her melt, lips that she knew could kiss like a god; he was dressed casually, waiting for her to say something.

"Hi."

"Can I come in?" His hair was shower wet and the stubble on his cheeks cropped close. Sexy in a way she couldn't ignore but needed to.

"I'm not sure that's a good idea." She had a very thin line of sanity when it came to him. One touch, one kiss, and she'd be ready to make another mistake. That last mistake still made her shiver, but their previous interaction in this room had been a lecture on returning stateside.

His jaw flexed. "I have my reasons, but... I shouldn't have been in your face."

A tickle of surprise caught her off guard. "Is that your version of an apology?"

A beat passed. Javier licked his bottom lip then nodded. "Yeah. Yes. I'm sorry."

It shouldn't have been so easy, yet Sophia stepped back, holding the door open as an invitation. "Fine."

Javier stepped into the shadowed room. Without the door as a layer of protection, his overwhelming presence grew. They were alone, with a bed, in the dark. Her heart thudded as she waited to find out why he was there. What more than to apologize did he want? Sex? Someone to chat with? Just practice working on his manners? Wow, he was gorgeous… and more than that, he was *Javier*. His scent, even his height, affected her. He'd rubbed her back as she drifted to sleep months ago. Why on earth she chose that moment to remember that, Sophia had no idea. But she did remember, and it had been sweet and tender, very much like the look on his face now.

"I'm sorry for how I said those things earlier." He cleared his throat. "But not what I said."

Her warm, ooey-gooey man melting *stopped*. "Oh, for God's sake. Go."

"I was out there." He threw his arm toward the window. "And it's hell."

"Well, it's not when I go." Except sometimes it was, and that was why she needed to continue her work.

"Bullshit." A soapy-clean heat emitted from Javier as he bore down on her. Everything about him was enticing—the way his damp hair fell and how the barely toweled-dry mess made her wonder if he'd rushed to see her.

"It's not."

Much softer, he whispered, "You know that's bull."

A slip of moonlight from her tiny window illuminated him, handsome and angry, emotional and cold—things that never should go together, but they did—as Javier towered above her.

"You have to know that, paixão."

She couldn't breathe. Her pulse jumped, and the most feminine part of her body came alive. A current of desire and electricity bounced between them, both their breaths quickening. He stepped closer until they touched. Her chest rose, and his fell. Javier's hand moved to her bicep, drifting, sliding. He caressed up her neck—so careful, so delicate that he gave her pinpricks until he captured the back of her head with the force of his strong fingers threading harshly through her hair. Sophia sucked a breath and resisted him just because… hmm, just because his grip was iron strong and sure.

"You want to move?"

The tenor of his voice sent trembles straight to her nipples. "I don't."

Javier leaned toward her neck. His breath was hot, his lips even better. They were close enough to feel the heated tickle of skin on skin.

"No?" Gently, he tugged her hair. "Sophia Cole…"

Oh, God. He pulled again, firmer, tilting her face so their eyes lined up. She felt as though he could see her every thought without her speaking a word.

"Mmm, nice."

She couldn't stop arching and making that same *mmm* sound he did. Her eyelids slipped shut, letting the feeling run through her veins, awakening every nerve.

"Paixão." The whisper of the word contrasted with his hard body, which backed her to the wall. "So good for me."

His weight pinned her and, despite the dominant hold, nuzzled her neck. Stubble scratched her as the scent of his shampoo made her weak.

Scratchy and coarse, his fingers flexed into her scalp. "It kills me you're here, and I don't believe what you're doing is about aid work—"

"It is," she barely whispered.

"Liar." His teeth grabbed her earlobe. The bite stung, and the pain skipped straight down her neck, igniting an erotic fire in her blood, making lust fire in her veins. She wanted more, needed to feel the bite again. But he released and licked the tiny spot and gave it a kiss, and all Sophia could do was tilt her head, a silent plea for him to do it again, which went unanswered. "Tell me, are you lying?"

Melting at the protective, truthful accusation, she let sanity leave her. If only he'd give her a biting smack of a kiss again. "Maybe."

Javier moved faster than she could anticipate. His mouth took hers. A reward. Better than she imagined. His tongue probed, hot and needy. Wanting. His hands crawled over her body, but God, her mind spun so fast she couldn't place what was where or how it happened, just that he kissed like a man who could set her insides on fire and make a kiss turn into a touch passionate enough she could've been floating.

She cupped his rough cheeks, and Javier moaned. As if something *she* did was *anything* as amazing as what he was doing to her. Their tongues tangled, and his hands clawed her, pulling her to his muscular chest, eating her mouth as though her lips were the only things that could keep the world turning. This tough, strong man telling her *good girl*, calling her paixão, was worshipping her body, and whatever she had done to deserve it, she wanted to do again.

Javier growled again. Or maybe this time the masculine sound was a groan. Whatever the noise, he responded because of *her*. He gripped her hips, backing them again, this time to her bed. The mundane, utilitarian bed was nothing like the last bed they'd been in, and she couldn't wait to jump into it. Thread count didn't matter, just the man who gripped her body and made her cunt pulse before he'd even stripped her panties free.

"We have to be quiet."

Javier dug his fingertips into her butt, and she squeaked, jumping into his lap, making him chuckle quietly and her giggle.

He raised an eyebrow. "I can, but what about you?"

Superintense Javier was not always that way. It was almost too much that he could joke around at the very moment that she was going to crawl out of her skin if she didn't come in the next ten minutes. "*Yes*, I can."

"We'll see, gatinha." Javier pulled her to straddle him.

"Oh, *not* fair." He was massively aroused, and her yoga pants let her feel everything.

"Hm?" His breaths were hot against her neck, and Javier pushed her shirt up and over her head. "Too beautiful."

He did away with her bra before she could so much as help with the clasp. At once, his hot, wet mouth sucked her nipple deep, and it was her turn to make a noise.

"You don't really want me to answer that question, do you?" she said. Whimpering, she couldn't help but rock against him.

He plucked at her nipple. "What question?"

Sophia laughed and clawed at his shirt. His biceps flexed, holding her hips in place.

"Javier," she whispered into his neck, kissing the salty taste of his skin and dragging a three-syllable name out forever. "That's so very good."

"Good girl." He dropped her to the bed, pulling his shirt over his head then laying his weight over her, supported on a forearm, while he took as much care of her other breast. The tip of his wet tongue played circles with her nipple. So soft. Easy. His hand kneaded the mound until he scraped his teeth. It was exquisite, the back-and-forth, the sensations, the extremes. Easy and hard, pleasurable and pushing the edge of what she should like. But hell, she liked it. No, she loved it. She wanted him to pluck, to pull, to make her moan then smooth his loving tongue over needy flesh again.

"That's…" Breath catching, she squirmed—or tried, but he didn't let her make much headway in escaping his onslaught. Not that she wanted it to stop for a single ever-loving second.

"You like this, Sophia?"

"Yes. Yes." She nodded, scared if she didn't convince him adequately, he'd ease up. "*Yes.*"

The needy ache that had grown between her legs was out of control. She couldn't move against him. Friction wasn't happening. Javier tortured her with a flex of his hips, grinding their clothed junctures together.

"You want more?" he asked.

"Yes."

"Are you sure, Sophia?"

"You like to hear it said?" she hissed.

Javier's low laugh purred against her. "By you? Absolutely."

"Ugh." She groaned. "Yes. I want more."

"Good, gatinha. I do too."

Anytime his native tongue rolled off his lips, she melted.

Javier slid down her body, slipping her athletic pants and panties off and pushing her thighs wider. "*Tesão.*"

Whatever that meant, it worked. Brazilian Portuguese and his tongue flowed together in a beautiful symphony between her legs, and she died when they collided with that sweet spot and his long fingers curled inside her. "It's…"

"Hmm?" he murmured against her skin, barely stopping what could only be considered a natural talent.

"God, it's…" She panted, almost bucking as his fingers searched inside her for that G-spot. "Been too long."

"Since?"

She wanted him to never stop talking and never talk again. Just keep going. "Since you've touched me."

This time, he didn't say a word, but he pushed her thighs open further and pressed himself into her pussy deeper. He lapped and loved. Javier's whiskers tickled and scratched, his face went back and forth, and his cheeks teased her folds… he *loved* this. He did. He wasn't just doing it. And as Sophia bucked and gripped the sheets—as she thrashed and cried—he played to every one of her moves.

The quick-building climax swelled through her, and she let go of the last of her aggravation and embraced all that was Javier caring for her. His fingers took her harder; his mouth sucked her clit until her muscles rippled at his demanding command. She reached for him, knotting her fingers into his thick hair, and prayed to remember the moment because this orgasm was as good as it could possibly be.

His mouth slowed as her body did. Muscles relaxing and with eyes pinched closed, she let her hands trail down his neck and his powerful back as he crawled up her stomach. She locked her arms around his neck, nuzzling into it. "Baby."

He turned his face and touched his lips to hers. "I like that you call me baby."

Her cheeks heated. Had that been out loud? But more importantly, he liked it.

"Baby," she whispered.

Minutes slipped by, and Javier held her, caressing her skin with his fingertips. "Last time we were in a bed together…"

It'd been so good. So needed.

"It might've seemed like I was there to take care of you." His forehead touched hers; his lips whispered across her cheek. "But it was the other way around."

She held the hardest, toughest man she'd ever met, and for a slice of time, he was allowing a vulnerability to show. "What does that mean?"

He leaned up. "I never planned for that to… go down that way."

Her lips quirked. "Yeah, me neither."

He kissed her lightly, letting his tongue slip along the seam of her lips. Sliding her hands down his back, her fingernails scratched on their way to his belt. Sophia hooked her thumbs inside the waist of his pants. "But we can again?"

"I'm the asshole who wants you to leave."

She laughed quietly. "You're the guy I don't want to let go of."

"Something about you. I swear…" Chastely, he kissed her lips then removed his wallet and took out a condom.

The way his muscles moved was magical. The heat in the room rolled from him, and their eyes were locked as his hands went to his waist. Her mouth watered, and her heart pounded. The teeth of the zipper slid open, and there was nothing sexier than that primitive, primal expression that showed he was hungry for her.

She nodded as if the world was playing in slow motion. "I feel how you look."

"Molten." His fist ran down his cock—one stroke then two—before he sheathed himself.

"Javier." Her word was a breathless whisper, and her body hummed, alive.

Javier leaned over her in all of his muscled glory. His hands cupped her face, and his thumbs swept over her cheeks as their bodies fit together. "So beautiful."

He was, too, but a man like Javier would never accept that as a compliment. Her thighs spread to allow his hard body to slip into place. The blunt head of his erection pressed against her ready opening, and even in the moonlit room, she could see him watching her, paying attention to every breath and blink.

"Easy." The exotic accent rolled off his tongue. Every inch of him slowly speared her as Sophia nodded against his neck, urging him on.

"Yes. Please. I need…" Her jaw dropped. She needed everything. More of him—in her, on her, kissing her mouth, whispering in her ear. She breathed him in and tasted his skin. She needed more of him than she could comprehend.

His breaths were ragged, his face strained. Before, on her wedding night, they hadn't taken their time; it had all been instinct and a need to escape. This time was so different. He was diligent about her, watching and listening. More expressive than she'd ever seen or imagined, and *how* she'd imagined him. But now, this… it was a connection beyond the physical. She had no idea what exactly it was. But it made her lungs tighten and her head swim.

Javier rocked their bodies, murmuring words against her lips she was sure were not in English. The fullness and his intensity could destroy her. With each thrust into her, he worked her body to the edge all over again. Their rhythm was long and relishing, and their build together was mind erasing. Her body obeyed his as though he held the secret to instant climaxes.

"Hold onto me, Soph." The sexy-sounding words ran through her. She did as she was told. Stronger and deeper. He held her as she clung to him, climaxing again.

"Baby," she moaned.

And that one word was all it took. He went into overdrive. His hips moved like a piston.

Their bodies were desperate and hungry. She pushed into him for more, arching and aching until a third wave of orgasm readied to sweep through her. Javier ground into her, holding her tight and clamping his limbs around her. They came together and went boneless as he rolled her to the side.

The tips of his fingers traced down her jawline, skipping to her arm, then hip. His touch lingered before he got up and removed the condom.

"Are you leaving?" she whispered into the dark.

"Do you want me to?"

Now was the chance she could protect her heart. Yes. She wanted him to leave. She wanted him to take that accent and all his sexiness and walk away because that was the only way this would go. He was on assignment, working for the same company that Colin worked for as well. They didn't live on a schedule, and they didn't reside in one place. And he could die just as her brother could.

Heck, she was in the middle of Honduras. It wasn't as if she could date.

If he lay back in bed, given the way she was already feeling, it would hurt more when he left, which would happen any day now.

"Soph?"

But she couldn't tell the man she'd dreamed about every night since their one time together to leave. "Stay."

Silently and smoothly, he joined her back in bed. Javier pulled the covers from under them then tucked her against his hard, muscled length just as he had wrapped the blanket around her half a year ago.

"Night, Sophia," he said with his accent purring softly in her ear.

"Night, baby."

His arm pulled her closer. Whatever happened tomorrow, she'd happily fall asleep with him there.

CHAPTER THIRTEEN

DAWN BROKE AS morning light spilled through the window in Sophia's room. Javier's eyes were open. They'd been open after a couple hours of sleep against a beautiful woman, and he didn't move. He just watched her. Unlike Sophia, he had no family that he had a claim to. He'd walked away from his family the moment he could. *Not like they noticed.*

Work called, and he needed to get a move on, but he didn't want to roll away. The woman in his arms was sweet. He'd never done sweet before. He'd done a lot of everything else but never anything like Sophia.

And it was worth lying with her until the very last second—which was now. He had to move boots. Brock was liable to knock the door down if Javier didn't report in on time.

Her eyelashes fluttered as he pulled himself from around her. "Gotta run."

Sleepily, her eyes opened. "I'm glad you were on the team here."

Warmth hit his chest, and the pleasant reaction made him want to dive back under the covers. But that was a no-go. He needed to keep that reminder in the forefront in his mind. Delta had to hit the ground today. They were moving equipment then bugging out in a day or two, leaving someone as soft and sweet as Sophia in this hellhole part of the world. He sighed, tucking the covers around her, brushing the hair off her cheek.

He gave her a gentle kiss then donned his clothes and left to meet up with the team. Their voices bled through their makeshift war room, and Javier grabbed a cup of joe and a chair. Three sets of eyes landed on him.

"What?" he said though he knew what was up.

Brock bit down a half smile and shook his head. "Nothing."

"So you *slept* with her?" Ryder asked, one hand under his chin as though he was deep in thought.

"Fuck off."

"No, man. I mean you went to *sleep* somewhere. Not where you shoulda bunked. So?" His brows arched.

Javier shrugged.

"Dude." Grayson chuckled into his coffee, not doing a decent job of hiding his shit-eating grin.

Javier shrugged again. "Not my style to gossip like you women."

"It's not your style to see the same woman—"

"Twice," Ryder finished. "Or catch Zs with her."

"Right. Get it out of your system. Give me hell. Bring it. Whatever." He focused on his coffee, ignoring the jabs. The thing was, they were right. He'd never slept with the same woman twice. Never. Something was inherently wrong with him. He knew that, and it seemed his team did too. And he *never* bedded down with anyone. Never in his twenty-some-odd years walking the earth did he have any idea that sleeping next to a girl was as much fun as screwing the girl.

Except maybe Sophia wasn't just any girl. Shit. Javier burrowed his knuckles into his eyes and then downed a gulp of black coffee. It didn't matter. They had a job to do here, then they were off to the next op. That was the lay ahead in his world, what he'd signed up for, no matter how eye-opening last night had been.

THE SECOND DAY in which Sophia watched the four men walk out the embassy gates and disappear into the city, she grabbed her binoculars and searched for where they might go, what they were contracted to do.

A knock hit her bedroom door with a muffled, "I'm coming in." Janny waltzed in without waiting for a response. "You and those damned binoculars. Bet you're not looking at the village people this time. I'd say there's a fine piece of Delta ass walking his fine fanny out of here—"

"Janny!" Sophia put them on the desk. "I was just—"

"Lordy, I'd be watching those sweet behinds too, honey."

"For real, Janny."

"Pfshh." She tossed her hand. "So, you gonna give me the lowdown on that sexy piece of sweet-sounding man candy, or do I have to take a page out of his book and interrogate you?"

"There's nothing to—"

"Don't tell me we're gonna go the waterboarding route, because I'm not in the mood to clean that kind of headache up."

Sophia dropped to the bed she'd recently made—after taking a moment to realize that her pillow had a hint of Javier's scent on it—and she covered her face with her forearm. "I slept with him."

"Tell me something I don't already know."

"Oh my God, you heard us?"

"No, child. But the second he walked in, all growly alpha bossy, and chased you up the stairs, there was no doubt someone was having a sleepover."

Sophia groaned. "Wasn't the first time."

"Coulda guessed that too."

"He's sweet."

"Now, that I wouldn't have guessed."

Sophia propped herself up on her elbows. "Right? And he was. So dang sweet."

"Alright then. Badass can do sweet. Mark that down in the pro column."

"He works with my brother, Colin. Javier and I… were together shortly after my wedding went the way it did. He had a lot going on, and I needed the distraction. We both needed to forget the world around us and just feel nothing."

"Nothing but an orgasm."

"Janella!"

She shrugged. "I speak the truth."

"Yeah, I guess you do."

"So last night?" Janny sat on the foot of the bed. "No life-altering disasters, and you two hooked up again."

"He doesn't like that I'm here. I'm pretty sure that his initial intention in storming my room was to lecture me all the way back to the safety of the

States."

Janny rolled her eyes. "Don't give me that."

"I—"

"Nuh-uh. Neither of us believes that."

Sighing, Sophia stared at the ceiling. "I think…"

Janny waited a few minutes then gave up. "You think what?"

"He's the guy that I'd want to fall for. Strong, protective." Or maybe she'd already fallen before she even hooked up with him. Colin used to tell her stories, and he had so much respect for his teammates. They were all heroes, doing what they could to save the world. How could she not fall for a type like that? Then when she met Javier—the accent, the tattoos, the muscles, and the looks? There was no chance she'd not have a thing for him.

"Oh, Lordy. Put that in the con column. Honey, there's no way a man like that domesticates. There just isn't. I've seen my fair share of Rambo boys come through these doors and leave. I'd be lying if I said I didn't have my own sleepover or two, but they leave. They always do. Those boys are made of a different fabric than we are."

A sad curl of agreement made her stomach drop. "I know."

"Can't have a man who doesn't come home."

"I know."

"Can't want a man that won't need to come home."

Sophia turned her head. "What does that mean?"

She shrugged a shoulder. "A man that fine will never lack for companionship, and given who he's running around with, he's talented at something. The world's always at war, and he'll always have a job. Not at home."

The truth was going to give her early wrinkles. Sophia's forehead furrowed, but then she studied Janny's face, knowing there was something about her friend that she should have learned long ago. "Why are you here, Janny?"

" 'Cause I wanted to know the juicy details, none of which you have shared yet."

"No, I mean in Honduras."

Janny's face went taut for a moment, but she smiled sadly, turning it around on Sophia. "Why are you?"

"I totally used my dad to post me here."

"Those are the logistics. But *why?*"

Sophia bit her lip. "Because I'm fighting for something that is a basic human dignity that all people should have. I can't imagine going home when this exists out there."

Janny's eyes went soft. "I had a son. He never came home."

That hit Sophia like a grenade. "God, I didn't—"

"I don't share it. This place isn't where we lost him. But this is the best I could do to dedicate my life to what he died for. I cook. I clean. I bleed red, white, and blue for my baby. I can't leave this life. But, child, you can. No one wants you rotting away in this place."

"I'm not rotting."

"You're not living."

"I'm working for something I've become very dedicated to."

"True." Janella patted her shin. "Enough of that. The juicy bits, please."

Sophia's cheeks heated as she laughed. "Javier—"

"Did I mention how sexy that name is?"

She raised her brows. "Agreed. And he is very, *very* talented."

"And?"

Sophia smacked her lips together. "And that's it. No kiss and tell. Just that he can deliver."

Janella playfully smacked her knee. "No fun." Then she stood up. "Alright, I'm off to do my thing. Try not to perch in the window all day long. You'll catch a sniper round in the brain."

"I won't."

"Yes, you will. When you're not looking at a fine piece of soldier ass, you're checking the scene, so keep tabs on whatever you're really here doing."

Sophia shook her head, staying mum.

Janella pressed her lips together and smiled. "I know all."

She probably did.

Janella pushed off the bed and headed out. Sophia glanced at her binoculars and notepad but decided to reach for her bookshelf. At least she could quietly read, undisturbed. But as she looked at the cover of the current romance novel she was reading, it was clear that her favorite heroes—the brooding, tall, dark, and deadly soldier type—were all played by Javier in her mind.

CHAPTER FOURTEEN

T HE CLOSER DELTA drew to the gates, the stronger the pressure in Javier's chest grew. The guys made small talk around him, always with their eyes up and watching for danger, but he didn't have anything to say. All he wanted to do was scan the perimeter, but instead, he wondered what had caused him to spend the night. He hadn't wanted that. Yet he wouldn't have budged under threat of mortar fire.

The gates swung open, and his eyes bounced to Sophia's bedroom. There she was, and that tension in his chest jumped. Javier readjusted his gear.

"Your girl's got her eye on you." Grayson nodded his head upward as though Javier hadn't already noticed.

He grumbled.

"Nothing wrong with having a nice girl," Grayson said.

Another grumble. Grayson had two nice girls, a wife and daughter. Both smiled when he walked into the room. They laughed and joked alongside Grayson, who lived the American dream. Javier didn't have a dream so much as he had a life purpose, and it didn't involve a homestead and family.

Brock cleared his throat. "Not sure someone who gets his therapy through street fights and tattoos is a man who's going to make that woman happy."

"Fuck you," Javier said. "If I wanted a nice girl, I'd have a nice girl."

Ryder put his hand on the embassy's front door but turned before he pushed through. "You had her last night. *Spent the night* with her."

"I know what I did last night." He shouldered past Ryder, who gave him a good-natured, albeit *hard*, pat on the back.

Even if Javier wanted a girl and place to call home, his life was on a collision course with the Primeiro Comando. He wouldn't want those people anywhere near Sophia—or near anyone special.

They went down the hall to drop gear, and Janella was already hollering for them to head to chow as soon as they were ready. It was late, and the residents likely already had dinner. Sophia was awake, that much he'd seen in the window.

Hell. Screw food. He was showering and heading up there. One thing cleared his mind, and that was pain. Tattooing and street fights were his go-to activity for alleviating his mental stress. Except that right now, he didn't crave that adrenaline burst, that addictive bite of a needle or force of a punch. What he was jonesing for was sweetness.

Javier hit the shower, thinking about life in Honduras. He was here short term. He had no idea how long Sophia was here for. He had the Delta training hell that Brock had forced him through when he transitioned from fighter to mercenary-soldier and joined Titan. Sophia had what, exactly, that would keep her safe?

After a quick soap, shampoo, and dry off, he pulled on clean clothes and didn't bother heading for grub.

"Sleep tight," Ryder laughed as they passed in the hall.

Not giving a response, Javier bound up the stairs and headed to Sophia's bedroom. He took a breath, trying to calm his ass down, then knocked. His pulse pounded, lungs slamming in his chest as though he'd run a marathon. It wasn't as though he couldn't run up stairs. It wasn't an athletic issue. It was a Sophia Cole issue. His damn heart was racing as if he were readying to go to blows in a fight.

The adrenaline he craved was an addiction. But that *she* was making that jolt of excitement run through his veins? It was trouble that he couldn't stay away from.

The door cracked, and his heart punched it up a notch. Holy hell. Better than the anticipation of that tattoo gun or a right hook that he absorbed on purpose, Javier wanted her lips on his skin, her fingers sinking into his back, the noises she made, and the way her tight pussy clamped on his cock when she came.

"You okay?" she asked in a way that killed him.

"Am now."

Opening the door farther, she stepped aside, and he walked into her bedroom, sweeping his arms around her. Damn. She smelled good. Felt soft. His mouth watered, and his cock hardened. He had an instinctual need when it came to her.

"I saw you guys come in." Her cheek was pressed to his chest and her arms wrapped around him, not in a worried way but more as if she needed him too.

"Saw you looking." His lips dropped to the top of her hair, pressing a kiss. "Liked that you were looking. Even if you shouldn't."

She tilted her head back, and her cheeks blushed. Her grin made him want to smile, which totally screwed with his head, and he couldn't get enough of the feeling.

Her hands knotted in the back of his T-shirt. "Glad you guys are back safe."

"Glad it's done." He dropped his face, forcing her to meet his gaze. Her eyelashes fluttered, and he put heat into a kiss. Her mouth opened, and her tongue touched his, slow and sexy. Her lips on his were the definition of *welcome home*. "And I'm back here with you."

An angelic expression softened her features. "What'd you do?"

He shrugged. "Nothing worth talking about."

"Oh."

Despite all the lines he'd thrown down over his life and all the ease he normally found talking to women, this wasn't like that. The other night, he'd charged in and gotten in her face. Now he had no excuse, just a simple desire to hold her.

She sat down on the edge of her bed, nodding as though giving him permission to join her. It never occurred to him that this type of situation would be different than other interactions of the down-and-dirty variety. But now that he was here, not on a mission to get in her face or with a smooth line ready that could walk the pants right off her, he was almost ready to clown himself.

"What'd you do?" he asked.

"Read, mostly."

"What'd you read?"

She giggled. "Romances."

That caught him off guard, and he laughed with her. "Alright, then. Didn't see you as the Fabio type but—"

"No!" She laughed harder. "Not 1980s bodice rippers."

"I had no clue there are different types."

"Like the action-packed, supersteamy kind."

He rolled his lips together, amused and not sure he was ready to admit his curiosity about what made a book supersteamy. "What else did you get into?"

"There's drama in the village, but I don't know what about."

"Oh, yeah." He could've told her that and assumed she was prying for info, but he couldn't give it to her.

"Yup."

"And how do you know about that if you haven't been sitting in your window?"

She shrugged. "I may've sat in my window."

He shook his head. "Yeah, I bet."

"Probably nothing."

Shifting on the bed, she dropped her eyes as though she didn't know what they were there to do, and the truth was, he wasn't in a familiar spot either. "You came up to hang out?" she asked.

"Something like that."

She gave him the evil eye, half joking, half scowling. "To get some?"

"No—well, yeah, if that happens. But no, not why I came up here." He rubbed his hands over his face. "Shit."

"What?"

Javier pulled his hands away. "You're beautiful, Soph. You're sweet and unlike anyone I've hung out with."

"Oh, um—"

"I always have the right thing to say, but with you… there's something that throws me off my game."

She blinked, innocent eyes widening in surprise. "You don't have to have game with me, Javier."

Only a few inches separated them on the bed. He needed to respond, but instead, he simply studied the slope of her cheeks, the grace of her neck. He knew what she tasted like and what she screwed like, and he wanted more of that and the simple truths of statements like there didn't have to be game. With her, it wasn't a woman in a bar dying to go home with him and just having fun. It wasn't taking his pick from the groupies that stalked the dark corners of the underground to nab themselves a battle-hardened street fighter for the night.

He scooted closer, scooping his arm around her side to move her next to him. Instead of kissing her, he palmed her cheek, swiping his thumb to her lips and back up again.

"I'm just me," she whispered against his thumb. "I think we met under... very honest, raw circumstances."

Javier had had nothing but cold revenge in his heart that day. He hadn't been able to breathe for the disappointment until Sophia walked in and caught him in the middle of dejection. And she'd hugged him. *She* hugged him—the girl who had a shittier day—and at that moment, he felt warmth. Her smile, the sound of her voice, and the carefulness of her touch had made everything right.

"I wasn't honest with you, Sophia." His throat stung, not wanting this to end. "Your brother told me not to go near you."

She pulled him into her arms, and unready for that reaction, he tensed until he breathed in her lavender scent and absorbed the tenderness in her hug.

"Javier." She pulled back enough to kiss him, doing so harder than he expected and hungrier, too. "When my lips are on yours, everything is okay."

Yes. It was true. He kissed her back as he laid her down, threading his hands into her hair. This wasn't even about fucking her but was just the relief that ran through him when she said shit like that. He felt the same calm after getting new ink or after walking away, in the quiet night, as the winner of a bare-knuckle brawl.

They kissed and then stopped and stared until her eyes started to drift.

Their fingers were tangled together, and he shifted to give her his bicep as a pillow.

"I grew up too fast. And angry," he said while staring at her ceiling. "I'm good at what I do, but Colin is a marine just like our team leader. US Marine. Grayson, American Army. Ryder, Australian Special Forces. But I'm foreign. I'm a fighter. I'm just… deadly."

She didn't move. "You also have a good heart."

He blew out a breath, not believing that he was mentioning any of this. "Probably not."

She pivoted to her side, and her hair brushed his skin. "Why do you say that?"

"I want to hurt someone. A group of somebodies. They hurt my sister, and I want to hurt them back. I want blood."

They stared forever, and he was sure this was the moment that sweet, innocent Sophia would kiss his cheek then kick him out.

"I'm sorry for whatever happened to your sister."

And…? But nothing more came. He chewed the inside of his mouth then picked up his arm and pointed to the scrolling letters. *Revenge.*

Sophia glanced at what he showed her. "I hope you get it."

He wrapped the arm inked in a promise for blood around the most understanding woman he'd ever met and didn't want to let go.

CHAPTER FIFTEEN

J AVIER WOKE UP with his arms still holding Sophia. Hours had passed, and he'd never let her go. He checked his watch and listened to his stomach remind him he'd skipped dinner. Food would be available by now, but instead of sating that need, he turned to his priority.

Trailing his fingers over the edge of the comforter, he brushed strands of hair away from her sleeping face. "Morning, Soph."

She stirred and snuggled close. Warmth that had nothing to do with the blankets or her body ran through his blood. She warmed his heart and his insides. She brought a smile to his face without lifting a finger.

Javier kissed her cheek. "Paixão."

Her sleepy smile broke before her eyes opened. "Good morning, baby."

Yeah, he liked that word on her tongue—almost as much as he liked his tongue on hers. She stretched, still not opening her eyes, and he couldn't resist. Javier pressed his lips to her startled ones and kissed her awake. A raspy growl purred through his lips, and Sophia's chin tilted as she kissed him back.

"I like waking up in your arms," she whispered, curling hers around his neck. "I like this more than I should." She rolled into him, pressing their torsos together and locking an ankle behind his knee. "Way, way more than I should."

"You start that," he murmured, "and we might miss breakfast."

"I'll make sure you get lunch." She loosened her grip around his neck and tugged the back of his shirt up.

"Didn't you promise I'd get breakfast?" He pulled the shirt from his arm then turned his attention to her. With a quick slide up her sides, he had her topless as her shirt landed on the floor with his.

"Make it fast."

"Challenging me first thing in the morning. Seems you have a few lessons to learn." One arm grabbed her, the other did away with her bottoms, and he had her naked. "Pretty sure that's a record."

"Note to self: get what I want by just asking." Sophia's honey-brown hair fanned on the pillow. Her legs were long and her skin a milky cream color, contrasting to the darkness of his. Her curves made his hands want to trace her limb to limb, and the sweetheart pout of lips that were kissed swollen made him harder than he'd been in his life.

"Crazy, it being that simple, huh?" He winked but kept his eyes locked on her as he bent to her thigh, kissing her hip bone. "Spread your legs wider for me, Soph."

Her breath caught, and she gave a slight nod as she obeyed.

"Good girl." Javier let his thumb massage her clit, gently dragging his knuckles across her folds, but all the while, he watched her face. What did she like, what did she do? She was like an adventure; everything he tried elicited a new reaction.

"You're staring," she whispered.

"I know."

"I'm naked."

He smiled. "Which is why I'm staring."

"Take off your pants, Javier."

"You're just using me for sex." He delved his fingers into her pussy. "You like it nice and slow."

"Yes."

"I like what you like, Sophia."

"I like that accent. Keep talking while you strip."

"Bossy and beautiful." He maneuvered to do as ordered, snagging a condom from his wallet. Once, then twice with Sophia hadn't been enough, and he knew the third time wouldn't be the charm. But he didn't care. He tore the packet open and slid the condom down his aching shaft.

She straddled him, her full breasts swaying with the move. With sexy confidence like that, Javier didn't care if he came back for fourths or fifths. Though they'd have to scavenge the embassy for protection.

His eyes sank shut as Sophia slid her tightness down. "Paixão."

"Javier?"

He blinked and focused. "Yeah?"

"What does that mean?" Her jaw hung, and her eyelashes fluttered. "Tell me."

"Soon." He didn't want her to know. He wanted it to be his secret, how he felt. Why he'd used it on her since day one, he had no idea. It rolled off his tongue and fit. "Promise."

"Promise." She leaned forward, tilting her hips. The change was like a stroke, but he didn't dare move until she said yes. She caught his lips, dragging a kiss across his cheek where her tongue teased his ear. With that, he draped one arm around her waist and placed a hand at the back of her head and thrust into her.

Her back arched into his hold. "God, yes."

He did it again, and she pushed back.

"More." Sophia worked her hips and rode his cock. The deeper he went, the tighter she felt, the more her teeth scraped his neck and his shoulder. A moan that he thought would never end started as he held her bucking body to his. Her teeth latched onto him, and his climax roared through him as the sweetest thing he'd ever held cursed and bit his skin.

She collapsed on him, and his arms went slack, still holding her. Her pussy muscles clenched and released, rippling over his shaft. They were out of breath; sweat kissed their skin. His mind was spent, and they hadn't even left the bed. Javier didn't want the morning to start, because eventually the day would end. Time would pass, and he'd be gone, doing what he was supposed to do. What he lived for. But with her in his arms… he only wanted to stay.

"I'm starving," she said into his neck.

He squeezed her tight, ignoring his confusion. "Me too. Let's go grab grub."

And with that, they stood up and dressed. He snagged her hand, and they followed the scent of brewing coffee.

WALKING HAND IN hand into the dining room wasn't the smartest move. Her bosses wouldn't give two hoots, but Janella, on the other hand, looked ready to have a coronary.

"Oh, Lordy. We've got hand holding."

Nothing was sacred. Of course, Janny would narrate to the room. Thank God they were the only ones there. Still, Sophia's cheeks caught fire. She planned to give Janny an earful later.

"Good morning, Janny." Her warning voice was low but didn't wash away any of her friend's amusement.

Janella stepped close, eyed Javier, then smiled at Sophia. "Good morning to you, little miss nothing's gonna happen, he wants my ass back in Pennsylvania."

"Janella!"

But Javier squeezed her hand before letting it go to grab a breakfast plate. "I don't want her in Honduras. No secret there."

"I've heard you're sweet." Janella batted her eyelashes at him in the most obvious, annoying of ways.

"Janny!" Sophia snipped.

Javier turned to her, tucking her under him in a protective agreement masked with a playful tease. "I'm sweet? Yeah?"

Sophia stuttered to respond as Janella continued. "And *I* like the way you talk. Pro column for that."

"Seriously." Sophia picked up a mug. "I'd like to make it through coffee, maybe even breakfast, without having to die from embarrassment."

Janella laughed as she headed from the dining room to the kitchen. Javier leaned into Sophia's ear. "Sweet?"

"When you're not being a jerk, maybe."

"I am sweet. To you."

His voice traveled straight down between her legs, and if she hadn't been so irritated at Janny, Sophia might've given up her own *Oh, Lordy*. "Whispering against my neck isn't fair."

"And the accent works for you?" he teased.

She turned on him, taking any excuse to be closer, batting his chest just to feel his warmth, and gave a deflecting smile made of saccharine and self-preservation. "We both know your accent is your secret weapon."

He tugged her close, kissing her neck with more tongue than she would've expected—even from him—in the middle of the embassy's formal, albeit empty, dining room. "No, gatinha. Secret weapon is my mouth."

Oh, Lordy. Oh, Lordy, Lordy, Lordy. He held her against him and kept his lips to her skin, working his way to the perfect spot at her hairline so that all she could do was tremble. "Okay, you win."

Another squeeze and a chaste kiss to counteract the serious tongue action on her neck, and he asked, "Coffee?"

"Um, yeah." Or a quick run to the room for another orgasm. Or both.

His eyes smoldered, intensifying as though he could read her mind. Which, at that point, he wouldn't have to do, because she was sure every thought and emotion was lit up on her face like a neon sign.

"Whatever you're thinking, Soph, don't forget it when I come back for you."

Melt. God, she was a puddle of woman. "Okay."

He laughed, kissed her cheek, and turned toward the buffet. "Let's get our grub on."

Janny came back, and from the other hallway poured the voices from Javier's teammates. They all eyed Sophia, but no one said a word other than a couple of curious hellos. Really, all four men were stupidly hot. How was it possible that they worked together? *Like there was a superheroes convention and they teamed up.*

Jensen and Brackster arrived, and when all their plates were piled high, Janella joined them. Delta could put away some food, which Sophia was sure pleased Janny to no end. But mostly, they ate in silence, and they must have shared some kind of commando joint look when they were done because they basically finished at the same time. The men deposited their plates on a tray despite Janny shooing them away, and Brock led their exit, followed by Grayson. But Ryder lagged, keeping an eye on Javier, who walked over and smacked a kiss on Sophia's cheek in the most sincere and sexy way possible.

Yeah, she was done. This was the kind of guy she wanted to hang onto.

"Later. Whatever that thought was, paixão, don't forget."

"Oh, Lordy," Janny whispered loudly enough that Ryder chuckled all low and manly then slapped Javier on the back as they walked out the door.

Sophia fell into the chair as though swooning so badly her legs couldn't support her gooey, mushy, Javier-soaked brain anymore. "Oh, Lordy."

"THAT WAS INTERESTING." Ryder gave Javier an eye as they geared up with the rest of the team.

"She's interesting."

"I bet she is." His Aussie accent dragged as he laughed.

"Shut your mouth, bro."

Grayson laughed, Brock grumbled, and Ryder didn't listen, mumbling, "What are you doing with her?"

"Nothing."

"Kissing her see-ya-later isn't nothing, friend."

"Christ." Brock grumbled. "Gear up, Ryder. Let's go."

Javier ran through his mental checklist. Working in Honduras was a crucial point in his search for the PC. Payback was the only thing he should focus on, the only thing to be hungry for. Yet as he checked his weapons and strapped them to his chest and thighs, his mind was on Sophia and how she would stay safe and what she was really doing in Honduras.

CHAPTER SIXTEEN

BORED AND READING her book, Sophia lounged on the couch as Ambassador Jensen walked into the multipurpose room. His brow was drawn, and his usually tightly cropped gray hair needed a trim. But other than that, he looked ready for business. "Sophia?"

She placed the e-reader in her lap, hopeful that he had an update. "Yes, sir?"

"Can I join you?" he murmured, sitting before she could speak.

Oh no. Bad news. "Of course."

He leaned back in the couch. "You've been here for several months now, right?"

She nodded. "About six."

"And in that time, we've had our share of... guests."

Oh. The awkward vibes of a father-daughter talk crept up her neck. This was embarrassing. "Yes."

"I know your father very well, and if I were him, I'd want to tell you to..." He shifted on the couch. "Not to get your feelings hurt."

Ambassador Jensen was trying to do her father a solid. She got it, but he didn't know her history with Javier, as off-the-wall as it might be. She swallowed an uncomfortable knot. "He's a friend of my brother. I... know him."

"Be that as it may." He cleared his throat. "They're here, and then they're gone. I think you've done a great job with Hana Ferrera and do not want you to lose your focus."

"Okay." What to say to that?

"But you're also young, and this post isn't where you stay for a long time in the prime of life. There's no telling how long Whispering Willow will last. Two weeks, ten months. Who knows?"

"Um, okay."

"What I'm trying to say is, make sure you're happy, but don't fall in love out here. It doesn't go anywhere, and if you were my daughter, I'd want you to know that."

God. Her head pounded. This conversation would never end. "Yes, sir."

"No *sir* needed right now." He shifted again. "And onto another topic, you're free to go back into the field. Unrest has quieted."

Even though Delta was still in the field? "What about the team that's here?"

"They're working on something outside the city. And what they do, if they can do it, will actually help our relations here while at the same time protecting what you're working on. Very circular. But if you want to go search out Hana, you can. Their ongoing operations will not commingle with yours. Publicly."

Sophia's heart jumped. Javier was still here and not going anywhere. At least not immediately. Realization smacked her sideways. She needed to quiet the reaction, tone it down. "Thank you."

"No thanks necessary. Just, as always, stay alert. I suppose you want to head out?"

Her grin might've reached her ears. "I'm itching to."

He nodded. "Safely."

"Of course." She hurried upstairs, dressed for the occasion, texted Hana to meet her for sushi, and waved to Janny on her way downstairs. Her phone buzzed with a reply from Hana, agreeing to meet in an hour. Perfect. She could get out, stretch her legs, grab some caffeine, and meander to dinner. Setting eyes on the city, not through her binoculars, always gave her a sense of calm. She might be in the murder capital of the world, but a quick look around showed a normal, bustling South American city.

As she crossed the lobby, Brackster rounded the corner, a cellphone pressed to his ear. "Sophia?"

She turned, ready to explain that Jensen had given her the A-OK to get out of the building. "Yes, sir?"

He pulled the phone away from his ear. "Have you—"

"Ambassador Jensen gave me leave to go."

His face twisted. "When?"

"Just now."

Scouring his face with one hand, he looked at his phone then her. "Just now?"

"Yes, sir."

"Stay close. Keep your phone on."

For all the good that did sometimes. Cell service wasn't a guarantee outside the building. "Is everything okay?"

He gave her the look that said his response was classified. Despite her work on Whispering Willow, she was still out of the loop on pretty much everything. "Should I stay in?"

A dry, heavy sigh blew through his lips. "I wouldn't speak against the ambassador's orders."

Right... something was going on. "I'll just be down the street."

His gray eyes narrowed, and again he did the face rub. Then he nodded, rejoining the call, mumbling a response as he headed upstairs.

Weird but not unheard-of. Just to be safe, Sophia revamped her plans. Instead of walking the endless loop of blocks, she'd hop on the bus that ran the avenue almost every ten minutes.

The reinforced door groaned as its foreboding, protective weight opened. She smiled at the RSO guards who stood post as she passed, and the heavy, armored door clanged shut behind her. Perfect timing: the bus was half a block away and slowed toward the stop. She jogged to the post as it drew near, and moments later, she pushed through the too-warm, overly packed bus crowd.

She settled into her seat, glancing out the window as Jensen pushed open the embassy's front door. The bus jolted forward, and she lost sight of the building. It was odd for the ambassador to walk out before his car had arrived. He certainly wasn't the type to ride the bus like staff might.

A twinge of uncertainty scratched at her senses. Did he look as though he were searching for someone, for *her*, instead of arriving before his driver did? Sophia pulled out her phone, hating the closeness of all the people on the jam-packed bus. No texts, no emails, no missed calls.

If someone from the embassy needed her, they didn't have to send the ambassador running after her.

Still… her parents hadn't raised a fool. Dad would appreciate the seat she'd chosen despite the at-capacity bus that insisted on hitting *every single* pothole. And her mom… what would she have appreciated? The smartness of her clothes—they didn't scream *Wealthy American; please kidnap me.* Sophia broadcast no tourist signs. So maybe her mom would appreciate that. Though the public transportation she wouldn't like so much.

Checking her phone again, Sophia tapped the pad of her finger on the smart phone's screen then tossed it into her bag as the bus neared her stop. She pulled the string and pushed through the overly warm crowd, even grunting without too much commotion when someone accidentally elbowed her on the way out.

Seriously. She shook off the icky feel of too many people in too closed a spot and hit the familiar path down a congested street. Shifting her purse from one shoulder to the other, an awkward awareness hung heavy on her shoulders. It was as though eyes were on her even though no one met her gaze. Her sixth sense rocketed into high gear in a way that she hadn't experienced in Honduras. The charged air crackled at the back of her neck, pin pricks of anticipation keeping her focused on constant surveillance.

Women looked away as she continued down Av. República de Mexico, and the men looked right through her. Whatever had had the city in a bustle for the past week was tainting the overpopulated community.

She stopped at a cafe for a coffee. Other patrons knew her. Some were poverty stricken, some aligned with the PC, but mostly, they were hard workers, raising their families and socializing with their neighbors. They were people who, over the last six months, she had come to chat with or say hi.

"*Querría un café Americano.*"

The barista nodded at her regular coffee order, and Sophia shoved her hand in her purse—her *empty* purse. Shit.

She snatched the bag down, pried it open. No wallet. No cell phone.

Nothing worth a cup of coffee. Damn it. *"Mantener mi pedido por favor."*

Her mind raced back to the bus and how diligent she was. On the bus… the man who'd elbowed her. It must have been a team, because he'd been in front of her. Apologizing. Taking her notice away from the weight of her purse…

Of all the dangers that she'd prepared for, of all the bad feelings and the weirdo juju that had her head turning somersaults, a pickpocket was *not* what had been her concern.

No phone. No money. No way to check in with the embassy or let Hana know she was running behind. It was pointless, but it was also a matter of self-preservation. Her ID, credit cards, and whatever cash she had were all gone. Visa and AmEx would handle any rogue charges, no problem, but she needed to call them. On what phone? And she needed a police report to go along with her stolen driver's license and work identification.

She shook her head, sighing, as the barista offered to cover her coffee for the day, and she turned as the cafe door's bell jingled. Finally. A splash of good luck. *"Disculpar?"* she said, politely getting his attention.

"Yes," the familiar policeman said in English.

Sophia took a calming breath. He knew English. This would be better than her futzing through intermediate language skills that were more effective for political-climate analysis and less so for reporting petty crimes. "My wallet and cell were taken from my purse. I need to file a report."

She needed to notify her cell carrier, too. There were lots of things to do. Okay. One step at a time. Police report first because he was in front of her, then track down Hana and use her phone to look up the credit card and cell phone numbers.

"Have a seat." He gestured to a small table and placed his order at the coffee bar. Two minutes later, he joined her and started the tedious process of filing a report for her stolen goods.

No, Sophia didn't remember faces.

Yes, she knew they'd likely never catch the guys—a team, she assumed.

Maybe it was a bad idea to report it first because as nice as this man was, he was slow, and all she could think about was how fast someone could order a warehouse full of appliances and electronics before her credit-card companies caught on.

A blaring car horn and then a second one stole her attention from the police officer. The jarring noises, longer than what could be expected in normal congestion, took the officer's attention too.

They both stared out the window. He shook his head, mumbling something. But she caught "PC."

PC? Her head tilted on its own accord as a stronger, more urgent voice came from the radio on his hip. It crackled, and she picked up words but was most struck by the immediacy of the policeman's tone, his mumbled *PC,* and his stiffening demeanor.

"What's going on?"

He shook his head. "I have what I need. You should follow up with your credit card and phone company." Standing, he closed his notebook and tore off a page from his carbon copy notebook, handing it to her. "*Gracias.*"

"Uh, okay. Thank you."

Without so much as a grin good-bye, the man had morphed from pleasant neighborhood friendly face to a no-nonsense brute ready to enforce the law. Whatever that particular law was.

Sophia wanted to follow him, more from nosiness and instinct than anything else, but the commotion was most likely a convenience-store robbery or dispute. Right? Or someone had died. That happened all the time.

But she was sure the car horns had to do with the Primeiro Comando. She needed to find Hana.

Sophia pushed out of the cafe, speed walking around the corner. A loud interruption of angry voices carried from what was a known PC breakfast and lunch spot that served *baliada*, *pastelitos*, and gossip. A small group of men were banded close, grousing and grumbling boisterously enough that despite walking down the street, eyes straight ahead, she could feel the tension leaching into her. No question. Something was going on with the PC.

In front of the sushi restaurant, Hana's chauffeured sedan waited. Or it should have been, would have been Hana's ride except for the disconcerting three men who leaned against it. Against Marco's wife's ride. Panic clutched Sophia's heart.

Between what she saw ahead and at the lunch hangout, unease crept deeper. She needed to talk to Hana. She really wanted to call her, but what option did she have? More men approached the sushi restaurant, the crowd growing at a concerning rate.

Her heel caught in a sidewalk crack, and she tripped forward, righting herself as she came face-to-face with the shopkeeper of a boutique Hana frequented. The woman jumped back as though Sophia radiated an infectious disease. Her eyes were wild and wide, and her mouth formed an O but no words came out.

"What's happening?" Sophia straightened her shirt, righting herself from the almost tumble as she pushed the pointless purse to her shoulder.

The shopkeeper gave her a painfully slow, panicked—no, scared—head shake as she stepped backward, bumping into the boutique's door.

"Please tell me." The air crackled with uncertainty, with foreboding. Sophia's skin prickled with an uneasiness she couldn't classify.

The woman paused, looked toward Hana's car, and then scanned across the street. "*Traidora.*"

"Traitor?" Her stomach sank as thick dread pushed heavily through her heart.

"Hana Ferrera." Her hand reached to the doorknob. "And you."

Oh no. If Hana's assistance to the US had been discovered, the PC would likely kill her. As the mob formed around the car and in the area where they were going to meet, Sophia picked up the pace, needing to get to Hana, needing to shut down rumors and play her part as an American aid worker.

Sophia picked up the pace, jogging to the group, which was growing louder with angry conversation. This was still in the gossipy stage of unknown whispers and guesses. The embassy could play this down. Couple that with the fact that an attack on Hana might as well be an attack on Marco, and they could defuse the unrest. Damn, she needed her phone more than ever. All she had to do was get inside and use the phone there—

talk to Hana and find out exactly what the hell was going on.

The front door to the sushi spot was a few feet away, and Sophia pushed into the tight group. Angry jeers encircled her. Specifically. Shit, how much did they think they knew? Sophia didn't know their exact words, between the pace at which they flew and the anger behind them, but the intention was clear.

As she pushed harder toward the door, there stood Hana, tears streaking down her face. She wasn't inside? Where was her driver?

A man Sophia didn't recognize shouted into Hana's face. *Traitor. The United States.* Those were the words that stuck out.

Shit. This was a bigger issue than Sophia realized, and the crowd became thicker with each second. Across the street, police cruisers sat—doing nothing—and Sophia needed to get Hana inside or to the police car.

"Stop! You're scaring her!" But as she looked to each face, she realized that was their aim: to humiliate her. Hurt her. An eerie voice in Sophia's head said no, it was more like they wanted to *kill* her. "No! Don't do this!"

A large man grabbed her arm, pulling him to his chest. His elbow trapped her in a throat hold, and his voice rang in her ears. "The American!"

That got Hana's attention, her hands reaching toward Sophia, shaking her head, shouting "No," proclaiming a misunderstanding.

The scent of perspiration and anger loomed in the area. Sophia was jostled, and vitriol-lobbing men pushed her toward Hana as their heated taunts surrounded her. Sophia gritted her teeth together, dragged into the melee, to the front of the circle, and her heart shredded as she was thrown toward Hana. *The traitor and the American.*

Her mother's disappointed face flashed in her head, cold chills of terror running down her arms and spine. Sophia had failed.

She'd failed Hana. Her country. Her parents. Herself.

And she was going to die for it.

CHAPTER SEVENTEEN

One Hour Earlier

"I'M SORRY. *WHAT?*" Javier's arms hung numb as he tried to wrap his head around the words their team leader had said in perfect English. It could've been perfect Portuguese or Spanish, languages he understood perfectly, and Javier still would have needed the repeat.

Brock's forehead pinched, a mixture of annoyance and understanding clouding his eyes. "Jensen can't get ahold of Sophia. Whispering Willow—and a shit ton of other classified operations—have been compromised. Classified documents were leaked online, and they've gone viral. Her name and contact have been publicly identified."

"I thought she was an aid worker." Ryder stepped forward.

Brock grumbled. "Guess she's not."

The steady pounding of his heart echoed in his ears. Processing straight facts wouldn't compute. This wasn't like a normal op. It wasn't even like being thrown into a street fight where he had little intel on his opponent nor a surefire map to victory. The unknown was terrifying, and Javier couldn't remember feeling like this ever before.

"Sophia's *missing*," he murmured. "And working on Whispering Willow, which has been compromised."

Brock nodded.

"*What* exactly is Whispering Willow?"

Their team leader's jaw flexed, restraint and resolve as evident as aggravation in his demeanor. "Whispering Willow has been classified as *need to know*. Which we don't know."

Motherfucker. A growl began in Javier's chest, quietly seeping through his grinding teeth. "Okay."

Brock pushed his sleeves up to the elbow. "What we do know: Sophia was on her way to meet Hana Ferrera. As you're probably familiar with the name, she's the wife of Marco Ferrera."

What? "How is this need-to-know, and we *don't* need to know what she was working on?"

"Not my call, Brazil."

Ryder slapped Javier on the back, a cue that he needed to take it down a couple hundred notches. Brock wasn't the bad guy. He was working off what they had, which wasn't much. But Delta didn't need much. Give them a high-value target and a general idea of where in the world it was, and they would find it.

But the target was Sophia? And within a few miles of his location? It was as if he couldn't have enough intel to make the operations happen swiftly or surely enough. Couple that with anything PC related, and his mind was spiraling, hungry to destroy those assholes.

And Sophia was working on something with the PC? How did he not know that shit?

Brock's phone chirped, and the team waited, agitated that Colin's little sister, that his... interest had become the focus of their work. Brock listened and made notes, requesting coordinates as Javier prayed to get to her.

"Roger that." Brock dropped his phone back into the holster. "Titan's HQ pinpointed her cell phone and credit cards. They're running a mile a minute, likely stolen. They've got suspicious activity near Calle República de Ecuador, police and PC both on scene, locals doing what locals do."

Fuck. What locals did was let mob law take place whether the police were there or not. "So we go?"

"We have to," Ryder added.

Brock nodded. "Hostile urban environment. But yeah, we go. Sophia Cole will be back to the embassy, safe. No alternative."

No shit. With locations and a working plan of attack, they loaded into the vehicle and sent gravel spinning as they headed west with Ryder at the wheel, Brock riding shotgun.

Grayson watched Javier in the backseat as though he could read his mind.

"What?" Tension pushed through Javier's veins with each eager breath.

"She's fine. She's a Cole. Smart."

His fists bunched. "Yeah, I know. She's also in a lynch mob that we have crap for intel on."

Gray nodded. "Which is why she has us."

It was Javier's turn to nod. Anxiety was unfamiliar and clouded his thoughts, but there was no time for that. It wasn't who he was or what made him good at his job. Javier turned off the emotion, returning to ground zero of the cold, emotionless epicenter he had for a heart—a heart that noticeably still pounded.

He flexed his fists, bunching and cracking knuckles in silence as they pulled closer.

Brock turned as Ryder began to negotiate the traffic, honing in on the danger zone. "You good, Brazil?"

"Yeah, of course."

"She's important. We get that. It will be fine. Just keep your head on straight."

"Straight as a motherfucker. No one else could be more calm."

Brock gave a nod that said *bullshit*. "Whatever you say."

Ryder stopped and slammed into park. Their earpieces were in and comm equipment checked. Javier was the first one out. One, two, three, four doors opened and slammed. The men swept the streets and identified their target. They were armed to the teeth and looking like a Hollywood action movie, strapped with an arsenal and wearing clothes that showed they were no strangers to blood or war. Delta walked en force toward the center of a PC hurricane, focused only on Sophia and not on a single goddamn Primeiro Comando piece of trafficking shit.

PARKER BLACK'S WORDS crackled. "Got you on sat feed. Looks like tangoes have clued in to who she is."

"Roger that," Brock replied.

Who she is... Parker hadn't meant to disturb Javier's thoughts, scoring terror into his soul. But it was there. Her cover was likely blown. Some major world fallout was happening across the globe, and his girl was trapped in the middle.

"How deep's the shit she's in, mate?" Ryder mumbled as Brock pointed to them to fan around the unaware crowd.

"Deep, brother. Get. Her. Out."

Fuck. *Deep.* Definitely, that word would haunt him—maybe for the rest of his life. The ache, the panic, and the pure, 100 percent need to get to Sophia made him faster, smarter, and more ready to kill than he'd been in his life.

The small crowd pulsed with angry energy. He understood every harsh, deadly word directed at Sophia and Hana.

Javier got the go from Brock and pushed hard toward the humid, sweat-stinking center, finally setting eyes on both women. One attractive brunette was pressed against the wall, the barrel of a 9mm pushed into the soft spot under her jaw, and then there was Sophia: strong, angry, scared, and trying to protect her point of contact more than herself.

What he'd known of her was soft and delicate, hidden and unsteady. But here she was, putting herself at risk for a woman she didn't really know and a cause that she might not understand. She might deal with the ins and outs of the PC world, but Sophia didn't know what they were capable of outside of headlines and safety reports.

With complete tunnel vision, Javier went in strong, knocking jeering men aside as though they were weightless obstacles. Ryder moved in the corner of Javier's peripheral vision with more finesse. Grayson did the same from the other side. But Javier was on a mission: get to Sophia, removing any obstacle in his path.

Voices surrounded him. But their directed shouts were simply white noise. He focused on her, connecting his eyes to hers. Sophia Cole was the only thing worth focusing on in this angry melee of PC supporters that he otherwise might want to destroy.

Their eyes locked. Awareness dawned on her face. He was her savior in the surrounding hell. "Coming for you," he said.

She likely couldn't hear him and didn't smile. But her fight stalled as though she knew he was there to protect her from trafficking scum.

Sophia jolted, pushed from the side into Hana. As much as he didn't want to care about this ally, he had to. Hana was important to the Americans. Important to somebody. She had to be saved from the business end of the barrel under her chin whether Javier could find it in his heart to agree or not.

Ryder came broadside from the right, ripping the gun from the man's grip and disarming the asshole before he saw it coming. Javier let his fist fly into Hana's aggressor. Damn, it felt good to throw the left hook—the impact, the power, and the gutted, unexpected sound of defeat. Adrenaline surged in Javier's blood as he took a breath, embracing the high of the hit, and only then was he able to turn to Sophia. Like a junkie, he'd had to get his fix before rescuing her. He didn't even know he was craving it. But she as much threw herself to him as he grabbed her, and damn again, having her in his arms was better than a punch to a PC piece of shit.

"Target acquired," Gray said loud and clear through Javier's earpiece. "Hana Ferrera too."

What else were they going to do—leave the woman to die by a criminal mob because she'd helped the United States?

Javier needed to interrogate her to know what she and Sophia had worked on. But with Sophia clinging to his body, all that could wait. The world could hang tight so long as he held her close. His hold wouldn't last nearly long enough, and he couldn't explain the desperation in it, but for now, he'd savor it.

Grayson ran crowd interference. Ryder had Hana, and Brock ordered them to get a move on.

"Javier. God. Thank you."

Holding Sophia's weight soothed a rip in his chest he hadn't realized was tearing. Between the exasperated, horrified tears and her hands gripping his chest, he wanted to kiss her calm. "Take a breath, paixão. You're okay."

"It happened so fast. I don't know what it was, but God, thank you."

A man faced down Javier. The anger emanating from Javier and the growl that promised a painful encounter made his potential combatant step aside. "Anything for you."

He saw a glass bottle flying toward them out of the corner of his eye. Javier hunched over Sophia, turning as it hit his shoulder with a heavy impact. *Freaking mob law right now.* The police were meters away. *This* was why the PC had to go down and why Honduras had the reputation it did.

The bottle shattered at his heels when it hit the sidewalk. More bottles bumped and bruised them.

"What is wrong with people?" It was less a question and more exasperation. Whatever Sophia had done to earn this job, she'd likely never been the center of a throng of angry criminals.

"Just—why?" Fright scratched her words, and fear made her hiss rhetorical questions that he had no answer for.

"It's over now," he murmured, cradling her like a baby as they pushed through the last ring of the crowd, his lips brushing her temple. "I've got you."

He knew every calming word said to her was broadcast by his mic, but some things didn't matter.

"Those *assholes*." Her snap was muffled with the sniffle of tears. Her bravery was fast fading, and the shock of it all was hitting with brutal force. One second, Sophia was thankful, and the next, she gripped him, sobbing into his shoulder as he carried her away from hostiles, giving no fucks that she could get down and walk on her own.

"God, Javier." Her voice cracked, and he held her tighter.

"The world is ugly, Soph." It was the only thing he could offer, because he wasn't in the right frame of mind to acknowledge her risks and the worthiness of her being in danger, or school her on how miserable the world really was. He could teach a class on that, the PC, and how the two were intertwined. But now he just had to hang on to her. Revenge for this, just like for his sister, would come later.

"I hate this place sometimes," she whispered into his chest.

"Me too." *Not for the same reasons, but still.* Hatred had grown where his heart should've been.

The earpiece crackled. Brock gave Ryder directions for how to handle Hana. She was to go to a different location. Who or where Hana would be protected by wasn't Javier's interest. Sophia would flip—he'd bet on it—but returning her to US territory, to the protection of the embassy's sovereign ground, was his top priority.

Grayson flanked him as they rounded a corner. There was their ride. Brock manned the driver's seat, and in one smooth move, Gray opened the back door for Javier and Sophia then jumped in behind. Brock hit the gas, pulling a U-ie in the middle of the road. Ryder appeared, hustling down the sidewalk sans Hana, and jumped into the front passenger seat as Brock slowed enough to make it happen.

"Wait." Sophia stiffened against Javier. "Where's Hana?"

"Safe," Brock replied, not turning his head and turning down a side street.

"*Where* is she?"

Javier squeezed his arm around her, hoping to calm her down. Hana could be in any number of places: in a safe house, with an auxiliary team, or with a friend or ally. Delta wasn't going to let her die by the hands of a street mob, but that didn't mean Hana and Sophia were afforded the same protections.

"She's safe, Soph."

"I need to talk to her."

"Later."

Tense seconds hung in the air until her shoulders sank. "What in the hell happened to cause all this?"

"Don't know much," Javier mumbled. "Leaks move fast in an electronic world."

"We were outed?" Her gaze shifted from him to Grayson. "Well, obviously. Okay." She took a deep breath then slammed her hands into her hair, hunching over and groaning. "Damn it! Damn it."

He let a hand rest on her back, wishing there was a better way to offer comfort.

"No." She shook her head. "You don't understand. They're going to *kill* her. And I failed." Sophia's head snapped up, and her eyes locked to his. "I *failed.*"

"No. I promise."

She shook her head, dropping it again, burying her fists into her eyes, and tried to hide the sniffle. Whether this round of emotion was fueled by anger at the world or anger with herself, he didn't care.

"All I do is let her down."

"Hana? There's no way she's blaming you for this." It was clear that if the intelligence breach were Sophia's fault or if she wasn't strong enough for the job, she wouldn't be in the field with an asset of Hana's caliber.

"No. Not Hana." The smallness in her voice shook the car. "My mother."

JAVIER TOOK SOPHIA'S hand and exited the vehicle. He tucked her in front of him while Gray and Ryder flanked, Brock leading their charge to safety inside the embassy.

The guarded doors swung open, their arrival expected. Brackster and Jensen waited in the lobby, both of their faces tight with remorse, but it was Sophia's disappointed voice that offered apologies.

"Nonsense," the ambassador said, but Janella took over the situation.

"Upstairs." She bustled through the pack of suits and soldiers. "Unless it's a matter of international security, this girl is coming with me."

Air conditioning rolled over Javier's skin as he took a step, uneasy to have someone pulling his girl from his chest.

"Are you alright?" Janella's worried pitch sounded like the way his insides hurt. "Is she alright?" she asked him, not waiting for Sophia to answer.

Javier grumbled. "Too close."

Grayson and Ryder peeled off as Javier stuck with Sophia and Janella.

"Report in later," Brock ordered, following Gray.

Javier nodded but never slowed as he and Janella shuffled a silent Sophia toward her bedroom suite.

Janny opened the door and stood back, letting Javier lead Sophia in. Sophia shrugged out of his hold and made for her bed, crawling on top of the covers, a desolated emptiness haunting her eyes. "They're going to kill Hana."

"Focus on you right now."

Janella nodded, taking a throw blanket off the chair and tossing it over Sophia. "What hurts on you? Did they touch you?" She turned to him, one eyebrow cocked high.

He shook his head. No, they hadn't hurt her physically. But she'd been touched in a way that was certain to change her. Fuck the PC for that. One more reason to make his hatred for them grow.

"Everything hurts, Janny," Sophia said. And then the devastating reality of this fucked-up part of the world took over. Sniffles and tears wracked her.

Javier perched on the floor to stay eye level with her pillow as Janny moved to the opposite side of the bed and rubbed her back in silence. Together, they let her cry until she had nothing left.

CHAPTER EIGHTEEN

JAVIER PERCHED ON the edge of the chair while Sophia slept. After she cried, he'd let her drift away. Janella had slipped out quietly, leaving him to watch her tear-stained face. Her tangled hair sprawled against the plain pillow, and her pink lips were cracked as though she had nervously bitten the bottom one.

Even after she slept, the tear-stained marks remained as a reminder that she'd been terrified and he'd almost been too late.

What if he hadn't been there at all? But he had, and—

Sophia's eyelashes fluttered, and her hands slowly lifted to press her temples. A tiny whimper left her lips as she woke. "Hey."

Her scratchy voice was too quiet, and he knew by the worry in her gaze that she was thinking about the ugly side of life that she'd witnessed.

"Hey, you."

A half smile flickered. "I don't want to be here."

"Paixão, I don't want you here either."

She closed her eyes and rolled to her back, stretching her legs then tugging up the blanket. Her face tilted toward him. "Do you know what happened to Hana?"

He sighed. "A lot happened today. There wasn't just a leak about your work with her. It's more global than that."

"Is she okay?"

Javier nodded.

"And protected?"

He nodded again. "Yes."

"Good. That's important."

"Jensen's itching to talk to you, but I'd say Whispering Willow is done."

Her mouth parted. "You know about that?"

Javier shook his head. "No. Just that you are more than an aid worker, and she's part of the problem."

"Opposite, really." Sophia sat up, leaning against the headboard and tucking the blanket over her knees. "It's important we get back to work."

"If your op is done, won't you head home?"

"I want to stay."

His chest cranked tight. "Sophia…" Now wasn't the time to wage this battle, and she might not have the stamina to put up with it. But Sophia on a job in Honduras, doing more than humanitarian aid or fluff? That didn't sit with him well. "Talk to Jensen, and deal with that later."

"I guess." Her fingers fidgeted with the edge of the blanket. Beautiful brown eyes jumped to him then away, then back again. "So."

"So."

Her eyebrows went up. "I…" Brows dropped, but her shoulders went up instead, shrugging. "I don't know."

"What do you need, Sophia?"

"I need…" She straightened her posture, smoothing her hair as though suddenly aware that she looked as though she'd been dragged through a mob. "A shower."

"You'll be okay to do that? We didn't talk yet, but you didn't hit your head or anything, right?"

"Right."

"Okay, give me a minute." He pushed off the chair, muscles aching from his hours-long watch, and walked to the attached bathroom. With a quick look around, he turned on the shower to let it warm up and returned. "It's steaming up. I'll be out here just in case."

"I'm fine. But—"

"Give me this. I'm not trying to make a move. Just worried. Okay?"

Her eyes went wide.

"Let me be here to make sure you're okay."

"Javier—"

"I guess I could wait outside, or really just come back, so—"

"Join me."

Oh. Damn. A dozen thoughts rushed. Most notably, he didn't have a condom, nor did he want to screw her as much as he wanted to hold her, naked against him, and reassure himself over and over that she was safe.

"Please?"

"God, you don't have to say please, *tesão*."

"One, two, three; we take off our shirts."

He laughed and stripped it off before she could say another word.

"Cheater," she said.

"Overachiever."

Finally, a smile. A real one. God, it felt good to see such an unguarded moment.

"Okay, overachiever. I'll give you that."

He laughed, taking a step closer. "Do *you* need a countdown?"

"No." Her eyes raked across his chest. He'd had more than his share of females eyeball-fuck him over the years, but her focus was different—less on him and more on what he'd inked on his body. "Do they all mean something?"

He nodded.

"Maybe you'll tell me sometime."

Maybe he would share his secrets. Of course he would. Most of them. He nodded again.

"You sure about that? Looks like I just asked for your firstborn."

"For you, yes." He took her small hand in his, appreciating the delicate softness that he remembered from their first night together. How long had he appreciated her from afar? So many times, he'd thought she would be this gentle, this giving, yet remain fierce.

"Thanks." She leaned against him, her shirt still in place, and Javier wrapped an arm around her back. Their eyes held one another as their bodies did. He could feel her breathe, see her pupils react, and absolutely sense that she felt what he did.

With no words to share, he walked her into the small, steamy bathroom and shut the door. The humid warmth engulfed them, and he took the hem of her shirt in hand. "One, two—"

"Three."

"Three." Javier lifted it over her head and dropped it to the floor. Underneath that plain-Jane shirt was heaven. Her curves made his mouth water, and the curve of her neck made him groan. Javier stepped close, resting his palms on her bare shoulders and letting them drift down her biceps. Soft skin; strong woman. Not fragile or frail but the very definition of beauty. He breathed her in, and the faded scent of her shampoo pulled him closer. Forget that she'd been through hell that day—he couldn't wait to comfort her and hear her sound the way he felt.

His lips touched her neck, his tongue sliding along in a wet kiss. And she did moan, that simple, perfect noise that made his erection stand and reach for her. Javier flicked her earlobe with his tongue. He tugged it with his teeth. Sophia stepped closer, her hands firmly on his stomach, searching and gripping, scratching and exploring. When her fingernails flexed into his skin, he breathed softly into the shell of her ear. "I promise you."

"Hmm?" she purred, letting him nuzzle her neck.

Javier went back to her ear. "The only thing you'll remember about today is how you're about to feel."

She sank against him, nodding. "I'd like that."

His hands went down, tangling their fingers together. He squeezed their handhold, kissed her neck, and smoothed his palms up her back to the strap of her bra. Sliding it from her, Javier held her out, memorizing the sheer sexiness, the absolute perfection that stood in front of him. There was never a woman he'd dreamt of more than her. "God, you are beautiful."

She blushed and turned her head, but he caught her chin and directed her to face him again.

"Beautiful."

Her eyes brimmed, but she blinked it away. "Thank you."

His palms ran lightly down her arms, over the hairs that stood on end and the goose bumps that appeared despite the steamy warmth. Then they rested on the waist of her pants. His fingertips drifted from her side and across her stomach as she sighed, shutting her eyes.

"Like when you make that noise."

"I like everything about you." She let her head hang back as though it lolled on its own.

"Good." He unfastened the button. "Eyes on me."

Sophia languidly rolled her head back, but her eyes were a dark contrast to the lazy move. They were on fire. Just like he was.

"Good girl."

"Mmm."

Javier smoothed his knuckles from the loose-hanging pants over her stomach. Her skin prickled under his touch, and Sophia swayed ever so slightly into him.

"That noise too."

"Promise I'll come up with some new ones to make for you."

He laughed—actually, from the bottom of his soul, *laughed*. And so did she. That was the thing about her that no other woman had. Yeah, she was sexy, but she had more... dimension to her. Sex wasn't just sex. It was for her, and him, to get those sounds, those sighs and whispers. That could keep him wanting her again and again.

He didn't do things like that. Just like he never fell asleep with a woman. Or put a woman's safety ahead of his PC intentions.

Her hand covered his on her stomach, pushing south. He took the cue and took charge, lowering the zipper and sliding them down along with her panties.

"You got me naked, Javier." A playful smile tugged on her mouth. "What are you going to do about it?"

"Killing me." Taking her hand, he jerked her close. "One second sweet, the next, not so."

"I'm a puzzle."

No kidding. At the moment, they both were. He turned her head to lightly kiss her temple then kissed her lips, sliding his tongue down her neck. "I'll enjoy figuring you out."

"Out of your pants, baby."

He laughed. Again. "Bossy."

Then he ditched the pants and pulled her into the hot stream of the shower. Sophia wrapped her arms around his neck, pulling herself close to kiss him. It was more like a charge than a kiss. Her mouth opened to his, her tongue lashing, and their hunger bled together. His hands skimmed her water-slicked body. The pert tips of her breasts brushed his chest.

Sophia arched against the water, letting her lips hover as her dripping eyelashes fluttered with his. "We feel good together."

Amen, they did. Such a natural connection. Brushing her hair away from his target zone, he focused on kissing the neck that would be his undoing.

"That feels even better," she murmured and wriggled.

Again, he agreed, his erection pressing between them. Their bodies clung together as water fell. His palms roamed her wet back, smoothing up and down, cupping and squeezing her ass. *Cristo*, making love to this woman felt right.

"I'm starting to forget about today." She dropped her head back.

"Just what I'd thought."

"Yes," she breathed.

"Now, my plan." He turned his attention to her chest, massaging her perked breasts and gently rubbing the nipples that colored his fantasies.

"I like the way you think. Everything about you…"

"You—" He nipped at her neck. "Too." Everything except her job. He liked what she thought and how she reacted, how she seemed quiet, almost shy sometimes, but in the bedroom or in front of someone who needed help, she roared to life. He liked the sounds she made when she came, and he loved the way she said *baby* and watched him when he was intent on diving into her pants.

Sophia moaned for more.

"There are so many things to like about you, paixão. Too many to count." His stubble-covered cheek brushed under her jaw as he went for her ear, and Sophia whimpered, almost buckling into him. "You like that, huh?"

"Uh-huh. Yes. Please."

"Good to know." He was making a mental checklist of what got her going, even though he was probably leaving the next day. If only tomorrow would never come and they could stay hidden in this room. Maybe one day in the future everything would be different.

But then he'd fail his Delta team and his sister. He'd give up on his life's mission—to destroy the PC—and where would that leave him? With nothing. No purpose. Or a lost, abandoned purpose—

"Hey, you okay?" Sophia inched back.

He blinked, brought back to the moment. No. He wasn't okay. "Of course, why?"

"You growled or something." She bit her lip. "I think."

He didn't want to leave Sophia. Simple. Didn't want to abandon his goals over just a girl. But he'd be stupid to call Sophia just a girl when she was anything but that. "It was nothing."

To distract her—and him—he slipped his hand between her legs and listened to her gasp as he circled her clit, sliding deep to stroke into her pussy. When he added a second finger, her pant turned to a groan. She rocked against his palm. "Such a good girl, *coração*."

He kissed her neck, leaning to her breast, and ran his tongue against her dark-pink, pebbled nipple. So sweet and beautiful. She arched when he sucked, riding his hand as he dropped to his knees.

"Javier."

He hushed her, kissing her stomach and moving his hands to her hips, on a mission to taste her. She backed against the shower wall, hands splayed against the tiles as though she needed to grip them. He kissed her mound, nuzzling his chin against her folds. She arched her back, and he flicked his tongue against her. Water streamed over them as he urged her legs wider, lapping against her seam. Javier put a hand on her ass cheek and tossed her opposite leg over his shoulder. "Paixão."

"What does that mean?" She moaned, flexing her hips.

"Just a word that makes me think of you." It meant passion. Everything about her was passionate in some way—from how she tasted to how she fucked to why he wanted to spend the night wrapped in her arms, her body safe against his.

"God." Her hands left the wall and knotted in his hair.

Javier thrust his tongue inside her body and worked her clit with his fingertips. She bucked against him and rode his kisses as if she might die if she stopped.

"Please... Javier." She moaned and moved. Gasping, her words were lost in the cascading fall of the shower. Making her beg—that was his paradise. Sweet God, never let her stop.

Sophia's leg clamped on his back, and she pulled her other leg onto his shoulders. His forearm supported her weight. Her tightening orgasm started on his tongue. She moaned and thrashed, and he owned every sound, every ripple of her sweetness until she clawed into his hair, bucking against his mouth, and promised it was the world's greatest orgasm.

Damn. He was done for this *gatinha*.

THE HUM IN Sophia's head rivaled the most intense fall she'd ever had. Her mind blanked, her muscles relaxed, and the soothing massage of hot water, mixed with Javier's dangerously careful lips, gently ran across the inside of her thigh. "Spent" didn't begin to describe her state of mind.

"Hungry" did. She was hungry for him, for this, them, together.

Sex was sex. Except with him, it was like *whoa*. It wasn't just another level of amazing; it was as though he redefined the galaxy of her understanding. The man's tongue was intense and everything she wanted and needed and craved—all with him on his knees in front of her.

Despite the hold he had on her, Javier dominated from the floor. But there wasn't a question of who was in charge, of who made her feel this way.

Sophia wanted to thank him, to promise him the world if he could make her fly like that again. Javier's strong hands ran up her sides as he blocked the water, standing over her, his erection jutting between them, and she tingled at just the thought of penetration.

"What?" he asked.

How could she put into words the visceral hope of feeling the silk of his shaft—the amazing, breath-stealing spearing of his cock? "You. Just... *you*."

"I want inside your body," he promised against her lips.

She kissed him, tasting herself, tasting him, opening her mouth as his tongue probed inside. "I want you there too."

"I don't have a condom."

A shot by her ob-gyn four times a year said she didn't have to use a condom, at least to keep from getting pregnant. But his words made her take pause. Why did he say it as an open-ended question but without asking? Maybe it was an excuse for not wanting her to cling to him any more than she already was.

"My loss," she said because that was the safe response, one that let him know exactly what she wanted while still putting some distance between him and the truth.

"Sophia." He cupped her chin, guiding her gaze to his. "I'd never hurt you."

"I know."

"Are you on the pill?"

Her mouth hinged open at the straightforwardness. "Well, yes." Basically. "Birth control."

"Trust me to be safe for you?"

Oh, God. Him, skin to skin. "Yes."

"Are you safe for me?"

She nodded. "Even with my ex-fiancé, we used condoms."

"I always have too."

"He was a cheater. Josh. My ex."

"I know who Josh is. And that he cheated on you."

A nauseous feeling at the memory made her itch to forget Josh and scream because he'd been brought into her moment with Javier. Josh might not have left her with any physical reminder of his cheating, but the mental recaps popped up at the absolute worst times.

Javier's thumbs swept across her damp cheeks. "So, yes?"

"Yes," she whispered.

He kissed her lips, letting his tongue guide him to her ear. He bit her earlobe. "You're going to let me. Inside your body. Me in you. Nothing between us."

Oh, God. "Yes."

"Say it." He flexed his shaft between them, making them both groan at the erotic slide of their slick skin together. "More than understanding what we're doing, Sophia. I want to hear you *say it*. You like how I sound?"

She murmured, knowing she blushed into the shower's stream.

"I like how you sound."

Sophia's eyes jumped to his. That hadn't crossed her mind. "Really?"

Javier nodded. "Words, tesão." He tweaked her nipple. "Use them for me too."

Leaning into his hand, she swallowed away the gasp. Instead of begging for a harder touch, for him torturing her vagina, Sophia inched closer. "I want you inside me."

He growled in approval under the hot rain of the shower. "Tell me more."

Her heart jumped, and her pussy clenched. She took a breath. "I want to feel you bare inside me."

"Good."

"How my mind stutters when you split my muscles."

His hand dropped and fingers went into her needy entrance. "Yes."

"That first thrust. When your eyes are on my eyes. That's what I want from you."

"Such a good girl."

"God." She grabbed his biceps, holding him to steady herself. The cold tiles pressed to her back, and lava-hot excitement raced through her. "I like when you say that."

"Good girl?"

"Yes, sir."

His smile went half-cocked in a way that was teasing and pleased and a thousand things in between that she couldn't define. "Like when you say that too. I like when you say all the words."

"Always remember the feeling is mutual." Steady on her feet once again, she let go of his arms and circled his cock. Sophia locked her hands on him, stroking as he groaned.

Javier dropped his mouth to her neck. His stubble scratched the slope of her skin, making her arch as he pinned her against the wall, lifting her leg and wrapping it around his back. The shower sprayed on him, raining heavy, hot mist around them. Sophia's eyes sank shut as Javier's hand took over on his shaft. She circled his neck with her arms and anticipated every microsecond with him taking charge and guiding himself against her needy flesh.

The head of his cock urged against her, and it was nothing like she'd experienced before.

"Damn."

Her eyes fluttered open, and his opened too, his teasing erection pressing against her, Javier's eyes seeing *into* her. "You okay?"

"Yes," she promised.

His weight shifted, moving her from the wall, into the hot spray. His back took her position against the tile as the hot shower rained on her. Too good. The sensation of him toying with her, teasing and testing, coupled with the warm hold pressing her to him, was too good.

"Better."

"Eyes on me," he ordered.

Just as she'd said she wanted. "Yes, sir."

"Paixão. My good girl." Javier tilted his hips and thrust into her body.

Sophia's head rolled back, crying at the heat and intrusion. He gripped under her ass as her knees angled up and took over. All she had to do was exist.

"God, that's good." Javier held her weight. He fucked her, held her, lifted her, moved her. He was everything for her, and all she had to do was enjoy him as tight, low growls of Portuguese spilled from his lips.

"I can't," she cried, fighting the pleasure.

"You. Can." The slapping noise of his pure strength manhandling her body onto his would forever be her favorite sound.

"God." Her pussy tightened. Her arms squeezed around his neck, making his cheeks abrade hers.

Javier used each gasp and word as directions to bliss. He worked her faster and harder as she did nothing. She was just a vessel for him to fuck and give pleasure to, and as her climax crested, tears filled her eyes. He'd never know about them, not with all the shower water. But she felt so effortless and so intense. He pushed her beyond words, beyond trust. He made her feel a way that no man had before.

"Help me. Please." An orgasm had never hurt so much and never felt so good.

"Come, Sophia. Now."

Simple magic words that only he could order. Her muscles rippled on his driving shaft, and he met her groans with primal thrusts, coming simultaneously, lava hot and inside her body, a fire within that she couldn't describe but could feel with crystal clarity amid the climaxing chaos.

They battled for breath and milked their orgasm together, lips pressed together, sucking and kissing, probing and biting in one deeply connected moment. Heaven.

She went limp; his greedy, hungry kisses melted to sweet and slow. Carefully, Javier released her legs, and as her toes reached to the tile floor, she limply hung to his hard-breathing body.

"Thank you." Javier kissed the top of her head. "For giving me you."

And she was in love.

CHAPTER NINETEEN

M IND-NUMBED AND WOMAN-FOCUSED, Javier pulled a towel that wasn't good enough for Sophia around her then stopped to wonder when he'd ever thought about towels before. His bigger problem was that she worked a job he knew nothing about, and his protective instinct, which had only ever had been self-serving, was inserting its opinion into *anything* having to do with Sophia—apparently, including towels.

Javier stepped out to grab his own. She followed him to the counter as he rubbed his hair dry and wrapped the towel around his waist.

Her arm hooked around his bare side. "I know you're leaving soon, but if we could stay in here and pretend the rest of the world had disappeared, I would."

His heart seized. It simply hurt. The sweetness of her words and the conviction in her face hit him like a grenade explosion—fast and destructive. "Me too."

Her gaze dropped to his chest as she took a sad breath. "What's this one?"

"This?" He touched the ink over his heart.

Nodding, she tilted her head to study it. "Like a very masculine, screwed-up arrow."

Javier forced his gaze down. "Almost. Do you know what a malin is?"

"No."

"Malins are Swedish." He gave her a playful wink despite what he wanted to say. "Opposite of me, right? Normally very clean lined, not as..."

"Ornate?"

He nodded. "But it basically means you have to deal with setbacks before you can move forward."

She pressed her fingers to the arrow and traced the lines, sending shivers across his flesh and reminding him of his goal and every setback he'd had.

"What are the setbacks?" Sophia asked, having no idea that she was touching something that could rip him apart.

"Life stuff." Stuff that would hurt to talk about and that hurt to remember. Those things suddenly seemed less important since she entered his world, just days ago. He didn't know how to justify his shift in feelings or the way his prioritization was fluctuating.

Her lips curled in a sweet smile. "Do you care to share?"

"Not really."

Gone was the sweet smile, and that cut like a serrated blade, needlessly painful and messy. His jaw ached to keep talking, and it was clear that he should've kept all mention of setbacks to himself. He cleared his throat. "Sorry—it's not something… I'm protective over it. I don't know how to explain it to… others."

Her cheeks had flushed in a way that had nothing to do with the shower-soaked orgasm. "Really, I get it. I was prying too much. No worries." The shift in her manner erased the star-struck expression in her eyes, and in its place was the same hardened look he'd seen before—when she marched down the aisle, groom-less and holding on to her dignity. That Javier was able to classify that look and lump himself into the same category as her asshole ex served only to make the situation worse.

"Sophia?"

"Yup." She pushed out the bathroom door and headed to a dresser. In a perfunctory fashion, she pulled out clothes and focused intently on dressing.

He followed, feeling the loss of their sanctuary as the bathroom opened. Cooler air and reality coated him, making him feel chilled both inside and out. "Soph?"

"Hmm?" But her voice was cold as his freshly dried skin, not that he blamed her.

"Sophia?"

She stopped midmotion, her shirt barely tugged down over her bra. "Yes?"

His hand rested on her stiff shoulder, then he pulled back. "Remember that I said someone hurt my sister and I wanted revenge?"

Her brows softened, lips upturning with perhaps understanding and recognition. "Yes."

"That's been my life's focus." He stretched an arm up then squeezed the tendons at the back of his neck. Sharing wasn't comfortable, but necessary after the reaction she'd had when he'd been too damn abrupt. "To track down every person involved and eradicate them. That's what I'm moving forward toward."

"Sorry, I didn't mean to—"

"I don't tell people because I'm nothing more than a cold-blooded tracker. My job, my life, my world is dedicated to…"

"Revenge."

"Yeah, revenge." He took an uneasy breath. "My dad, mom—they were bad stock. First roadblock in life is overcoming biological roots. That was easy. Soon as I could support myself, I did."

She shifted, her posture not as harsh and angry as it had been. "What'd you do?"

Memories of his first street fights and the handfuls of money he made flooded him. Javier leaned against the wall, still only in a towel. "It wasn't a job. More like a hobby. At first."

She pulled up her pants, smoothing her shirt into place as though she had to focus on anything other than his nonanswer. "I don't understand."

How best to describe what was simple ruthlessness? He'd been an animal. A savage. Even though it was a makeshift career for an essentially homeless boy, he loved it—needed it. The fights, the thrills, the wins.

Explaining something so dark to someone so innocent was impossible. He turned and escaped back into the bathroom, using the precious seconds to not only snag his clothes from the bathroom but also find words that made him less of a predator.

There weren't any. The truth with her was the only way to go. She'd sense a lie and deserved better than that even if the truth disgusted her. "I fight."

Her brow furrowed. "You fight?"

"Since I was half my size and weight." He laughed uncomfortably at what he was and what he'd become then shook his head and re-dressed. Boxers, pants, shirt. When he focused back on her, she stared, waiting.

"I was good at hurting people. It brought in the money I needed. But my problem, my setback was… damn, I liked it. The attack, the triumph. The blood, the pain, the win. I loved it too much. It made me forget, made me feel alive. It's my addiction."

She bit her lip, not taking a step back as she should have but, rather, an inch forward. "You're addicted to fighting?"

He rubbed a hand over his face. "Not the actual, physical action of it. But yeah."

"So you like to hit people? Like abuse? Or like a sadist?"

Kind of. But… "No. Just… it won't make sense."

"Try me." She took another bare step forward. "Please."

With the distance between them shrinking, he wanted her to realize what she was standing in front of—a brute. But her inquisitive eyes waited.

Javier cleared his throat. "It was the only outlet I had. Some kids grew up watching TV. I didn't. Fighting was entertainment, release. And survival." He cracked his knuckles then jammed his fists into balls. "So that's me. Not the good, upstanding soldier like you might be used to in the Cole family."

His gut check didn't come in time to soften the words as they fell off his tongue. Even he knew throwing the perfect Cole family up for comparison wasn't fair.

"Don't act like that." She closed their distance but didn't touch.

He could feel her warmth, smell her sweetness, but couldn't touch her without permission, not after what he'd just confessed. He was a barbaric villain compared to the political royalty of the Coles. "You have good parents. A strong brother."

"That doesn't matter to me where you're concerned, and you don't always know what you think you see."

He blinked, taking in the sometimes timid, sometimes pushy puzzle piece of a woman who made his insides calm. "Fair enough."

"Good."

Nodding and uncomfortable, he pinched his neck again. "Okay. So, do you have any other questions—about me?" He dropped his hand, trying to read her blank face. "I won't be an ass about it, Sophia. Promise."

Her simple smile lit, too sweet and forgiving, and it made him want to hug her against his chest. "How did you join Delta?"

"They grabbed me off the streets."

Her eyes went doe wide. "Oh."

"Not like I was homeless. I mean, I was a man on a mission. Fighting and hunting and—"

"Hunting?"

"For the men who hurt Adélia."

Sophia's face gentled, and a strand of drying hair fell across her cheek. "I didn't know her name."

"I never share it." If he could push that wayward piece of hair behind her ear... if he could touch Sophia and hold onto that feeling... Javier wondered if he could do that when he was long gone. That way, he'd always have his time with her.

"Her name is beautiful."

"Is. Was. I'm not sure if she's alive. It's better if she's not. But her name is not close to how pretty she was." Words shaking, he took a step back, needing a deep breath. "But Delta. I was a street fighter with intelligence on South American cartel traffickers."

"Is or was?" Sophia's teary eyes were wide, and she hadn't switched subjects along with him.

"I can't talk about it."

Nodding, she whispered, "Okay."

Javier swallowed around the rock in his throat. "Brock found me. Knew I had skills, trained me for weeks. He broke me down and built me up. Made me as good with an AK as I am with my fists."

"Wow." Her tongue ran over her bottom lip as she processed the toughest years of his life. "That's... crazy. Are you okay?"

"I am if you let me talk about Delta."

Sophia nodded.

Thankful that she didn't push it, he continued the genesis of how the Brazilian street fighter was part of an elite American private security team. "Brock found the one guy with a hard-on for fucking up a cartel in South America. Crazy. But that's Titan. They could find anyone they want, anywhere. They found me."

"Just like you found me and Hana."

"Yes, paixão. But I promise you I didn't need Titan or Delta to back me up when I went after you." Javier nodded and sat on the bed, patting next to his thigh. "Sit."

She snuggled into his side, and Javier shifted, wrapping an arm around her. "Whispering Willow. The PC. What are you actually doing out here anyway? You're, what? Intelligence?"

"Something like that."

A different tightness in his muscles made his chest ache return. She faced risks, probably more so than he already knew. He'd be gone within days, off to fight the good fight somewhere else in the dark world. Sophia would be here without him, maybe walking into city scuffles, maybe unaware of the danger of political climates. There'd be no one to haul her out of trouble and take her home when he was gone. No one was as passionate about her safety as he was. "Promise me something, Sophia."

"Hmm?"

"Whatever you're doing, make sure it's worth it. And, paixão, walk away. Walk away when you see the ugly, when you realize you can't stop the hell. Turn your head and pray if that's what helps you, or curse if that's how you'll survive. Cry and scream, but Sophia, please don't do what you did today. Don't try to protect Hana." He pressed a kiss to the top of her head. "Can you do that for me?"

Sophia nodded, tucking her knees to her chest and wrapping her arms around her shins. "I screwed up. I know."

"Huge," he said quietly.

"They were going to kill her."

"You too, and that's reality in this part of the world. You know that."

"But I *know* her. She trusted me. I was the reason she was in danger."

He stiffened. "No. The reason she was in danger is because that's how she lives her life. With the Primeiro Comando."

"Life doesn't give us the choices we want, Javier."

"No one knows that better than me, but it doesn't matter, Soph. You have one person to look out for in Honduras. That's *you*. Everyone else is secondary."

Her head tilted as she studied him, and he knew that whatever was about to spill from her pink lips would be his hell. "What?" he asked.

"If that was you?" She tugged her lip with her teeth, letting the question hang. "I'd walk over again. I'd drag you out, somehow. I'd stand by your side if we couldn't leave."

His heart imploded as though forced to cave under a rain of shrapnel. "Soph—"

"How is that different from what you did for me?"

Because we're clearly feeling each other in a way you and Hana can't. But that wasn't something he could share because he didn't know what it meant. "I'm trained. That's what I do."

"So, none of it was about me?"

Damn. Right on the bull's eye. All of it was about her. "You're too good for out here."

She lurched back as though the words had been an assault. "That's a double standard."

Whatever she wanted to call it. "Promise me you'll watch out for yourself when I can't."

"I did just fine before you got here, Javier. I'm not changing what I'm doing, *which is important to me*, just because you asked nicely."

There it was—the famous Cole family stubborn streak that was rooted in patriotism, just as her brother and father had. Javier should respect it, but the idea of her in the line of fire made his palms itch. "Fine."

"Fine?" Her beautiful eyes narrowed. "Just that simple?"

"Ha. Hardly." She was the only thing walking this earth that he wanted to protect and keep alive. Her eyes pinched, back to angry and annoyed. He would have given up the hunt for the PC cartel to ensure Sophia walked away unscathed.

Wait—what?

His stomach lurched. Guilt and realization twisted in his mind, forming an instantaneous headache. *She* was the *higher* priority?

No question. *She was.*

Shit. What the fuck was he supposed to do with that realization? Javier pulled at his collar and tried to swallow the boulder of guilt closing his throat. He coughed, failing to clear the discomfort, and stood abruptly. "Alright."

"Alright?" Sophia's surprise mocked his own.

How could he do that to Adélia's memory—to the very reason for his agreement to join Delta? His knuckles bunched. Irritation scraped down his spine, like nerve-ending-coated nails down a raw chalkboard. He needed to get out of this room. The ceiling was falling, and the walls were collapsing. Decades of fighting, living, and surviving became a crushing weight as he spun helplessly in a room that was losing oxygen. "I have to go."

Sophia's confusion couldn't have been more apparent. "What?"

His gut swam with a nausea he refused to accept. Anger rapidly joined guilt, and the speed of his emotional transition nearly knocked him on his ass.

"Seriously? You're leaving?"

The only thing that kept him standing was the need to run away from Sophia and toward the memory of Adélia. "I'm done with this conversation."

Hurt darkened her face, along with shock and surprise, disappointment and devastation. "Just like that?"

"Yeah. Sorry." This was why he didn't need a personal connection. Everything about him was screwed up. Seriously, how did a guy go from *never* sleeping next to a woman unless he wasn't ten kinds of screwed up to *this*? Whatever this was.

This was her. It was perfect. It was something people wanted, searched for, and dreamed of. *This* was *never* supposed to happen to him. Never.

Javier rubbed his temples. Therapy would've been a good thing a decade ago, but the streets had given him their own version of how to deal.

And now he was hurting a girl because he needed to run back to their memory, where blood and brawls would center him, where he could find peace in a search for vengeance. How else could he survive with not protecting his sister?

Javier stood up, hating every fiber of his being as he rose off the bed. He didn't want to go but couldn't stay. His skin crawled; his mind tumbled. Panic and tension grasped his throat, squeezing the oxygen and sanity away. "I have to go check in with my boss."

"Wow. Okay, then." She pressed her lips together. "See ya."

He stepped into his boots and felt Sophia's mental daggers slice into his back. Every painstaking sting was deserved. *This* was why he never slept with a woman more than once and why he didn't spend the night and play house: he didn't need the judgment or confusion. He didn't want the ache residing in his chest.

"Bye." His boots might've well been soldered to the ground for the effort it took to move from her. More than a decade of a tight focus, one goal, and a pretty girl came along to shake his world up and make him want something else?

Nope. God, he needed this job done so he didn't hurt Sophia anymore and so he could become a ghost and disappear until Delta was called up for duty again. Fists bunching, he needed to fight and fight and fight until everything but the pain and his reason for breathing disappeared.

Right before the door shut behind him, he heard the faint whisper of her good-bye.

CHAPTER TWENTY

GO TIME. FOR the first time, Javier leaving a job location physically hurt. There'd been jobs he'd had to walk away from before, when he thought they'd find intel or learn something but he came up dry. But this was the first time the job was finished and a personal reason had him dragging his boots.

But leaving was part of his deal. Delta did jobs. They came in fast and left when the mission had been accomplished. Simple. Or they'd leave when there was a larger job to do, *which there was.* Mass chaos was breaking out across the world as the ramifications of US intelligence leaks manifested. Delta had been lucky to have been in Honduras when Whispering Willow was compromised. Javier's presence had been fortunate for Sophia's sake.

All Titan teams were expected to clean up Uncle Sam's mess, and Delta was on their way out. Dread thumped through his veins. Not once, not *ever*, had he wanted to stay on the job, but especially, he'd never wondered whether saying good-bye would ease the discomfort of missing a person.

Not. Ever.

The guys he'd grown up fighting with in Rio had never crossed his mind. He didn't know who half of them really were, how they lived, where they lived, what they did outside of their brawls.

His Delta teammates? Javier could say "peace out" to his bros and not think twice, because they'd always be there when it was time to work again.

But Sophia? She was upstairs—or wherever—feeling hurt and angry at him. All of which he deserved. It sucked. He was a ghost operative, and she was stationed all the way in Honduras, not wanting to leave. So the idea of this—of *them*—happening for longer than just a few days was impossible.

"Brazil?" Brock's voice boomed down the hall where Javier had posted himself against the wall, teetering on the edge of a mental moment.

His tongue pressed to the top of his mouth, thick, with too much to say and nothing worth trying to explain. "Yeah."

Brock's boots echoed at an angry pace before he marched into the room. "Get to the room."

"Yeah, coming." As with tearing off a bandage, Javier needed to act fast. He cleared his throat and followed as ordered to their group rendez-vous, where Ryder and Grayson sat, bullshitting.

Brock's phone rang, and when he answered, all eyes watched, wait-ing—Javier's stomach churning—for their team leader's final report. Brock gave a thumbs-up. "We have a green light. Let's roll."

This was it. He was leaving Sophia, maybe never seeing her again—unless there was another Cole family event the team hit up, and even then, he shouldn't go. Not after how he'd left things with her.

"Brazil, move your slow ass."

Javier turned to Brock, but his muscles ached as though he'd gone thirty rounds with a heavyweight. His mind was equally heavy. "Shit. I need a minute."

"Goddamn it," Brock muttered while Ryder and Grayson chuckled, and everyone knew where Javier was going.

They knew it before he did. His mind was at war, but his boots were hauling ass. He bounded up the stairs, not bothering to knock on Sophia's bedroom door. He burst in. *Empty.* "Soph?"

No answer. Retracing his steps, a panic gripped his thoughts as he rushed without a plan. "Sophia?"

The dining room? Also empty. The kitchen maybe? He pushed through the door—

There she was—*Cristo.* Her eyes were red rimmed, and Janella gave him a look that would make a lesser man take a step back, guarding his balls as well as soul.

"Soph, can I talk to you for a minute?"

Her gaze dropped to the floor, and her cheeks heated pink as she shook her head, hair draping over his view of her sweetheart face, trying to hide the heartbreak and hurt. "Just go. I'm fine."

"Yeah, well." He wasn't fine. "One minute?"

She wouldn't look up. "Say whatever you have to say, and go. Okay. I get it. I'm a big girl."

Janella made an "mm-hmm" noise of agreement, still glaring as if to say he was a dick. Which he was, so the noise and look were deserved. But still they stung.

"Can we have a minute?" he asked the source of the unrelenting eye daggers.

Janella smirked, not sheathing or slowing her deadly glare. "Not a chance, honey buns."

He took a deep breath. He wasn't one to like an audience unless they were strangers howling at his street fights, but instead of leaving, Javier inched closer to Sophia. "You're *here* whether I like it or not."

Her chin came up, but her tear-stained eyes rolled. "Yeah, we've been over that."

"And I'm nowhere, every day. I live off the grid. No home base. A job that could kill me. Where I have to kill to stay alive. And I have one purpose in life right now."

"I get it. You're fine. You can stop explaining, Javier."

"No. You don't get it. Because never, not one time in the two decades since Adélia was taken, have I *ever* wavered on what I should do, where I go, what I think."

Sophia's sad gaze rounded as though something he was about to say could change their reality. That was the opposite intention of his one-sided conversation. He needed to solidify in her mind that they had no business thinking about a coupling of any sort because of logistics and because his focus was screwed up when she was on his mind.

"What I'm trying to say, Sophia, is that I have to concentrate." His head dropped back, hearing the flatness in his own voice. "I can't when I'm with you."

The ceiling was as bare and drab as his heart. Slowly, he took an uneasy breath and brought his stare front and center. There was a flicker of emotion in her eyes, different from the teary irritation and post-fight sadness. It brightened her frown from hurting to uncertain. "I'm in your head?"

"No. Yes. What I'm trying to say is…" The hope that shined in her eyes would be his death. "My team is leaving this second, and I couldn't walk out the door without coming to see you."

Sophia blinked, her mouth opening slightly, and Janella's face softened. He wasn't saying the right things, wasn't detailing why they shouldn't—they shouldn't *what*? He had no idea. "I just can't, coração."

"Can't?" she repeated softly.

Janella repeated her one-word question, though not softly, but more incredulous and biting.

"You…" A knot lodged in his throat as he searched for an explanation that either of them could understand. "Distract me."

She didn't respond, and time ticked. He didn't want to walk away with her staring at him as though he'd lit a charge that could destroy her smile. Memories like this would rot his insides. "Sophia. The only thing I'm supposed to do is take out the fuckers who hurt my sister. It's the reason I live for, the reason I have this job."

"Okay."

"And when you were in that crowd yesterday? When I couldn't see you? When I knew you were in trouble and couldn't get to you fast enough? You were the only thing I wanted to take care of. *You*. Not my sister. Not for Colin's wishes or my boss's orders. Not my team. *You*." He shook his head, scratching his stubbled face. "I just can't."

Sophia hopped off the counter, taking two steps so they were face-to-face, then her hand rose as she poked him in the chest. "You chickenshit *bastard*."

"Wh-what?"

"God!"

"Soph—"

She slammed her hand against his chest. "Get out of here. Don't throw your loss or my brother in my face. Don't you *dare* say something like that as a reason you can't do *this*. Whatever *this* is." Her hand went back and forth between them. "Because whatever this is, I felt it. And you did too. So screw you for playing it up then playing it down."

"I—" He had no response. No idea. No clue how to deal with the tension in his shoulders and the ache in his eyes.

"Go away, Javier."

"Yo, Brazil," Brock yelled from another room with timing that couldn't have been worse. "We gotta roll."

"*Go,*" Sophia snapped.

"Paixão."

She flexed her fingers and straightened her arms as though exasperated with him. "Just *Sophia*. No more cute names, no more sweet words. No more of any of that."

"Brazil! Now." Brock's muffled voice echoed through the wall.

Javier didn't have a choice but to follow after his team leader. "Okay." Taking one last look at what he hoped wasn't his biggest mistake, he slammed a fist against the wall and walked away.

CHAPTER TWENTY-ONE

SOPHIA'S NIGHTMARE SHOOK the walls, the bed. She couldn't place whatever she'd been dreaming about, but it had come crashing down with vibration and an alarm. She thrashed, a light sheen of sweat soaking the covers with a mix of anxiety and dreamful fears.

The booming growl of an explosion hit too close to her bedroom. Wait—what? The faint scent of smoke made her skin prickle. Sophia sat up in bed, panting and blinking into the night as the wailing of a second alarm started. Another flash lit her room from the tiny window she'd been barred from perching in. And then more lights and booms. Growls.

Holy crap. They were under an attack.

Was it because of the intel leaks or Delta? But Delta was gone. Okay, think! She needed to get to safety. They'd drilled on these things; she knew what to do and where to go. This was so real, though. Adrenaline flooded her veins, and her mind was clear as suddenly each noise became distinct: different alarms and the return fire of the stationed guards.

But gunshots and grenade blasts versus whatever had attacked the embassy? The embassy didn't have massive manpower, especially after Delta left. The men downstairs were screwed. Done. Soon to be dead.

Think. She needed to—

Another rattle came as the books on her shelf clattered to the floor. Shit. Sophia rolled out of bed, one arm over her head, another one catching her fall. Protocol for attacks had been instilled in her since she was a child, traveling around the world with her family. She should've known better. So much for adrenaline-fueled clarity. Those thirty seconds of frozen fear in her bed could've cost her life.

Staying down and crawling to her closet, she ignored the explosions outside the embassy buildings and pushed to grab a helmet and a mask that she never expected to need as another blast hit the building.

The scent of smoke, no longer faint, carried through the air vents. Something close by was on fire, and she needed to get to the safe room. Why hadn't any of the armed guards been to her room yet? Easy answer: they were busy. This wasn't a drill, and Sophia needed to get her ass in gear.

Keeping low, she covered her face with the mask, praying to God there weren't chemical weapons in play, and then pulled on the hat and tied the chin strap. Another blast rocked the building like an earthquake.

She put her palm to the doorknob, testing for heat, and carefully turned the cool metal. The hallway was dark. They had generators to keep from having outages, but not even the emergency lights blinked. Janella's room was to the left, and the way to the safe room was on the right, down the stairs closest to Jensen and Brackster's bedroom suites.

Sophia ran to Janny's closed door, slamming her fists hard. "Janny!"

No answer.

"Janella!"

There was no way that she would've passed Sophia's closed door and not checked to make sure she was moving. What time was it? Janny woke up far earlier than Sophia, and maybe she was in the kitchen or the laundry. Both were near the safe room. Where was everyone? God!

"Hello?" She needed someone she recognized to appear for a moment of reassurance. But there was nothing. The place was like a ghost town under attack.

Sophia ran toward the stairs, and another blast hit, throwing her off balance. The hits were powerful, like grenades or bombs. The intensity level was far past a gunfight.

Didn't intel see it coming? Why weren't they more on guard, and why did Delta leave?

"Hello?" There was no response in the growling darkness except for another shake of the very stout building. It tossed her up, and Sophia stumbled on the stairs. Her shoulder slammed, biting into the wall, and her grip slipped. The face mask went up, and her helmet went down.

Vision obscured, Sophia fell. The edge of each stair bit into her as gravity tugged her down. Her face smashed as she came to a stop.

Stomach swirling, pain spinning—everything hurt. Blood seeped into her mouth. Her cheekbones ached as much as her body stung and cried silently for help. Empty, airless lungs made her mind rush in panic, and each limb was bruised, scraped, and maybe broken.

Coughing, she gasped as oxygen reinflated her lungs. "God. Help me."

For a moment, all she could hear was the wail of the warning sirens. The blare bounced off the walls. She tried pushing up. Her throbbing wrist was of little use, and her elbow screamed in pain.

Sophia coughed and swallowed awkwardly. Her ribs hurt as she wheezed in the acrid air. Where were the people who were supposed to protect them?

A loud, close bang hit the front door. Her head jolted up, her eyes narrowing on the locked, reinforced door. Words she couldn't decipher shouted on the other side. Whoever was out there had passed the gates and the guards and was physically trying to enter.

She needed help. She needed Javier.

For a long moment, she knew he would be the man behind the door. There was no doubt that the shouts she didn't understand would stop because he would protect her. She knew without a doubt that Javier was a superhero who could arrive in the nick of time and wipe out the bad guys—lift her up, heal her injuries, shield her from the hell of being in a blacked out, siren-screaming embassy under attack when she had yet to see *anyone* else, either staff or soldier.

Fear made her shiver. But the high-pitched shouts that she heard behind the blaring alarm struck her as different. They were excited but backing away—damn it, they were going to blast the door. Why wasn't Javier here?

Oh, to hell with him; he didn't matter. Sophia pushed through pain and half stumbled, half fled down the hall toward the kitchen, gasping and coughing. "Janny!"

No one responded. She moved through the pantry area, still watching for her friend. No light reached back there.

Sophia tripped, slamming to the ground. Everything hurt. Her head spun, and as she yelled and kicked at what had taken her down, she heard Janny's hoarse voice pleading to be left alone, to be given help. Her breaths were fast, her gasps loud enough that Sophia could hear them in between the beats of wailing alarms.

"Janny." She bit her lip as she crawled into the darkness, reaching her friend. "What's the matter?"

"Oh, Lord." Gasp. "Sophia." Gasp. "This isn't good."

Shit. "Are you hurt?"

Did she fall? Was she hit on the head, or had something broken her ribs? Janella was heavier, older, and not nearly in the kind of shape that she needed to be in. That was part of her charm but also part of why she couldn't move.

"Chest."

"Something hit you?" But with the commotion and the mask, no one would be able to hear her.

"My." Janny sucked a deep, painful breath. "Chest."

"Your chest?" Oh, shit. "*Your chest.*"

"Yes."

She pulled up the mouth piece to make sure Janny heard her. "You're not having a heart attack, Janella. No, ma'am."

"If you—ah—say so—"

Okay. Whatever they had to do, they couldn't sit in the dark in the pantry. They needed to get to the safe room, where there was a medical kit. Surely there was something in their supplies that would help—aspirin to start with or glycerin. Whatever they gave heart patients for pulmonary distress.

A loud explosion ripped into the front of the building. The front door would be breached soon if it wasn't hanging on hinges already. Sophia ripped her gas mask down, taking the risk and needing to communicate. "We have to get to the safe room."

Janny nodded, hearing the same thing and coming to the same conclusion. Sophia grabbed Janny's sweat-soaked body and hooked under her armpits, tugging and lifting, grunting through the muffled groans of pain.

Janella didn't budge.

"Go." The order came out as a gasped whisper.

Sophia pushed her weight into Janella, acting as a human fulcrum. "Like hell. Get up."

"Soph—" Gasp. "—ia."

"Shut up and try, damn it."

Sweat poured down Janella's face. Fear and pain, exertion and desperation made her shake. Janella leaned into Sophia, and together, they gritted through their agony, growling their intention to survive.

"Ain't good," Janny mumbled.

"It'll be okay." The only other option was to die, and there was no way that was happening today.

Between their arms and the walls, they managed to round the corner of the dark hall, heaving and breathing on their fight to the safe room.

"Almost there, Janny. Come on, honey."

Janella grunted a response. They had ten feet to go—just a few yards, but it seemed like miles.

The access panel was next to the hidden door of the safe room, which was more like a safe bunker; it could be entered via a keypad on a separate power source. So even if the lights were out and the ventilation system stopped working, they could still get inside and safely stay put until the all clear was given.

"Here we are." Sophia leaned an arm onto the reinforced door, sweating and exhausted. Her trembling hand punched in the code, and the red light flicked to green. A pressurized release sounded, and she tugged the door open.

Empty. Where were Jensen and Brackster?

"Come on, Janny." Sophia heaved the woman in behind her then pulled the door shut. They both collapsed on the floor, breathing in gasping tandem. Janny rolled to her side, and Sophia pushed to her knees. Medical kit. They needed to find that. A well-stocked shelf of supplies stood in the corner next to tanks and medical equipment. There was definitely not time for a defibrillator or oxygen. Rows of prescriptions, all labeled but meaning nothing to her and didn't do shit. They were knocked down and out of order. The room looked as though it had been tossed, but it was probably just the intense vibrations from the attacks.

Nothing was where it should be. Panic made her mind spin. Uncertainty made her next move unclear. She needed a shit's-gone-down-now-do-this manual. Sophia forced her hurting hands to her sides and breathed deeply until she could control the piercing, debilitating fear.

Her heart rate slowed. She opened her eyes and focused on the scattered, unorganized mess of supplies. The bottle of aspirin would help—no manual needed for that. She'd been educated by TV commercials enough to know that Janny should suck down some of those babies. "Janny, open up."

Sophia fumbled the bottle open. Her hands shook. She doled out two baby aspirins, having no idea if that was fruitless or enough, then popped out another one. Without questioning, Janella took the offered pills and swallowed them down.

"Okay." Sophia sank back to the floor.

"Okay," Janny mumbled.

"Are you still having a heart attack?"

"Child," she wheezed. "Lord. Maybe a panic attack? Don't think heart attacks just stop, and I didn't die."

"No, you didn't." Sophia laughed flatly. "Thank God for that."

"We're the only ones here."

"Yeah," she whispered. "What do you think that means?"

"We're in trouble. That's what that means."

"Is there a comm system in here?" Sophia spun to inspect the room again. Outside, the sirens still blared. There was still live action happening, and their enemy had breached the embassy. Even if there wasn't a way to communicate with the outside world, help had to be on its way.

"Do you pray?" Janella asked.

For an angel. For Javier. To a God that wouldn't let them die that day. "Yes."

"We need to pray."

They fell silent, the world around them loud and brash while, in the safe room, there was nothing but the sound of breathing and sniffles. And

Sophia prayed. Hard. Her fingernails bit into her palms as she squeezed her fists tight.

Dear Lord. Help me. Help us. Save us. There's too much good to do, too many ways to do it. Let us live. Give me the chance to fight. Think of Hana. The women and children that need a voice. I can be that. Let me be that. Let me survive.

The building shook, and her eyes pinched closed. Janella unsuccessfully stifled a yip of fear.

I need your help.

All she could picture was Javier. Javier opening the door. Javier knowing how to help Janny. Javier whisking her into his arms, whispering that it would be okay, and walking them out of the building that had been made safe under his protective eye.

Beep.

Sophia's eyes flew open. Janny twisted for the door. There was another beep. Beep. Beep.

Access *denied*. Shit. The safe room had been found.

Janella inched back onto the floor. "That's not good."

"No," she whispered. "It's not."

Bam!

"Shoot!" Janella pushed back again as though a few inches would save them from a breached safe door.

"It's bulletproof. They can't get in."

"They know we're in here."

"No one knows we're in here except our guys, who will get us out."

"Where are they?" Janny's voice jumped pitch.

"I don't know!" Sophia's heart slammed in her chest, fear leaving her weak, but she wouldn't show that. Never. All she had to do was calm down.

The light flickered and failed. The room went pitch black.

"Shit!"

"Oh, Lord. They know we're in here."

Her pulse pounding in her neck, Sophia nodded. "We need those things."

She dropped to her knees and crawled over the supplies on the ground, searching blindly for glow sticks or flashlights. They shouldn't be hard to find, and she should have located them after she gave Janella the aspirin.

Crawling on screaming hands and knees, Sophia fumbled through boxes and supplies. Finally, she found a flashlight.

She pressed the button, and nothing happened. "Damn it!"

She took a breath and dropped her hand. The flashlight made a noise as she turned it over, frustrated. The weight shifted as though a piece inside had rolled to the opposite part of the handle.

"Maybe there's another one?" Janny whispered.

Maybe they didn't need to look. Was it self-creating energy? Sophia shook the light, holding her breath and ignoring the pangs of strain in her wrists and ribs. Out of breath and painted in a sheen of sweat from a benign activity, she pressed the power button and hoped that it would work.

Dim light flickered on. Finally. They needed something to go right.

"Oh, thank you." Janny wheezed.

Sophia swung the flashlight to Janella. "Amen."

Their dismal light source didn't give them any insight into the happenings outside and nearby. But at least they weren't in the pitch black.

"You still having a heart attack?" she mumbled, holding the light to her chest and using the residual brightness to inspect Janny's face.

"Think so." Janny leaned against the wall. "Heart attack. Panic attack. Enemy attack. One of those. So long as I don't die, I'm okay with it."

"Me too."

"Brackster and Jensen are dead." Janella's voice was calm and factual as though she were reading the stock quotes.

"You don't know that."

"Don't lie to yourself now." Janny shook her head. "They weren't in here." Gasp. "The embassy is on fire. Explosions. People with guns." Gasp. "No one came to find us. Jansen and Brackster are top priority." Cough. Wheeze. "If they weren't in here, they ain't anywhere." Gasp. "They ain't breathing."

She bit her lip, agreeing but refusing to do so out loud. "We're okay, though. It's a safe room for a reason."

"The generator's cut; the air is going to run out. It's been at least an hour. More?" Hell, Janella sounded as though *she* were going to run out of air too. But she was also correct.

"What do we—"

Beep. Beep. Beep. Pfffsh.

Pressurized release gave way. The door unlocked, and Sophia's heart stalled. The room tilted as she waited for the other side to be revealed. If it were the enemy, she would die. Eventually. It wouldn't be pretty. She hadn't accomplished everything she wanted to in life. Had she made a difference? Maybe a small one, but nothing that she couldn't have done better. Fallen in love? Perhaps Josh had been a small love, but nothing compared to how she loved Javier.

Metal clinked and scraped as the door pushed open. The anticipation as to who was on the other side made panic flush over Sophia's skin, a rush of goose bumps coupled with a vomit-inducing stomachache.

Dim light cast a shadow as their safe room was breached. A glove-covered hand pushed the thick door open, showing a larger-than-life man above them as they cowered on the floor. A terrified whimper pushed through her lips.

"Oh, God," she and Janella both cried.

CHAPTER TWENTY-TWO

ELTA HAD BEEN back to the US for a few hours, waiting on their next deployment's instructions. Discussion was that they were heading to the Middle East to provide additional security for the Americans working with the Saudis on a project that had been leaked. Either that or Egypt, where life was hell more often than not. Either way, they were having a domestic moment: clean clothes, home-cooked food, and watching a ball game while they waited.

Except all that relaxation BS was over as Javier bolted upright, ready to charge across Trace's living room, reach through the TV, and shake the news anchor breaking into their show. Headline over his head: Embassy Attack in Honduras.

Javier's blood froze. "No."

"Oh, shit." Trace dropped a spoonful of cereal back into a bowl.

On screen, the news anchor nodded, adjusting an earpiece as he readied to go live into a press announcement. Every second ticked by, ratcheting a fear Javier had never experienced before.

"We interrupt your show tonight with just-breaking news. The US embassy in Honduras sustained mortar attacks."

Bile crawled up Javier's throat. "Someone call Colin. See if she was there." But of course she was there. He'd abandoned her fewer than twenty-four hours ago, crying in the kitchen of an embassy with minimal security. It had more than a US embassy somewhere like England but nowhere near enough to handle mortar strikes.

"Two US officials have confirmed local Primeiro Comando were warned late Tuesday against any violations of the diplomatic immunity of embassy staff and facilities when a staffer was accosted by a local mob upset by the leaked information on what's been called Whispering Willow."

"We should've brought her home." His molars ground, and he turned to Trace, who had his phone to his ear. "Who you calling? Colin? Brock?"

"Colin," Trace mumbled. "No answer."

"Fuck." Javier pulled out his phone and called Brock.

"The cartel-led uprising appears to be a continued retaliation for the leaked intelligence on a US-PC informant partnership."

"Brazil," Brock answered, obviously knowing why Javier had called. "Give me a second."

"What do you know?" Javier barked.

"A second."

One second, then two. Each took longer than an eternity.

"The embassy was closed for several weeks less than a year ago after the resignation of the Honduran president and cabinet. However, it reopened with a skeleton staff to assist in diplomatic efforts in the region. Routine consular activities have been on hold for more than a year. Known occupants of the embassy reportedly—"

Thump-thump.

Thump-thump.

Javier's heartbeat echoed in his ears. His blood slowed to the speed of molasses. His lungs ached, and he couldn't make time move fast enough to hear who resided at the embassy.

"—have not been accounted for. The building siege began approximately one hour ago."

Marlena walked into the room with a gallon of orange juice and a stack of cups, eyeing Javier and her husband. The mood of the room had drastically changed since she'd lost the game of rock-paper-scissors and gone to grab drinks. She followed their gaze and turned toward the TV. "Weren't some of you just there?"

"Yeah, babe."

Mar placed the cups on the coffee table. "Isn't that where Colin's sister is?"

"Yeah," Luke answered.

Javier hadn't talked to Luke about Sophia. He hadn't talked to anyone other than Grayson and Ryder, who'd witnessed him and Sophia in Honduras together. But Luke had heard what had gone down and knew better than anyone Javier's internal conflict. They were brothers in Delta but also brothers in tragedy.

Luke had lost an old girlfriend to traffickers, similar to what had happened to Javier. They both understood revenge and had an appreciation of pain. But Luke had found a way to handle both his need for revenge and a relationship—with a woman involved in the industry, no less.

Javier hadn't talked to Luke about his woman. There was no way they'd discuss Sophia. But they shared an addiction: they were both hungry for pain and the blessed distraction it brought. They were both covered in tattoos and reveled in fights—not just war or a job or a mission, but blood. Beatings. Brawls. They could take the pain, inflict it back, and triumph.

But not knowing about Sophia, more than pain or revenge on traffickers, Javier wanted news. Good news. He wanted it more than any other time he'd called Brock.

"Alright, Brazil."

The center of Javier's chest pumped as though his heart would brawl, no matter what the boss said. "Alright, what?"

"No one's accounted for yet."

The ground caved, and his vision crashed. Javier dropped to the couch, and fear unlike anything he'd known could exist tore his world apart. "What else do you know?"

"Damage was heavy. The closest SEALs team was given approval and a go for an extraction."

"What about the RSO?" They handled all American security on post or staff for the embassy, and Javier knew several of them personally. Good men. Talented. They'd give their life to protect Sophia.

"Last known communication was a request for additional assistance."

"*Shit.*" He rubbed his eyes and felt the room's attention on him. "Where's Colin?"

"Talking to Jared."

Jared owned Titan Group. There was no one higher up in their world. What every man on the team also knew was that Jared was working only the most important job—his wife Sugar was getting ready to pop out a baby in the next month or two—and if the boss man was taking time to have one-on-one conversations with Colin, things were worse than Brock was letting Javier in on.

Javier dropped his head into the palm of his hand. *He* wanted to know what Colin knew; he wanted in on that briefing. But he'd walked away from Sophia and staked no claim. Outwardly, at least. Everything on his inside was pressurized. It twisted, tore apart, and shredded as if hit by shrapnel. Yet all he could do was sit on the couch and clutch a phone. Helpless.

"Brazil, get to HQ. One way or another, you should be with us."

One way or another. Good news or bad. Meeting with Jared Westin to talk about Sophia Cole. "On my way."

THE WAR ROOM at Titan's headquarters was different than the ones Javier had visited across the globe. He'd been in the US location a half dozen times, and each time, there'd been a comfortable feel to it. Not to take away from the security systems, weapons, and manpower that the single building offered, but some of the men from Titan's main team lived nearby, and there was more a sense of coming to work than, say, dropping by a command center in the Middle East or Asia. Jared even had a dog that stayed on-site.

Thelma, the drooling bulldog, sat at the end of the large conference room. She had a pink, palatial dog bed where she knew her place as queen. She chewed on what looked like a grenade-launcher plastic dog toy.

That was what Javier concentrated on—Thelma and her bazooka—because sitting across from Colin and Ambassador Cole, and next to Ryder and Trace, he didn't know who thought what or who knew about Sophia and him. It would have been awkward if he hadn't been scared of out his mind.

Luke sat at the end of the table, working a paperclip, and Grayson alternated between rubbing the back of his neck and tapping his fingers on the table. Jared, Brock, and Titan's war-room genius, Parker, waited stoically.

What they knew: SEAL Team 6 had been activated. The live-mic feed played on the speakers from the helo drop point, report after report of bad news.

Gatehouse: destroyed.

Wrought-iron gates: blasted with a car bomb.

A few bodies of PC combatants and all of the RSO were counted as the SEAL team moved forward.

"Passing through front door. Two blast detonation areas."

"Roger that. Keep moving."

"Clear."

"Clear—Jacobson, on your right."

The pops of quick gunfire and targets taken down should have been consoling, but if the PC was still in the embassy, it wasn't a good sign. Javier's gut tightened. Sweat dampened his collar as they continued to listen to the SEAL team's comm. Never had he felt so helpless.

"Approaching the safe room. Damn. This motherfuckin' building saw action." The quiet crackled, and hushed orders fell through the mic. "I've got a dead panel."

Javier had known the building had lost power. But the safe room would be on a backup generator. If that had gone down, no one could get through the door. A conversation bounced with the boots on the ground, and someone named Jacobson had the tools to jimmy a power supply. Minutes ticked by.

"Update?" the CO asked.

"Almost."

"That should do it. Code?"

The numbers were listed over the air, and a muffled noise bounced off the war room's walls. Javier could picture the scene. What he couldn't picture was Sophia. Since the time of known attack, three hours had passed. If she was in the safe room, without ventilation, odds weren't good. But if she wasn't inside, then there were no odds and she was dead.

The man punched the code, each beep bleeding through the room, as Javier held his breath. *Please be alive.* His eyes closed, scrunched tight as he listened to every breath, every move in Honduras.

"We've got a negative on Jansen and Brackster."

Javier's throat burned. His eyes burned. Everything in him needed to believe that she was in that room.

"Got two live ones. Is one of you Sophia Cole?"

Oh, God. Javier's eyes flew open, his mind spinning, shaking, praying that whoever responded would say—

"Yes. I am."

"Oh. *Cristo.*" Relief shivered down his arms, his shoulders caving down as his head dropped. Silently, Javier prayed and rejoiced for the first time since before his sister had been taken. It wasn't a pleading to some greater power—Javier was in *prayer.* He felt thankful as his breaths shook.

He didn't care to join in the cheering conversation between Colin and the ambassador. All Javier knew was his soul had bled and exulted, and he thanked God for the first time in two decades. Sophia Cole was the reason for that.

CHAPTER TWENTY-THREE

Turbulence. Sophia jolted awake. A steadying hand stayed on her shoulder, and she focused on the familiar face of the medic who'd flown back to the States with her. The pieces of reality slid back into place. She was safe, on a plane, however many hours into a twelve-hour flight back home and under medical supervision as requested by her dad. Or probably her mother. Maybe both, considering that sprained wrists and elbow and a couple of cracked ribs weren't the nothing she continued to play the injuries down as.

"Doing okay?" the medic asked.

"Yes." She nodded, but her ears rang with the playback from her dream—or nightmare.

"Hello?" The voice was English. American, unaccented English. Thank God.

It wasn't Javier nor Brackster nor Jensen. But still, the men who broke into the safe room were saviors. "Is one of you Ambassador Cole's daughter?"

"Praise Jesus." Janny's head dropped against the wall as Sophia pushed up unsteadily on bruised bones and hugged her cracked ribs.

"Ambassador's daughter is secure," he said to someone else. "Either of you hurt?"

The man wasn't Delta. He was maybe a SEAL and definitely US military. Two others walked in behind him. There was still no sign of Brackster or Jensen, and the reference to "two live ones" confirmed that she and Janny were it.

"Janella's having chest pains." Sophia turned to her friend even as she felt the man's scrutiny on her. "I'm... fine enough to get out of here."

Sophia's gaze fell out the door. Secretly, silently, hopeful, she wanted to see

Javier walk down the hall to her.
It didn't happen.

"Sophia?"

She shook out of her memory. "Yes, sir?"

"I can give you more pain meds if you need them. Something to help you sleep?"

There was no way she would take a pill that would force her to sleep. It would be hell if she couldn't wake up from her stomach-dropping, chest-aching nightmare where she looked for Javier down the empty embassy hall. Her eyes had kept searching for him even as she and Janny were led away. Just around the corner, just at the airport. Just… nowhere.

Sophia broke from her pathetic trance. Lives had been in danger, people had died, and here she was, daydreaming about a knight in shining armor.

Her life had been in danger, and her last thought, wish, and comfort had been Javier Almeida.

CHAPTER TWENTY-FOUR

Two Weeks Later
Titan Safe House, Caribbean Islands

ANOTHER JOB DONE, another day closer to the epicenter of the PC cartel. Delta had dismantled a major player, and that was something to party over. The crash pad on this Caribbean island was a bonus. Or it should've been. But Javier wasn't feeling the crowd even enough to pay attention to where in the world they were.

Tiki torches outlined the sandy bar. Though they were staying at a huge beach home, courtesy of one of many Titan friends, the team had wandered to this resort bar, looking for whatever fun they could get into.

And tonight seemed to be the definition of fun. It was like the mecca of good-looking and gorgeous. There were ladies in bikinis with wraps—poorly disguised as skirts—around their waists. The bartenders had the drinks flowing, and the music even had Brock drumming his thumbs occasionally on the table.

Luke, Trace, Colin, and Ryder were kicking back at the table across from him, Grayson and Brock on either side. Everyone just chilled out.

But as dinner became a memory and the drinks continued, Colin and Ryder wandered off.

Luke had a woman he would never let go of. Trace was married. Grayson was married. Brock was married.

And Javier was miserable.

"This I never thought I'd see," grumbled Brock.

Javier searched the scene, checking out what could have caused the comment, but nothing caught his eye.

Grayson and Luke chuckled, and Trace sipped a beer, not cluing Javier in to what was interesting.

"What?" he asked, bouncing a bottle back and forth between his palms.

"You." Brock tilted his head toward him.

"Me? What?"

"Nothing." Their boss slugged back the rest of his drink and stood. "Alright, I'm out. See y'all mañana."

Is this what they did when Javier and the guys stayed out to party—talked shit, drank beers, and went to bed? That wasn't much to look forward to. Except, the four of them were happy as snipers in a city full of insurgents.

Grayson and Trace bantered back and forth, laughing about bullshit and talking ops and weapons. All those things should've been conversation worthy, but it'd been weeks since he'd walked out of the Honduras embassy and away from Sophia, and he was fucking miserable. Worse, it'd been fourteen torturous days since he'd almost lost her. Since then, his world had shifted on its axis, and he was too confused to do anything about it.

Adélia versus Sophia.

He had to choose family. There wasn't a middle ground. He couldn't give a sliver of his heart to anyone else. It wasn't fair to her—but which *her*? Javier's chest tightened, and he needed a change of scenery, something to stop the thoughts consuming and confusing him. "I'm out."

They nodded, and when he was a couple meters away, Trace called out, "J?"

He turned, still walking backward, wanting to get away from all the beachy BS. "Yeah?"

"Call her."

He stopped dead.

Grayson nodded.

Trace ran a hand over his chin. "You gave me advice one time, and it was solid. I'm not the guy that knows how to give that back as eloquently, but I will say, just call her."

Luke cleared his throat. All eyes turned to him. They hadn't sat down to hash this out like a gaggle of teenage girls, but words had been spoken. "Call her, bro," Luke said.

From one man ruined by a trafficker to another. Damn it. Javier pinched his eyes shut, turned around, tossed a hand to say good night, and kicked sand all the way until he was on the front patio of the beach house, where he knew he wouldn't sleep.

NIGHT AGAIN, AND Sophia had awakened from a dreamless sleep. How had she ended up back in her parents' house in Pennsylvania in the guest bedroom where she'd first been with Javier? It would've been much less torture to sleep in her own room—it was as cold and foreign as this one—except this one had a warm memory of him holding her, and that was the only happy thought she'd had in this house.

She'd spent two weeks talking with her father, trying to get back in the field because she was *angry* at the world and wanted something to do with her time and with her life. She wanted to make a difference or do *anything* that would keep away the drifting thoughts of the man she wished had saved her.

The phone's ring jarred her back from sleep-soaked thoughts. Unknown number. "Hello?"

"Paixão."

"Javier," she whispered, suddenly wondering if maybe this was a dream and she hadn't woken up.

"Hey, I'm glad you answered."

"Are you okay?" Why else would he call? Delta calls were for emergencies only. That much she knew.

Javier quietly laughed in her ear. "Yes. Are *you* okay?"

"Yes." She kneaded her eyes then checked the time. "It's the middle of the night."

"You're home?"

She pulled the charger from her cell and rested back against her pillow. "How did you get this number?"

"I can get any number. But you're home. Good." He took a long breath. "That's good."

"Colin could've told you that."

"I needed to hear you say it."

She'd been on US soil for too long. Of course, he had to have known by now she was safe. Her mind was sling shooting from one extreme to another: angry he wasn't there then missing him to the point of obsession. She couldn't get a handle on what to say or how to feel. "Did you need something?"

"Yeah. And I got it. You're safe. Sorry it took that for you to come home. But I'm glad you're there."

There, *here*, in the bed where they were first together. He had no idea, and still, she was just as brokenhearted and miserable as the day he'd left her in the kitchen. "Don't find too much comfort in it. I've got a new job." Or she would soon, hustling every lead and connection she had.

"Where?"

"You don't know?"

He laughed quietly. "Guess I could find out. But I'd rather talk to you."

Just like that, Javier could turn the conversation and make her melt. "It's late."

"I can't sleep."

She smiled. "So you woke me up?" That was fine with her even if she couldn't voice anything but snippy bitchiness. Where had he been? And he was worried about her?

"You want me to let you go, paixão?"

"Of course not." *Because when you say that word, my insides turn to liquid even weeks later.* She hated how there was an instantaneous reaction to him—to how he sounded and the thoughts of how he held her and made her body feel.

"Good."

"Good," she replied, curling into a ball with her phone pressed to her ear. "You hurt my feelings."

"I'm an asshole."

"It's not because you had to leave Honduras. I get it. Work. You're in;

you're out. But it was—"

"Talking in your room." Regret tinged his words. "About my sister."

"Yeah." The vivid memory of him hot and protective morphing into cold and mechanical made her stomach turn. "What… happened?"

"It was like a switch flipped. I shut down."

"That hurt, Javier." She closed her eyes, needing to forget that night but wanting to emotionally keep her distance.

"Hurt both of us." He cleared his throat. "When news hit about the embassy attack…"

"Yeah," she whispered. How to put into words what she wanted and couldn't have, what he had and wouldn't give? She would've died to have him as her savior as much as she wished to never hear from him again. "Where are you?"

He heaved a sigh, evidently of the same mindset and begrudgingly letting her change the subject. "Some vacation island."

"Oh, fancy."

"If I had half a chance to choose, we'd be in Pennsylvania."

Her heart clutched, and laughing quietly, she asked, "Really?"

"Yes."

"Not much here. Philly has some nice things to do. Main line. Pittsburgh and Primanti's if you like fries in your food. Or State College if you're into football."

"Stop, Sophia. I'm into *you*. Because I'd want to see you."

"Liar, liar."

"I almost lost you."

Sophia pinched the bridge of her nose, unable to take the back-and-forth but not wanting to play games or miss him more. "So, Delta's on a vacation island. Complete with beach time and coconut rum?"

He paused, taking in what she'd said. "Something like that. Work hard, play hard."

"I can only imagine what you guys were doing."

"Not what I wanted to, Sophia. I've done *nothing* I've wanted to in two weeks."

She let seconds hang on the phone. Her insides twisted. She needed to hear him say it. "And that was find me?"

"Yeah, paixão," he growled.

Her stomach dropped, fluttering. It was the command he had over such an innocent term. *Paixão.* When he said that, her body trembled as though the word was a tactile touch that swam over her flesh.

"Sophia?" he asked, bringing her back from a heated, needy moment.

She licked her lips and took a breath, needing to get a hold of herself. "What does a Delta boy do for fun on an island? I bet girls in bikinis flock like groupies."

Even if Javier hadn't looked as if he'd been blessed by an island god—which he most certainly did—all he had to do was talk, and panties would drop.

"What did I do for fun?"

"Yeah," she whispered.

"Call you."

"Oh." And *that* she felt all the way in her tummy. "You certainly know what to say."

He laughed quietly in her ear. "What does that mean?"

She closed her eyes and tried to slow her racing thoughts. Admitting to him that she was turned on and missing him worse than ever just because of a simple conversation wasn't the best strategic move. "Nothing."

Seconds hung on the phone again, as though he had more to say, and she couldn't hang up.

"Soph, I have some time off coming up. And you're home. So you do too."

Again, need swirled through her. What did she say to that? What did he want—crazy good sex? But how would that leave her feeling? Empty. She wouldn't be in Pennsylvania long-term, and he would never be the guy who stayed home, and she was already so caught up in him that it would hurt when he left.

That was what guys like Javier did. They didn't come home. They didn't fall in love. They didn't have families and babies and warm houses that were really homes, unlike the museum she was staying in at the moment. They didn't do what she wanted, so why was she mentally rejoicing over the opportunity to see him?

"I can't." Disappointed tears she wouldn't shed sprung into her eyes.

"Yes, you can."

Her arms ached to be in his again. Everything tingled on the inside at the thought of him kissing her, sliding into her, and it wasn't just her body that *really* appreciated how talented the man was. It was her swelling, aching heart that was seesawing between bursting and crying that very second. "We had a great week in Honduras. That's all it was."

What sounded like a determined rumble met her ears. "No. We had a great night months ago when I was lucky you were strong enough to walk away from the altar. That night stuck with me, stuck with you. That was a great night. Honduras was *more*."

She gulped but didn't respond.

"Nothing to say? *More* doesn't work? How about *intense*?"

"Intense. Good word." Her throat hurt as she choked down emotion that was too much to feel toward someone who wasn't boyfriend material. "But it was just a week."

"In a war zone, a week is like a year."

"No, it's not."

"Coração, tell me those days together didn't make something inside you feel."

She bit her lip, knowing that he spoke the truth. "Maybe so."

"Better," he said. "You know what I think? That I fucked up. That I missed out on months of hanging out with you. After the wedding, then leaving Honduras."

Tears slipped free. "Javier, stop."

"I want your arms around me, Sophia. I need them. Sinking into you, feeling your body come for me? That's my world. My... need."

Sex. That was all it would be: mind-blowing sex. Nothing would come of it, and she wanted a *partner*—everything she'd felt with Javier *but with roots*.

"Say something, Soph."

She wiped wayward tears away as she readied her defenses. "Where do you live? Like where do you pay rent?"

"I don't."

"And where is your car? Your truck? Whatever you drive."

"Wherever the job is."

"*Your* vehicle."

"Sold it."

She pressed. "Because?"

"Because?"

"Yes," Sophia shot back, needing to hang on to the fragile void she was pushing between them. "Because?"

"Because if I need a ride, Titan hooks me up. Wherever I sleep, Delta's bedding down."

All of that she knew. That was Colin too. She knew the lifestyle. "And now you have time off, you think it'd be fun to hook up—"

"Don't."

"Don't what? State the facts?"

"Play down what we have."

"*Had.*" Tears stung her cheeks as she tried in vain to believe her lies. "It was a week. A freakin' week. I know I'm way too messed up over it, but I also know that it was only a few days of awesome sex."

"Stop it. Don't do that to me."

"Do what?" She pushed herself up from the pillow. "We—"

"I have *very* few memories that I hang onto. That time with you? It's on the short list. Don't drag that through the mud just to make yourself feel better."

Was fighting him away worth protecting her heart, when her arms felt empty without him, and her chest housed an ache that she'd never before experienced? Her lungs hurt; her throat closed. Punishing tears burned down her cheeks. She'd hurt him while trying to protect herself. "Javier, I'm—"

"Stop. Okay?" His husky voice scraped over her with a rawness and realness that she could feel into her soul.

"Okay." She clutched the phone, praying that the back-and-forth of reality and wistfulness would even out and what hurt and what she wished for would level.

"I lost months of hanging out with you because I didn't know better. Now I do."

She sniffled quietly, trying to keep the truth of her emotions from him. "Now you know what?"

"Then I lost weeks away from you after Honduras and, shit, probably years off my life when I heard about the mortar attacks on the Honduras embassy."

Her stomach spun, and her mind melted, but just because the right words poured off his tongue, that didn't change who he was. He wasn't built for the life she wanted. Javier Almeida was emotional trauma waiting to happen. "You don't have a home. You don't have a car. We'd never work."

"Truck," he corrected.

Just like him to ignore the point, which made her smile and long for his kiss. "Whichever," she whispered. "You don't have one."

"No. I do not."

"I'm not made for a man like you. I'm not as strong as you need. I'm too much—too invested; too alive. I feel too deeply for something that you can't be. I'm just not... for you." Stifling a sob, she pinched her eyes closed, but it did nothing to slow her tears.

"Every indication says that you are, paixão."

With that, she couldn't hide the sob. Quiet though it was, it tore from her throat from the depth of her heart. "Javier, I can't. You're built to hunt. You said so yourself. You can't be what I need, and I can't give you what you're desperate for."

"I'm desperate for you. Sophia. Do you get that? *You.*"

"No. You breathe for revenge, and I won't hold you back."

"God! Throwing my words in my face."

"When you left, I was broken. Shattered into a thousand numb pieces. I didn't feel that way walking away from my stupid ex at the altar. It's scary. You're scary. To me. You've hugged me, held me. Made me forget about the reality of our lives. I can't give you anything like you gave me, and you don't deserve what I want. You want to avenge your sister. You should. I believe it in my gut. More than I believe that you should be with me."

"Sophia…"

"More than I have stupid dreams about you holding me in a house that looks like a home. Not this formal bedroom where you made love to me."

Silence hung on the phone. She never should have admitted that. Crap.

"Soph?"

"What?" She sniffled.

"You're lying in that bed? Now?"

"Yes, but what's the point? I'm miserable."

"Misery loves company."

"Wrong thing to say," she said.

"Look, I don't know—"

"I'm headed back out on a job again soon. It'll take my mind off you. You should concentrate on what you need." She stifled a sob. "Okay?"

"Stop it, Soph."

"I hope you get what you need, and after that, I hope someone hugs you, holds you, and puts you back together the way you did me." Then she hung up and cried herself into a dreamless sleep.

CHAPTER TWENTY-FIVE

JAVIER STARTLED AND blinked into the darkness, unsure of how he'd fallen asleep when his gut and head hurt. He scrubbed his eyes and stared into the dark. What had woken him up?

His phone chirped, and his attention turned to the culprit. A text waited to be read. He checked the time. Twenty after two in the morning. The guys were insane if they thought he was dragging himself out of bed to head back to the bar.

Javier swiped the screen and opened a text from Brock.

HQ has the intel you're looking for.

He sat upright, not believing the screen. Maybe this was something to help him torture himself after feeling Sophia's burn. Javier pressed Brock's name on the screen and put the ringing phone to his ear.

"We're a go this time, Brazil." Brock didn't mess with the bullshit of small talk, and for that, Javier was appreciative. "His name is Rodrigo Moreira, and he's the key to everything you want to know about your sister."

Excitement. Elation. Vicious, blood-hungry vengeance. They all played for top billing in his mind. "What's the plan?"

"Wheels up at oh-six hundred. Headed to HQ then off again. So pack your shit, and I'll see you in a couple hours."

The line went dead, and Javier fell back on the mattress, holding the cell and wanting to call Sophia to tell her there was progress. But that wasn't all his life was about—avenging Adélia. His eyes sank shut. Wasn't it?

The familiar jolt of anxious energy wasn't there. If this call had come at any other time, Javier would have packed up and waited at rendezvous until the rest of the team arrived on time. He'd have paced a hole in the ground, thinking of every memory and last moment. But the only thing that came to mind was the haunting assertion in Sophia's voice that they were headed down two different paths in life. And he wanted to be on her path.

BROCK STOOD NEXT to Jared Westin, both glaring down the war-room table. Alongside Javier was the entire Delta team: Grayson, Ryder, Luke, Colin, Trace. Parker Black, who ran the war room and logistics, had just stepped back from thermal images on the flat screen, and everyone was quiet. Even Luke, who had an eerily similar past, waited silently.

The mission was tough. Risk was high. The chance of casualties and equipment loss was outside their usual parameters. All were waiting for Javier to say his opinion. Every man in the room would walk into a hurricane of artillery for him. His lungs hurt, he noticed. Tension and unease that he had no experience with burned in his veins.

There was one answer. *Go.*

This was what Titan had promised him when he joined, what he lived and breathed for: to string up the men responsible for his sister and to crucify Rodrigo Moreira.

Brock cleared his throat. "It's your move, Brazil."

Jared crossed his arms over his chest. "You've got one answer."

Yup, just like he thought. So why the hesitation?

Sophia.

He didn't want to be the blood-hunting savage he'd always been—the guy she didn't want and couldn't imagine her life intersecting with. But screw it. She wasn't his goal in life. PC was. Avenging Adélia. Javier nodded. "Thumbs-up from me."

Brock and Jared reciprocated with a similar acknowledgement. Parker moved to a laptop at the head of the long table and started what would be the course of action. Logistics. Ammunition. Assault. Rendezvous.

They had two hours until they were headed to his home country,

Brazil, where Titan had made the connection with the Honduran and Saudi terrorists and the PC. They had to travel the world to find one asshole connection from his hometown. Titan had unraveled a giant hole in the knotted spiderweb of networking and funding of terrorist activity.

Javier should have been stoked—high-fiving, shit talking, and getting amped up. Instead, he sat in the chair, leaning back, and studied the thermos, ignoring the guys who moved around the war room. There was no bloodthirsty hunger that accompanied the job.

He had nothing except one question: instead of revenge, was it *Sophia* that was supposed to be his life goal?

CHAPTER TWENTY-SIX

Ten Clicks Outside the PC Compound, Brazil

THE NIGHT WAS muggy and hot, and the tepid breeze failed to feel good against Javier's perspiration-covered forehead. Again, his team leader's eyes were on him, and Javier was the last one to give a thumbs-up. "Ready."

Brock nodded as they all waited in the dark of night. The Primeiro Comando compound wasn't on lockdown. They were not alert to the fact that they were the hunted, the prey, or that they would die tonight.

Javier's blood pounded. He could taste the excitement coursing through his veins. The adrenaline kick from an op was always nice, but this was more. It was the culmination of every blood-soaked dream, every vengeful prayer and promise. Tonight was the night.

The operation was simple: dismantle the home base of Rodrigo Moreira, the PC's second-in-command, as cartel leadership played poker and drank *cachaça* and as Moreira smoked a cigar, leaning back, not realizing he was about to take his last breath.

Javier checked his weapons, running through the mental checklist of shit he'd already completed. Then they loaded into two armored Rovers, Ryder at the wheel. Brock sat passenger while both Luke and Javier brooded in the backseat. This job was as personal to Luke as it was to Javier. Trace was in the other vehicle. Three guys from the main Titan team worked this job as well: Cash and Roman were working a sniper-spotter angle on the opposite side of the PC compound, and Winters would go broadside, using as much brute force as tactical know-how to breach the back side of the house. Luke and Javier would have a similar plan while Brock maintained operational command.

The tense drive intensified as they neared the compound.

"Six clicks out," Ryder mumbled.

Luke cracked his knuckles.

Brock radioed the other Rover then checked in with Titan HQ back in the US. They were all monitoring satellite coverage with their eyes to the sky.

But Javier closed his eyes and pictured Adélia. Her sweet face, her innocent laugh, and the way his older sister watched out for him as he should have watched out for her. Blood thumping again in his chest, he opened his eyes as they slowed into the brush cover. The other Rover signaled radio silence as they separated.

In fifteen minutes, they'd link back.

They parked as planned and hoofed the remaining quarter mile. The night covered them in a thick blanket of darkness, but up ahead, the house and its lights came into view. Javier's pounding heartbeat slowed even as they hustled.

"In position." Luke led the second team, his focus laser sharp.

"Locked and loaded, my friends," Ryder called in from his sniper nest one hundred yards to the west, cradled in the limb of a cashew tree.

Javier took a knee by the door. Grayson stood tall across from him and Trace a few feet from them.

"In place," Javier replied.

"You have a go," Brock confirmed in their earpieces.

Three, two, one... a blast sounded from the back side of the house. Diversionary tactic in place, Trace breached the door. Thick wood splintered open. Grayson swung in, assault rifle high, searching the room as Javier went low.

Gunfire spat at the back of the house, and they swept room to room. A maid cowered in a corner. Grayson peeled off to ascertain whether she was friendly or foe while Javier and Trace continued.

The lights were bright. Music played in the background. Cigar smoke lingered in the air, mixing with the scent of blast charges. They went in blind, not knowing who was where.

"Hands on the ground! Hands on the ground!" The words boomed through the comm pieces.

Javier and Trace secured room after room, making their way to Luke upstairs.

The place was clean. The violence had started loudly and was quick to silence. He took a deep breath. Finally. *Finally!* He had what he needed: the sense of peace. Of revenge. Of a future and a life. Of Sophia Cole. One job had done it all.

Trace and Javier rounded the stairs. Three men were subdued. The poker-table pieces were scattered. Gunshots marred the wall, and PC security was down for the count. Gunpowder and blood smelled like victory.

Yet… Luke's face wasn't triumphant. "We lost him."

And all the peace and serenity Javier had experienced for the first time in his life dissipated. "What do you mean you lost him?"

Pure panic, stronger than anything he'd ever felt, hit him. Luke was right. The faces on the ground were not of PC's number two. They were high ranking, no doubt, but not the man he needed. Damn it!

Javier pounded down the stairs. His gaze swept back and forth. No Moreira. "Fuck!"

He kicked over a body, just to be sure. A sniper round had done this man in, and it was not who Javier was looking for. He moved to another room. And another. Roman and Cash's voices communicated over the radio. They had thermal up, night vision on. They had nothing.

Nothing.

"Shit." Javier came to a stop. It was a dead end. Nothing. He had nothing. Fuck!

Slamming his fist into the wall didn't change the outcome. He'd failed. Delta had failed. *Titan* had, and Titan *never* failed. But as Brock and Parker communicated with Luke about what they were finding, taking, detaining, and learning, Javier knew no one else would call this a failed mission.

This was success. They had inventories and shipping information. They had connection and evidence. They had shit that could stop a hundred sales and save a thousand girls. But they had nothing on Rodrigo

Moreira, the one and only reason he'd been on this team for years, and now that Javier had a name to go with his life's mission, it was all he could think about, not just the PC. But there was no Moreira. Blood boiling, temples pounding, he couldn't think, couldn't—

Trace walked in, slapping him on the back. "Keep it together, Brazil."

"Fuck that."

He didn't let go of his hold on Javier and gave him a shake. "Move. Let's go."

Javier bunched his shoulders as tension crawled down his spine. Rage made him an asshole, and desperation made him question everything and everybody. If Moreira had escaped during a highly planned, hyper-tactile operation, he didn't need a military team as well trained as Delta after him. Rodrigo Moreira needed the grim reaper. Javier could find him. He shouldn't have sidetracked with Delta all these years. No, he should've stayed on the hunt, tracking the PC until he discovered Moreira on his own and put a slug through the asshole's forehead.

He slammed a fist into the wall again. How the hell did that dude evade Delta?

Trace clamped both hands on his shoulders. "I see it in your eyes. You're questioning everything."

"Go away."

"Brazil."

"Trace, back off." Yeah, he was questioning the team. His decisions. Life. The PC. Sophia—*Sophia?* Hell. Javier turned and clomped toward the hall—his footsteps echoed. The dull thud of a hollow floor stopped both of them. Trace's eyes met Javier's, and their gaze dropped to the ground. Javier pulled the rug, falling to a knee.

"We've got a possible escape route," Trace called in.

False floor. How did it open? Javier studied the grain of the wood, knocking on the floor with the back of his knuckles. It was well construct-ed and virtually undetectable. In the flash and fire of a raid, it was easy to miss.

"How the shit does that open?" Trace murmured.

"Don't know." Javier shook his head and knocked farther down on the floorboard, then his eyes tracked the faint difference in wood slats.

Trace nodded to him. "Definitely a door."

"Let's go."

"Take it slow," Brock ordered in their earpieces.

Right.

"Ten-four." Trace inspected the opposite side of the hollow-sounding section.

Javier ran his finger on the ground, tracing the section to what had to be a corner piece. It was. He dug in, clawing into the corner.

Trace stepped closer, joining Javier in search of the door. "Slow down, man. It has to be easier than this."

No. There wasn't time. Just like he'd wasted time with years on Delta and months sidetracking with thoughts of Sophia. Time wasn't on his side tonight, and who cared if they tore up this place? Brute force was needed because stealth tactics had failed. Hell, Javier wanted to drop a ton of C4 and blast his way in. Moreira was probably halfway to Rio by now.

Trace clenched a hand on Javier's shoulder. "Chill. You're not in a good head space, Brazil."

"I am." He traced the floor until he found the edge of what had to be a corner to the trapdoor. Flicking his knife open, he pushed it in, jimmying the floor.

"Fuck, man. Slow down. This shit could be rigged—"

Pressure and heat blew them back. Smoke seared his nostrils and burned his eyes. The taste of it burned his throat and tongue as they both fell back from the blast.

Trace rolled over on the floor, pulling Javier back. The words were muffled, and his ears rang. Compression waves from the small blast were too much to hang through. Fighting it off, Javier closed his eyes to the night.

CHAPTER TWENTY-SEVEN

"IS IT SUPPOSED to hurt so much?" Sophia said, trying to smile but gritting her teeth.

"Sorry, darlin'." But the tattoo artist never looked up from her up-turned wrist.

The biting sting into her flesh wasn't the high she expected. It wasn't entertaining, wasn't exciting. If anything, it was heartbreaking. Sophia watched the man memorialize the tree losing its leaves into her flesh. For thirty minutes, she watched and wondered what made Javier like this as much as he did. An addiction, he'd said. Was the bite of the tattoo gun worthy of a craving? No. Because as much as it stung, as much as she tried to hide her grimace and focus on the simplicity of why Javier liked tattoos, she couldn't stop thinking that her tattoo would make her remember him. Forever.

The leaves were lifelike yet had a heart shape, and they were floating off the tree. They were meant to symbolize love found and then lost, but there were new leaves budding on the tree, a simple reminder that one day, she'd find her partner in life.

The gun stopped for a longer pause than what she'd established as the normal process. "Does it really hurt that bad, darlin'?"

She blinked, lost in her thoughts. "What? Um, no."

Actually, she'd been gone, lost in her memories, lost in Javier's smile and the gentle dream of his kiss. She thought of how he could almost order her to climax, and her body would obey. Her heart wanted him to feel love the way she did for him.

"You're crying." His brows were up as though he genuinely didn't want a girl crying while he worked on her. "We can start again another—"

No, she wasn't—whoa, she was. "No, that's, I'm... it's something else."

His face changed as though he understood. It couldn't have been the first time a tattoo memorialized an unrequited future. "You're sure?"

"Positive." Sophia wiped away her tears with her other hand, and the man went back to work. She was a mess and getting a tattoo that wouldn't do anything to calm the storm inside her.

Again, the gun stopped, and he squeezed her forearm, silently asking for her attention. Her attention he got. The work of art on her skin was... breathtaking.

"Wow," she whispered.

"What do you think?" he gruffly asked.

Beautiful. "That's..."

"No tears—come on." He gently placed her wrist down. "Whatever it means, we did it justice."

"You did."

He shrugged. "Just the conduit, darlin'."

"I love it. Thank you."

"Good." He went about swiping goo over the tender flesh, as manly and careful as a tough guy like him could be, in a few quick motions then wrapped her up and sent her packing with strict instructions.

As she walked down the street with the brisk night overhead, she couldn't let go of her Javier thoughts. She and Javier were under the same moon and stars, walking the same planet, but she'd never felt so alone, as though she'd lost something so important.

Taking in a deep breath, she found her Jeep and got in, aware that every move made her arm throb a smidge and that she was being a complete baby. Her phone vibrated in her purse as she turned the engine over, and she absentmindedly searched for it. She found it a second too late.

Missed Call: Unavailable

No voice mail. Part of her heart dropped as though it *knew* the missed call had been from Javier. She'd shut him down the last time he'd reached out to her, yet here she was with his memory indelibly inked into her flesh.

She should have gotten that tattoo with a girlfriend in tow. Then maybe she wouldn't feel so lost and empty. But no one understood how and why she felt the way she did about Javier—not even Tabby—mostly because *Sophia* didn't understand it. Even though Tabby would've been a good sport about it, her company at the tattoo parlor would have been less than genuine.

Sophia watched her phone's screen, praying for a voice mail, but none came through. Hell… she scrolled to the number she should've deleted, not knowing if it was really his number or maybe a burner phone, but she pressed the green button and—it was ringing. She held her breath until his voice mail picked up.

You know what to do.

His simple voice was her undoing. She couldn't leave a message. Couldn't speak. Sophia ended the call, hugged her wrist to her heart and, alone in a parking garage, let loose the tears she wanted to ignore.

THUMP. THUMP. THUMP.

Blood pounded.

Pain exploded.

An aching, hurting, crushing headache hit behind Javier's eyes. All of that could only mean one thing: he was still alive. If he could drop his head back and say a prayer of thanks, he would, but there wasn't a lot he could move at the moment. He couldn't hear much outside the ringing of his ears.

Javier blinked to figure out his surroundings. Trace had his arm around him, hauling Javier down the stairs. Alright, so he was moving…

His feet couldn't find purchase. His legs wouldn't obey commands to walk. His boots fumbled to find each step. All he could do was try to regain his bearings and ignore the squealing, piercing noise that rang in his ears.

Cold air hit his face as they burst outside, and Javier licked his bleeding, raw lips, unable to focus in the black of night.

The supporting hold from under his shoulders dropped carefully, and Javier was on the ground. Vertigo rolled over him. He wasn't moving; that much he knew. But he was falling. Sinking into the ground.

"Damn it." He groaned, trying to take inventory of his senses. He could hear his voice and some of the surrounding noises. Trace talked into his comm piece while he paced. Everything was coming back. He'd survive. A sigh of relief began.

Trace crouched down next to him. "You okay?"

Finally aware of a tingle in his fingers, then his arms, Javier brought his fists to his eyes, rubbing his knuckles to stop the pain. He understood and heard Trace's worry through the ringing. "I'm okay—enough."

"Can you move or—"

He huffed and ground against sore muscles, pushing up. "Yes, just a few minutes."

Time ticked before Trace offered an outstretched hand. Javier growled and grasped it, using more of his teammate's strength to pull up than he was accustomed to. Once on his feet, he removed his fried earpiece and tugged at his ear.

Trace grimaced. "Dude, since you're alive, Brock is gonna kick your ass."

Javier hoped their team leader wouldn't bench him. Not that he didn't deserve it what with rushing and putting Trace in danger. He'd put the whole team in danger, actually. Fuck. He'd screwed up. "Better get to it, then."

CHAPTER TWENTY-EIGHT

THE FARAWAY PULL of the ringing of a phone woke Sophia. She fumbled, grasping for it, and squinted into the brightness of the screen. *Unavailable.* Immediately, her mind jumped as she answered, simultaneously hoping and hating that Javier would call.

"Hello?" Sleep coated her voice, and she swallowed away what surely wasn't sweet or sexy but had to be expected because it was the middle of the night.

"Sophia?" Not Javier.

"Yes, this is." But there was a familiar hint she couldn't place, and her tired brain pushed through dreamless sludge to identify.

"Brock Gamble here. I'm with Delta."

"*Oh.*" Cold panic hit her veins like a freight train. "Is my brother okay?"

"Yes."

If not Colin... dread joined panic, cold and sickening, daring her to hyperventilate. "Javier?"

"He's alive, but he's not great. I need you to get down here."

"Here? Sure. Where's here?"

"Brazil."

"Okay." Her mouth couldn't ask the right questions about Javier's health or why Brock had called her. "Now?"

"*Yes.*"

"I can get there..." How did one get to South America in the middle of the night? "Soon."

"Drive to Virginia. Titan will get you the rest of the way."

Her eyes went wide. "Okay. I can do that." She nodded in the dark, processing his orders.

"He lost something he needed, Sophia. We *need* him. *He* needs *you.* That's how this is going to be. Get down here." He hung up—or so Sophia thought, but then he cleared his throat. "Please, get down here."

"I can do that," she whispered, more concerned that she was about to fail Brock than Javier losing whatever he needed.

"We'll get you wheels up in an airplane when you arrive."

Her fuzzy mind tried to make sense of the details. She didn't keep a "go-bag" on the ready as Colin did. When he was home, he was never far from a bag that he could grab before heading anywhere in the world, surviving for a few days without stopping at a convenience store—or, knowing her brother, an ammo depot.

Okay. She stood up. Things to bring? A passport. Contact solution. She paced, but her phone charger kept her from walking too far. She needed to pack that too, and her international adapter kit, but her list-packing mind was a poor front of her most basic concern. "Brock?"

"Yes, ma'am?"

Painfully, she swallowed her pride, letting panic and dread take a backseat to her desire for Javier to get better from whatever had him down. "I don't know that I'm what he… needs."

"I do, Sophia. Get up. Get moving, and *go.*"

Then, without question this time, the line went dead.

THE SUN BEAT down on her along with all the guilt and worry that Sophia beat herself with. It could've eased up, but the self-flagellation was fine by her. It was a distraction from the worry. Why she thought Javier would be in a hospital or a doctor's office, Sophia had no idea. Delta didn't *do* hospitals. And they certainly didn't *do* private jets staffed with people who could tell her *anything* about Javier's condition.

Private jet? Yes. White-glove staff from Titan Headquarters to the G-5 they were riding in? Yes. An update on Javier? Absolutely not.

They'd landed in Rio de Janeiro, and she was promptly escorted off the plane and deposited in an armored vehicle. Maybe an hour later, the driver pulled up at a monstrosity of a mansion. Covered in vegetation, the estate was like a cultivated jungle. There were greens and pinks and a smattering of yellows as if someone had placed flowers there for effect. In the background, birds sang. The scene was out of a movie, ten shades past what she would call gorgeous, and nothing like the medical sanctuary she had expected.

"Not a hospital," she whispered as the driver closed her heavy armored door.

The warm, fragrant air and lush greenery made her take an easier breath. The looming front door was equal parts intimidating and inviting, and she was unsure whether works of art were supposed to be actually knocked on.

"Ms. Cole." A butler swept his arm back, welcoming her in.

No knocking.

Her family had a mansion built for receptions. As Sophia stepped inside, she recognized this as a *home* that happened to be a *mansion*. The expansive space was filled with personality and love. It oozed the same warmth that was outside—very much not what she'd expected. From the vivid walls to the personal touches—both family pictures and religious art—the décor was abundant, overdone, and *perfect*.

"This way, please."

She nodded, following in awe, mesmerized. They walked up a grand stairway and padded down the gorgeous tile floor until they stopped at a door. The man knocked once then left her alone.

"Thank you," she said to his back and turned to see Javier's bruised and scratched face. "*Oh!* Um, hi."

His mouth parted. "Uh, hey."

Nerves crawled up her throat. "You look surprised."

"I am."

"They didn't say I was coming?"

He shook his head.

A hard, hot blush hit her cheeks. "Oh, okay. Brock said—told—kind of ordered me to come. I don't know. I'll just head back." *To North America.* "See you."

She turned, embarrassed and panicked, wanting to run and not having any idea where to go. No car waited for her in the driveway. She had no commercial round-trip ticket. What had she been thinking? Where was Colin? Maybe she should call Brock.

A strong hand touched her shoulder. "Wait, paixão."

Her legs went heavy at the sound of that one word. Fingertips tingling, she tilted away from his touch, but it pained her to leave his hold. Her mouth mumbled the ego-saving words so she might not cry in front of him. "No, this was crazy. I don't know what I was thinking. I'm sorry I showed up unannounced."

But he spun her to him. "Stop."

"I—okay." Embarrassed pain sliced in her throat. A white-hot coiling pushed the tears from her eyes and cut the air from her lungs. His eyes... oh, he pitied her. No, no, no. And yeah, she loved him. Wanted to be in his arms. Wanted to take care of him for as much as she was hurting.

"Take a breath, Sophia."

But she couldn't. It wouldn't happen. His bare feet stepped closer. Her bottom lip trembled. She searched his face. It'd been cut and bruised. He was in pain, but he cupped her cheek, letting his thumb slide on her skin, wiping away a tear.

"Hi, paixão."

"Hi," she whispered.

She swallowed, catching her breath, remembering how to breathe and that she needed to. "You're in Brazil."

"So are you." His smile was such a gift. Then he winked. God save her; she was melting...

"It's where I live."

Wait—"This is your house?"

Javier tossed his head back and howled—laughter and pain commingled. "No. But nice, right?"

She smirked at him, laughing as he hooked her under his arm. It'd been too long since they'd been in an embrace. "Are you okay?"

Nodding, he held her a little tighter, maybe thinking the same thing. "Bumps and bruises. Just my ego, I guess."

"Looks like more than bruises to me."

He shrugged.

"Why your ego?"

He tilted his head toward the room. "Want to come in?"

She nodded, and he took her hand, guiding her into a bedroom that was the size of her first apartment. "So…?"

"Need anything?" He slipped her bag off her shoulder and tossed it onto a chair.

"No."

"I'm benched." He shrugged, distant and dismayed. "Sucks. But I deserved it. And being the way Delta rolls, they stuck my ass here in posh and civility, under a doc's eye, until my team leader feels interested in talking to me." He shook his head. "And after the ass ripping I earned, I may be stuck in this palatial prison for-fuckin'-ever."

She smiled. "Hard life."

Javier raised his eyebrow. "You're here."

"I am."

"Thanks."

Sophia nodded. "So what happened?"

"Didn't think."

"Ran face-first into a blast zone?"

"Something like that."

"Are you… okay?"

He stared then turned, walking to the French doors that opened to a balcony. She trailed behind him, never having seen him in track pants and a T-shirt. It was interesting how formidable he still seemed in a room like this and dressed like that.

They stood on the balcony overlooking thick greenery. His hand found hers, and they stayed in silence.

With a squeeze, Javier gathered her to his chest. "Thank you for being here." His mouth dropped to her ear. "Stay?"

Tummy flipping and mind spinning, she nodded. "Of course."

"Best medicine yet."

Her cheeks warmed as his hands ran over her back. "How much medicine have you needed anyway? Thought it was just bumps and bruises."

Javier's lips found her neck. It wasn't a kiss but more like a taste. Every doubt and uncertainty washed away as a cascade of shivers ran down her spine, rocketing all the way to her toes. Sophia sighed, leaning into him as his kiss deepened. His tongue flicked, and his lips sucked. Even the gentle scratch of his teeth felt good. "God."

With the mumbled moan, Javier turned her. Their stomachs touched, and his hands ran down her shoulders until he interlocked their fingers. "I want to hear that again."

"God?"

"No. That sound. That sigh. The sweetness that fell out of your lips." Javier's hands stayed knotted in hers, but he pressed into her. Slowly, eyes locked in a trance, he pushed until Sophia's back hit the stucco wall.

They were in heaven, surrounded by the jungle, one of the most beautiful places on earth she'd ever seen. Yet it was Javier that had her mesmerized.

He tilted his head, turning his attention back to her neck. The gentleness of his mouth made her mind spin, but it was the strength of his body, pushing her against the grating wall, that took her by surprise. He dropped her hands, roughly running his up her arms and into her hair.

"Sophia." He breathed against her lips, threading fingers into her hair, tugging her head back, and opening her for a kiss. His tongue delved deep; his taste was sweet. Full lips owned the kiss.

That was what she needed: him, in the middle of nowhere, no pressure. Her mind calmed under the kiss, and everything she worried about and wanted from him and was scared of—*everything* was gone.

He pulled back, still holding her tightly in his hand. "Paixão."

Javier tugged her shirt overhead and dropped it, not wasting a second to stare. He removed her bra with the same efficiency. Exposed and aroused, they were outside in the middle of nowhere as the warmth of the sun hit her breasts.

He bent, taking her nipple into his wet, warm mouth. Tongue flicking and sucking deeply, he massaged her other mound as her head dropped back against the hard wall. With each caress, her heart skipped a beat. The sensitive flesh between her legs came alive, needing a touch as deliberate as he was doing to her chest.

"Javier," she breathed, and it was her turn to thread fingers into his hair. Thick, lush locks filled her palms, and as she held him to her, he pulled her pants down over her hips, taking with them her panties.

"Step out, Soph."

She did, hands still buried in his hair, bare to the world and pressed underneath a completely clothed man. Her shoes kicked to the side with the rest of her clothes, she pulled his head back, aware of how naked she was, and an exhibitionist thrill ran through her.

"Spread your legs."

She took a shy step apart.

"Further." He sank to his knees, dragging his hands—his tongue too—down her stomach.

God. He looked up, and she couldn't breathe. Her alpha man, down on his knees and—shit, his fingers went between her legs, stroking her wet folds. Using an elbow, he urged her wider. "Pretty little good girl."

Moaning, she nodded, liking how he said those words and how he appreciated her vulnerability. Javier pressed his fingers to his mouth. "You taste like mine."

A twist in her heart exploded, and she nodded, unable to speak. Her throat had knotted, and her mind had stalled. With no more warning than a smile, he kissed her stomach and continued to stroke her slit.

"Feel good?"

"Yes."

He spread her open and loved on her clit. "That too?"

Sophia's head fell to the side. "*Yes.*"

His fingers dipped inside her wanting body, and damn, it'd been too long since he'd touched her like that. She moaned at the intrusion, and he took that as invitation to press deeper, surer, stronger.

Sinking lower, he licked her hip bone, trailing to the trimmed patch of hair, then swirled his tongue around her clit. Sensation overload. Javier curled his fingers just enough to make her cry out, suckling hard enough to make her writhe against the wall, scratching her back, and she did not give a damn about that bite of pain.

His wet fingers pulled out, drifted back, and teased further. Then even *further. "Javier."*

The slick touch of his fingertip on her ass was more than she could handle. He nuzzled his face between her legs and circled her tight hole, which had never been touched. She shouldn't like it. But, God, she did. It was sensitive and erotic and forbidden, like having him finger her on a balcony.

"Easy," he whispered against her sensitized flesh.

Nodding, she whimpered, trying to be easy, to relax. Javier pushed his shoulder under her thigh and kissed her pussy. The stubble on his cheeks scratched the inside of her leg, his chin doing wonderful things to her flesh as he teased and circled his finger inside her.

"God." Her gasp shook; her body tightened. Parts of her that had never been touched begged for more.

Javier alternated to her clit, his lips encircling, his tongue wicking, and his scratchy chin pressed against her folds. One finger teased her ass; the others slid inside her pussy. A three-front attack stormed her as she gave herself over to him. Javier pushed and pumped, licked and kissed.

"Please." The impending climax was so good it almost hurt.

He leaned his weight into her, tilting her just right, growling against her clit. "Paixão, come for me."

The intensity slammed. The orgasm came as one had never come before. Sensations she couldn't get enough of and had never had before mixed with what worked so damn well, and Sophia lost her mind. "Javier!"

"There you go." He didn't let up, driving deeper, milking her response.

Sophia thrashed, feeling the scrape of the wall against her back. "God."

Her body quaked, and the wave of rippling muscles ran deep. Javier's lips and tongue gentled. His fingers did too. Even as her sensitive parts spasmed against his kiss, he worshipped between her legs, murmuring, kissing, and savoring. Everything about this man was perfect.

With the sun on her face and the warm breeze picking up, he held her, and she collapsed against him.

"*Gosto muito de você.*"

"What does that mean?"

"I am… gone for you." He scooped her into his arms and carried her through the French doors, leaving them open for the fragrant breeze to hit the air conditioning. Her humming body rode the aftershocks in his arms as they lay in bed. Javier pulled the shirt over his head, freezing midstrip and staring. He took her wrist, delicately holding it. "What's this?"

"A tattoo."

"I see that. Why?"

She blinked, shyness mingling with the magical feeling that only he could create. "I wanted to see how I felt about something and looked toward the future."

"What something?"

Sophia looked away, but Javier caught her chin. "Tell me."

Steeling her heart, she looked at the heart leaves—the ones blowing away and the ones growing anew. "To remember you."

"I'm here, Soph. I told you that. *I told you that.* That I want you."

"You want two things, and *one* you should have more."

Javier shook his head. "Sophia—"

"I didn't do this to upset you. I did it because I wanted to always re-member… you. When you go off to do your thing, and I'm doing mine. If this is supposed to happen, later…" Her new heart was blossoming on the unshakable tree. "But if it wasn't going to happen, I wanted to always remember."

How much I love you.

He wrapped his arms around her, hugging her as though she were his world, and curled around her body. "I haven't slept well in days."

That was the story of her life except when she was with him, but in his arms, her soul sighed.

Javier pressed his lips to hers, not kissing, just… touching. "Sleep with me."

She nodded, leaning into him. Javier adjusted the pillows underneath their heads then pulled the cover from the side, not bothering to crawl underneath. Seconds later, with the brilliant light shining and the fragrant breeze rolling in, he fell asleep.

With even breaths, she replayed the last twenty-four hours: the terror, the fear, the straight chaos of worry. Those feelings had morphed into an intense need, and now, there was nowhere on earth she'd rather be.

Javier cuddled closer, waking slightly and pulling her to him. "I'm in love with you, paixão."

Sophia's gag reflex jump-started. One second she was staring at Javier, feeling weightless, with her mind free, able to fly in his arms with no responsibilities, no focus, nothing except him and her and the warmth bleeding between the two.

Out of nowhere, harsh feelings she hadn't dealt with slammed her into the cold. Her mind wasn't with Javier. It was her awful ex, ruining the moment. Every time she had said the word love had been with Josh. Not once had she thought the word *love* for Javier. That headache had been reserved for Dr. Josh, the ex she couldn't forget.

Love you, Sophia.

Sophia. I love you.

Will you marry me, Sophia? I love you.

And she'd responded the same way every time—"I love you too"—because she thought she had loved him. The words were ruined. Her gag reflex wanted to dry heave all over Brazil knowing that phrase and sentiment had unknowingly been destroyed. Crap, she'd been so ridiculously slow to comprehend what love was.

And now *she was in love* with Javier.

She didn't want more, just the man in front of her. She loved Javier, and the words were ruined. They wouldn't come out of her mouth.

I love you. It didn't mean anything like the way she'd felt before.

"I—um—" Jesus. Physically, she couldn't vomit the words out. She should speak! Or instead, drop to her knees and pray. Thank God that there was a man like Javier who would offer to love her, and she was a stuttering, ridiculous mess. "Javier—"

He pressed two fingers to her shaking lips. "Shh."

"But, I—" Tears pricked her eyes.

"Sophia. Don't say another word."

She was ruining their moment. He must have realized it was insane to love a woman who couldn't speak and that she was a hot mess if there ever was one. She asked for so much from him and couldn't give him simple words. *My God!*

But his smile was—wonderful. Sweet. Caring. And, damn, so sexy. Just like the accent that rolled off his tongue when he said the simplest commands.

"Please don't hate me," she whispered.

"Only if you say something like that again." Javier wrapped his arms around her, pulling her to his chest. One of his hands threaded into her hair, and the other kept her clasped tight as she heard the steady, rhythmic beat of his heart.

"Javier—"

"Too soon? Too crazy?"

"No."

"Too what?" he asked.

How to explain that a simple phrase *wasn't good enough* to justify her feelings and that Javier wasn't worthy of what she'd wasted on Josh?

His fingers flexed into her, and her ear pressed on the broad, muscular expanse of his chest. She pinched her eyes closed and concentrated on the steadiness thumping in her ear. The calmness. The complete assuredness of him holding a shaking, fumbling her in his thick arms while he was the one hurt, the one who needed caring.

"Paixão?"

Sophia broke from his heartbeat trance and tilted her head, resting her chin on his breastbone. Her eyes asked, *Yes?* while she couldn't muster a single word.

"It's okay."

The burn of emotion stung in her eyes. "I—" *want to tell you. Want to share. Need you to know.* But instead of mumbling any half-assed thought, she clung to him, hugging him with the burning need to show him how she could not possibly love, need, care, and crave anyone the way she did him.

He stroked her hair, soothing away the surge of desperate panic.

"When it's time, I'm here."

And *it* was gone—the fear and uncertainty. He was simply the best. The sting in her eyes lessened, and the squeezer in her heart relaxed. Javier Almeida was a saint. And she'd been pushing him away for weeks because he couldn't commit to a picket-fence lifestyle.

"Thank you, Javier." A single tear spilled, and with it, she took a breath and kissed his chest in an emoting way, claiming him in the only way she could until she could find a way to say, *Javier, I love you too.*

CHAPTER TWENTY-NINE

T HE SMELL OF bacon and eggs pulled Sophia from an easy night's rest in Javier's arms. His strength and the memory of his words surrounded her. Yes, she was happy and willing to put aside her list of what she thought would constitute a happy life. What did it matter if he roamed the world? She too felt that need, and hadn't she given Josh hell for taking advantage of it?

Javier was what she wanted. Nothing about him needed to change. Silly things like where he might bank or sleep or what vehicle he might drive didn't matter. Those criteria were armor for her heart, an impenetrable coating that Javier would never get through because he wasn't that man. Deep in her soul, she knew that.

Wow. Good job looking out, subconscious, but it's time to ease toward another risk. She couldn't flat-out *tell him* how much she loved him, but actions spoke louder than words anyway.

"Lost in thought?" The scratch of morning-tinged words was quiet and powerful. Sophia felt each syllable massage down her body as the scruff of his cheek touched her shoulder.

"Yes."

"About?"

"You," she said.

"Ah." Deft hands turned her languid body to him. "Want to clue me in?"

"Should I?"

Javier nodded. "You should."

"What if I say something that scares you?"

His eyebrows went up, and he laughed, squeezing her into a hug.

"First, I don't scare. Second, that thing I said to you that I won't say again but still mean?"

Oh God. There the world went, spinning sideways even though she was safely tucked in his arms, in bed. "Yeah?"

"I'm not going anywhere."

"Okay."

"Tell me your thoughts."

"Bossy." Sophia smiled, blushing and biting her lip.

"Please." He kissed the lip she bit, taking a moment to bite it as well before sweetly, gently letting it go. "Tell me."

"Is this our version of happily ever—" A hot blush hit her cheeks. "Happily for now?"

"You want it to be? For now? If I try for you, when—" He shifted, uncertainty tightening his jaw. "When I don't know how I feel about you doing what you do—"

"And, *I* don't know how *I* feel about you not having a place in the world."

"Meaning?"

"No car, no truck, no rent, no apartment. No home."

"But I will have you."

Wow. Her mouth hung open.

His eyes locked to hers. "That's enough for me to ignore my concerns. Is it enough for you?"

"I already decided yes."

"We try?" he asked. "We make an *us* work."

"Yes."

Javier rolled on top of her, threading his fingers into her hair, letting her take the brunt of his weight just enough that she could feel his ownership, breathe in his happiness, and wrap her limbs around him, hoping to hug and share a tenth of how loved he made her feel.

THREE DAYS IN paradise had gone by in a flash. Now, in grand Delta fashion, Javier stood by Sophia on the runway next to two Lear jets. One was headed to Titan Headquarters to drop off Sophia and give her the opportunity to take on a job that she was excited about but that gave Javier heartburn. The second jet would take Javier to meet his team in an undisclosed location.

This was it. Time to say good-bye. The real world called, and their real world was a lot tougher than most people's.

"You okay?" she asked.

He was worried about her. Titan HQ was one of the safest places on earth, but what about where she went after that? Not that she was taking jobs that had her repelling out an Abu Dhabi skyscraper, but she had managed to find a decent bit of trouble in Honduras.

"I'm good, paixão."

Tension hung between them still. She shifted, and neither of them walked toward their respective jets.

"Oh, Hana is in the US."

Sophia legitimately looked thrilled. "Good."

"She'll be safe," he said.

"Never one hundred percent." *Just like you* was the part she didn't say. "But that's great news. Javier, tell me this will work."

He blew out a breath and looked down at the one thing in the world he couldn't stand to lose. Scooping Sophia into his embrace, he whispered into her ear, "I promise, paixão. Promise. We will make this work."

"Good."

"Besides, I've always wanted a girlfriend."

Her face lit, chin resting on his sternum. "I'm your girlfriend?"

Laughing, he shrugged. "I don't have a car, apartment, or mortgage. Have to start somewhere."

She hugged his chest and stifled a sob of nodding agreement. "See you soon."

Then the woman he loved planted a kiss on his lips that didn't last nearly long enough and took off for her jet, trying to hide her tears.

"I love you, paixão." Javier boarded his jet, torn apart, all because he'd found his reason for breathing and missed her already.

CHAPTER THIRTY

Four Weeks Later
Outside Kandahar, Afghanistan

BROCK CAME OVER to the team huddled on the ground, sitting in the sand, wondering what on earth had trumped their current job enough that he walked away midsentence during their ops briefing. They soon found out. Rodrigo Moreira had been found with a cartel trading partner in Saudi Arabia who had placed him in a safe house in Afghanistan. With this takedown, Javier would be able to finally ruin the PC, finally take out his revenge and dismantle the last slippery piece of the PC puzzle that he'd searched for his entire life. Tonight, his life's mission would come to rest.

But apparently, he'd have to wait until after Brock handled whatever had interrupted their final debriefing for what everyone was now calling Javier's job.

Never one to mince words, Brock stopped at the head of their gathering. "Colin, on your feet. Let's go."

Again, without another word, he left. All eyes went to Colin, who looked just as caught off guard as the rest of them. But he jumped up and trailed their team leader. From twenty feet away, under the cover of a quickly falling sun, Javier watched the two men talk. Colin's stance shifted. Brock squared, finished with whatever he had to say. Then they stood in silence, the tension evident.

Colin said a one-word answer, and Brock nodded, slapping the guy on the shoulder. Whatever that conversation had been, it held meaning. A beat passed, and they stalked back. Colin's hardened face was unreadable other than he was *pissed*. Murderous. Vengeful. One bad decision away from okaying a nuclear war.

"New priority." Brock dropped down, pushing what he'd been working on aside.

That pissed Javier the fuck off. They were closing in on a trafficker who they'd been chasing for months from one side of the globe to the other. His gaze flicked from Brock to Colin and back again. "New priority?"

"Yeah, asshole," Brock growled. "Stand down."

Javier's molars ground together as his fists clenched, but he kept his jaw wired shut and tried to focus, nodding his willingness.

"Sophia Cole was kidnapped four and a half hours ago in Paris. Algerian Combat Group has taken credit."

Javier's head swam. His heart sank. The last month had been the best in his life even though he and Sophia had often been ships passing in the night. More than that, terrifyingly, the ACG were the assholes who'd videoed beheadings and posted them on YouTube. They were the fucks who didn't negotiate. Not that there was a negotiation to be had. No, he wanted bodies.

Sweat brimmed on Javier's brow. His nostrils flared as he tried to maintain composure, and he wanted war. He wanted blood. He wanted them to pay. He wanted his woman, and he wanted in on the rescue. There was nothing to stop him from getting to her.

Brock continued. "Titan HQ is confirming with CIA and the Pentagon. We're the team closest to her assumed location."

"Which is?" Javier asked.

"Tunisia."

He growled. Tunisia meant mountains and desert in a country that might've had a democracy but still had jihadist attacks, where the ACG had their fair share of home bases. Delta could get there in a couple hours. If one drop of her blood had been shed, God help the men holding her. Had terrorist groups been put on earth to terrorize the women he loved? Eradicating them wasn't even an option anymore.

"We'll break up into two teams. Javier, you'll stay here, take a smaller team, and complete—"

His blood froze. "No."

Brock's jaw hinged before he squinted. "Excuse me?"

"I'm on Sophia's op."

Brock flexed his jaw and ran a hand over his chin, studying Javier. "You've been tracking *this* job."

"*No.* Sophia is *mine.* This is a *job.*"

Brock had made assumptions when he'd invited Sophia to Brazil, but that'd been over a month ago and primarily to focus him back on Delta. No one knew what'd been going on with them, and he hadn't shared. They were perfect as they were, doing what they did and living as they lived—quietly, happily, and figuring things out as they each took on jobs traveling the world, trying not to tell the other to stay home.

How had that that worked out for him? *Not. Good.*

Colin's confusion pinched to a glare, but with the stakes what they were, he settled back, more unsure of why Javier was claiming his sister than pissed that a stake had been made. "What?"

Javier held Brock's eye. "I'm on her op, with or without you."

All eyes fell on Javier, but he didn't waver from his demand. He knew their thoughts. They'd watched him obsess over the PC, and cartels in general, since Brock had brought him on board.

"I promised you one thing, Brazil." Brock's scrutiny intensified. "One. And this is it. The day I found you, I offered you this gig. Gave you a job on Delta, with Titan. I said you have the opportunity for revenge. The day has come, Brazil. This is your chance. Rodrigo Moreiro on a platter. Blood for blood."

"I understand that."

"You do?"

"I do."

"You miss this job, and someone else on this team will take your revenge."

It didn't matter. PC blood would be shed; the last piece of the cartel would be shattered. They would be dismantled. Ruined. Never to exist again. He might not deal the final blow, but they would be gone. "I'm on Sophia's op."

An eternity of a second ticked by. Brock nodded. "You're on Sophia's op."

CHAPTER THIRTY-ONE

S HIVERING ON THE floor, Sophia knew there was a bounty on her head that the US government would never pay, and even if they did, the Algerian Combat Group would kill her anyway. They'd behead her and make a YouTube video of it. Those sensationalist cell-footage shots were the hype that the ACG thrived on.

But at least her death wouldn't be pointless. Someone had to care that a girl from Pennsylvania went out that way. Someone would talk about the good she'd done in the world, how she'd fought for equality and basic human rights for women and children. Sophia sobbed, realizing that she was drafting her obituary.

The room was the size of a closet and smelled like the memories of victims. She leaned back, tapping the back of her head against the cement wall. Dirty light crept into the small space through large crevices along the ceiling and doorframe. The harsh wall crumbled into dust when she scratched and kicked at it, but judging from her brief glance as they locked her in, it had to be more than a foot thick. She could scratch and kick for weeks, turning her confines into a pile of gravel, but it wouldn't make a difference. There was too much material to go through and not enough time to enact a plan or room to hide her destructive process.

She breathed in the scent of death, not ready to die and not wanting her obituary to stop at only a few decades of life.

The ground rumbled. Gravel shifted from the top of the walls, letting tiny pieces of rocks break loose. She heard them hit the ground. Another rumble sounded. More wall dust and dirt loosened, some stinging her eyes.

Shit, they were on the side of a damn cave or mountain. Was this an earthquake? It could be a mortar attack or the repercussion of an explosion.

But the tremors didn't return. An eerie quiet hung as she listened and waited for the big one, an assault that would tell her they were being attacked. Then the walls would crumble and cave in, crushing her to death, pinning her into the ground. That would be much worse than a beheading—slow suffering and suffocation. Then there'd be no reason for her name to be in the news, not that she wanted fame, but she wanted justice and attention on the causes she had risked herself for over the years.

Sitting statue still, Sophia closed her eyes and listened to the roar of silence.

Not another sound.

Click. And then she heard the tiny whir of something slowing down as though a quiet engine or a fan had been running and she had only just realized it.

Now it was silent.

Her skin prickled as she anticipated Mother Nature as well as the ACG. The lights went black. Her eyes went wide, waiting and watching for the rush of men with cell-phone cameras pointed her way to blast through the door, swinging machetes, ready to slice her neck in the name of a YouTube video.

Or… a trickle of hope teased her. Had her dad pulled strings, made favors, paid a ransom, or asked Delta?

There was nothing more. No rattles. No shakes. No falling dust to sting her eyes. Just Sophia alone in the dark. How many seconds had passed? Maybe minutes?

She'd been alone for hours with someone checking on her every day, she figured. They threw in enough food to keep the hunger pangs and headaches away. Maybe she was cracking up. Solitary confinement could do that. The lights were out. She wasn't imagining that. Tremors and shakes could be a delusion—or, given the part of the world they were in, maybe just everyday life.

She took a sad breath. Nothing. It had been nothing. Her hopes had jumped, and her overactive—or maybe bleary—imagination had taken over. Now all she had to do was sit in the dark and wait to die.

The walls rumbled. They shook. The dust sprayed. The rocks crumbled. Surprised and scared, she twisted and fell. Disorientation wracked her. The blackness surrounded her as she fell onto the dirty floor. Her shoulder and cheek hit. Her elbow too. A wave of pain mixed with nausea sliced through her, and vertigo hit hard. She didn't know up or down. Her mind could confirm that her butt was on the ground, but her—

A close and loud boom struck. More dust and dirt rained down. The noise came the way of the exterior door, and then *her* door nearly bowed with the force of a knock.

"Clear, paixão. I'm coming for you."

"Javier!" She clawed to push off the ground, away from the door, but wanted to be closer to his call of safety.

A heartbeat later, a dull thump sent the door swinging off its hinges, and footsteps came toward her. All was dark—no flashlight, no sign of who it was—but hard hands wrapped around her. His face was covered with goggles, his head and neck not visible. But it was Javier. His glove-covered hands and weapons-strapped body pulled her close and swept her up.

"Oh," she moaned as her stomach turned and her eyes pinched at the sudden movement. "My head."

"It's okay. You're okay." With her still held to him, they moved fast. "Target acquired."

Her body jostled, and her stomach lurched. Voices blurred in her mind. Quiet but forceful updates and orders. She was the target. They'd acquired *her*. She was going to survive as long as they did. They always did. Always. So said Colin, and she believed in Javier.

Pops of distant gunfire echoed, and Javier never stopped moving but kept straight on his path, strong in his intentions. The man did not waver. Two of his teammates flanked him, and they returned fire. She jumped and lurched into him, but Javier hauled ass.

They exited a long tunnel into the night, and cold air hit her. It had to be freezing, but her system was so shocked by the sting of frigid breaths that she forgot to shiver. Javier was covered in gear and body armor. She couldn't feel his warmth or his muscles or the curve of his body holding hers, but she remembered it all, and from the inside out, she could feel her very survival becoming more certain.

Javier had saved her and Hana in Honduras.

He'd saved her from the ACG.

He'd taken care of her the night of her wedding.

He cared for her. Her eyes leaked, tears streaming down her face and biting in the cold. Harsh wind blew over them, and it took the night to pass for what felt like eternity before they came to a harsh stop. He dropped to one knee, propping her on his thigh, and tore off his headgear, pulling off the hat that also covered his face. He buried himself into her neck, holding and hugging her as though he'd saved mankind.

Her fingers threaded into his thick hair. The very essence of Javier Almeida captured her, surrounding her in a feeling of certainty and protection. She couldn't guard her heart from him, couldn't stay away from what he dreamed of. If he wanted to traipse the globe, searching for cartels to kill and criminals to bring to justice, that was fine. If he came home once every third op, that was fine. As long as it meant he was coming home to her, their definition of reality could be whatever they wanted it to be.

She clung to him, embracing his warmth, loving how he made her world safer. *Loving* him.

"Thank you," she whispered.

His arms tightened, and his cheek nuzzled against her neck. "*Estou com muita saudade de você.*"

"Whatever that means, me too." She kissed the top of his head and let the world drift away when he gathered her back into his arms and hustled to a lowering stealth chopper.

One, two, three, four of them hopped in behind her. The helicopter teetered and lifted, bumping her against Javier. The adrenaline high of an operation was in the air, and quietly, they whispered that it was a success. They stripped gear off their heads and leaned back for deep breaths. Her heart still pounded, and from somewhere in the helicopter, she heard a familiar voice.

"Target safely stowed. On our way to rendezvous."

They dipped down, and her eyes lolled in her head. While Javier was holding her, a hand reached out and touched her cheek. Her eyes opened.

"Colin."

He briefly smiled, his worried eyes saying more than he would ever voice. "Always have to make a scene when you need an exit."

She laughed quietly. "Always."

Javier didn't speak, and he never let go. They lowered down, and he deposited her in front of her father at the closest US Air Force Base.

With a nod, she was left alone. Javier, Colin, and the other men walked away as ordered. Javier had promised they'd be together as soon as they could, but her arms needed him at that moment. Instead, she was encapsulated in her father's well-meaning hug.

"I love you." The words weren't meant for how her father took them, and she cried inside, missing the man who had to go back to his job and hating that she hadn't told him to his face what he deserved to hear.

CHAPTER THIRTY-TWO

OUTSIDE JAVIER'S DOOR, Sophia stood, her fist raised, ready to knock, but did not know what to say. The ordeal had its ugly hold on her, and even if she pretended to be unaffected, she was traumatized. But that wasn't why she needed to be there. She needed him to take her, hold her, make love to her, and kiss her until the night melted to morning. She needed to be in his arms as though that were the key to her heart's next beat.

The door cracked, and she stepped back. "Um, I… hi."

"You okay?" Javier asked as though he knew how long she'd waited outside, trying to manage her thoughts.

She nodded, awkwardly dropping her knocking hand and unsure about what she wanted to say. Rehearsing would've been a good idea. Though when she thought of words she wanted to share, all she could feel was an all-encompassing need—for him. For more. For life. For *everything*.

"Come in." He backed up, holding the door for her.

His face was clean shaven. The T-shirt that stretched across his chest could've been painted onto his canvas of muscles. Even his jeans hung on his hips, as if he were the poster boy for sexy—in sheer, utter, absolute perfection. But more than that, her heart sighed when she drew closer.

"Thanks." Overwhelmed by the flutters in her stomach and desperation in her mind, she took a step inside the motel room. Her shoulder brushed his chest as he moved to shut the door, making her skin shiver. The spark zinged down her neck, sizzling to her fingertips, but her mind fell apart.

Yes, Javier was tall, dark, and handsomer than her wildest dreams. But he was also her savior. She was alive because of him. Sophia turned—not thinking—and she sobbed, collapsing against the protective cocoon of his body.

His strong arms wrapped around her. The door clicked shut, and he pulled her tight into a hug, soothing her with foreign-tongued whispers she didn't understand.

"I'm so sorry. I didn't mean…" *To break down and fall apart?*

Javier hushed her, walking them to the bed. "It's fine."

"No." But the cathartic release of tears and renewing sense of his touch was exactly what she needed. Just him.

He sat down, holding her to his chest. "Sophia. It's okay."

"God." She sniffled and wiped her cheeks. "All I do is cry around you. It's pathetic."

He gave an almost nonexistent headshake. "You've had a few shakeups. But we've had a few perfectly normal weekends when you weren't getting kidnapped."

Her face twisted.

"Okay, no jokes." Two of his fingers pressed under her chin, lifting her gaze. Fiery dark eyes held her, reassuring her. A calm eased through her, and he smiled softly. "You're safe now."

He was the reason she could agree to that. "Colin said you walked off a Primeiro Comando job."

He nodded.

"For me?"

"You're more important." He pressed a kiss to her forehead, letting his lips linger and drag to her temple, and his thumbs swept away the last trails of tears. "Because I had to find you."

She melted into him. "Thank you." But it was *I love you* that tickled the tip of her tongue.

Javier pulled her to his chest and lay back on the bed. Their arms entangled. Their legs twisted together. She could breathe. The heavy weight in her shoulders and the knot in her throat were transformed from on the edge of losing it to enjoying her very own heaven. Her eyes slipped shut, and the faint smell of his cologne made her warm inside. He surrounded her without smothering, raised her up from the fear she didn't realize had clawed her down.

"Open your eyes, Sophia."

She did, and he was beautiful. Handsome. Protective. Everything a man needed to make a woman swoon. And Javier did it unintentionally. He studied her as though inspecting her soul. Sophia leaned forward, eyes still open and gaze locked, until her lips met his. It was sweet, sensual, and soft, but he conveyed it as undiluted power.

Her tongue went to the seam of his mouth, and he breathed in deeply, opening for her kiss and wrapping his arms tighter around her.

Javier pulled her to straddle his hips. "I missed you."

Her hands cupped his cheeks. "Missed you, too."

"Don't stop kissing me, Soph. Don't stop at all."

He held her close and let her lead. She savored the velvet stroke of his tongue and the way his strong hands smoothed across her back.

"Promise." Drunk on him, she let the world slip away. Her palms ran down his neck, and she leaned back to tug his shirt up. Javier pulled the cotton tee overhead, and when he was bare chested, she dropped her kiss to the tattooed malin over his heart.

Despite undressing, it was her tree tattoo that Javier kissed. "Do you know what this looks like?"

Sophia let her tongue linger on the malin's lines. "The obvious. A tree."

"A Brazilian nut tree."

She smiled, drifting her tongue to the end of the arrow, and her soft touch turned to a scratch. "Is that a real thing, or are you making that up?"

"Real." He kissed her forearm. "You didn't know that."

"No." Her teeth scraped the inked flesh, then she licked his muscle and kissed it.

Javier groaned as her fingers explored the ridges of his abdominal muscles. Her tongue ran over the hard disk of his nipple, and he eased her onto her back. His bare chest rose above her, his hands on both sides of her head, caging her as she stared at him. "If I had lost you…"

"You wouldn't." She shook her head. Underneath him, she struggled to tug her shirt off, only briefly losing sight of his intensity when her shirt went overhead. "You won't."

"One of the strongest trees in the world, Sophia. Like us." Javier took her mouth. He probed with his tongue, urging her to kiss him back, kiss him as though she needed him to survive.

And she had needed him for survival. So she did.

Her legs spread, and his weight sank between them. His powerful thighs spread her wider ones, and his thick erection hardened as his hips worked against her. Every part of her body was sensitive. But with him sliding between her legs, Sophia's core was on fire. Arousal bled in her veins, making her wet for his touch.

Javier's hands were slow and methodical. He cupped her breasts, smoothing his thumb over her and pressing her lace-covered mounds into his mouth. Wet, hot heat enveloped her stiff nipples, cascading through her body as his mouth made love.

"Beautiful." His teeth tugged on the fabric as he slipped her bra off. Repeating the same moves, his lips encircled her nipple, without the fabric barrier, and nothing could be better. She arched and moaned. Excited electricity ran to every limb. They shared no words. It was an act, a dance, a moment where they needed to touch and feel.

He unfastened her pants, sliding them away with her underwear still in place, then Javier kissed and nipped his way up her leg, lavishing attention on the soft inside of her thighs. He toyed with the lace of her panty.

"Not fair," she murmured as his fingers danced over her clit. Heat bloomed inside her, and she ached for his touch to find her wet skin. "Touch me."

"Like this..." His fingertip delved under the fabric. He stroked her, languidly, watching her face, working her into a desperately slow frenzy.

"Yes," she whispered.

"Or like this?" Without warning, he sank two fingers inside her slick entry.

Sophia writhed against his hand, bucking for more, for deeper. "That. Like that. Please."

Javier tugged the lace away, leaving her panty hooked around one ankle as though he couldn't wait to get back to her fast enough.

"What do you taste like?" His tongue flicked over wet folds, and sliding his tongue inside her pussy, he groaned.

The vibrations tore her apart from the inside out. Her hands clawed into his hair, his thick locks wrapped around her fingers, and she pulled, and he fought it with another groan. Sophia went boneless. His tongue moved to the sweet spot of nerves as Javier spread her out then slid his wet fingers along her seam, teasing her ass then plunging back into her body.

"You're too much." The words were marred with pants and murmurs, and she never wanted him to stop. The pressure was perfect, his tongue magnificent. Her mind begged for more, and her breaths came heavier and headier.

Javier sucked her clit, thrusting his fingers and holding her wide with the breadth of his shoulders. Bliss pounded inside her body, begging for release as Sophia pinched her eyes tight and embraced the rapid fire of his fingers.

"Javier... oh, God." Her mouth hung open, breaths gasping as the roll of her earthquake hit her. Her legs trembled, and her hips bucked. She bit her bottom lip. Javier pinned her, forcing every second of this insane orgasm to pulse against his kiss and milk on his fingers.

Her fists dropped from his hair and clung to the comforter, and she breathed his name as though it were a prayer.

Javier hauled himself over her limp body, and her arms hugged his shoulders as though a simple move could reignite her. He breathed against her ear, kissing behind the lobe, letting his hand tangle in her hair, and telling her things she'd never know, in another language, that couldn't have sounded any better.

"I need you, Soph."

She nodded, and then he kissed her while somehow unbuckling his belt and downing his jeans. She clawed at him. Feeling him inside her was the only thing she needed. The thick crown inched into her body, and she was done. Nothing compared to this. "Please."

Javier thrust, and she bit his shoulder. His gasp burned into her memory, and the indescribable fullness that only he could provide was intoxicating. He pulled back slowly, every inch of him torturing her in the best of ways. Eyes locked to her, he plunged into her pussy again.

"You needing me, that's what I want to hear."

She nodded. "I do."

He fucked her hard and deep, controlling his rhythm until she cried for more, for him to let go and have at it, to never stop, never, ever. Sophia clung to his body, letting Javier lose control, and her orgasm slammed through her. She bucked and bit, and he never slowed down.

Until he did—with long, dangerous, delicious, strokes.

He growled as he came, straining as his head went back and his torso fell to hers. The sheer impact of his orgasm rippled and pulsed. She fell over the edge again, coming on his cock, clenching his release with her own.

He went lax, not moving except for the faintest of kisses on her neck.

CHAPTER THIRTY-THREE

THE SIDEWAYS RAIN hit the window in the Northern Virginia apartment, and Sophia watched the storm clouds, wrapped in the blanket she'd kept from the Cole estate in Pennsylvania. It was the perfect thing to curl up in on the overcast day when Javier had left her for work. She was eager to do something similar soon.

Javier wasn't what she'd call a phone guy, but he was putting up with her mindless phone chatter and hadn't seemed overly pained when she required him to accompany her on a mandatory Target run. After all, she couldn't pick out stuff for an apartment that he would crash at regularly when he was in the States if she didn't at least know his color preference. It was dark blues—something he hadn't known about himself either.

They were surviving dating domestic bliss. The next step was visiting IKEA and building something together. It was his idea. Who was she to say no?

"So, when do you get back anyway?" she asked.

No answer.

"Javier?"

"Sorry. I'm here."

"Were you listening to me?"

"Eh... blue."

Sophia tightened the blanket around her, laughing. "Close, but sorry. Nope. When do you come back after whatever it is you're doing?"

"Couple days. We're wheels up in ten, though Brock was just pulled off our job. So who knows?"

Her call waiting beeped, and Sophia didn't recognize the number on the screen. "Hey, gotta take this. Maybe it's a gig."

"Call me."

"Will do." She swiped the screen. "Hello?"

"Sophia?" Brock Gamble's familiar voice came through the line.

"Uh, yes?"

"Hana Ferrera's been abducted, and we have a location on her. If I can get you in front of her safely, can you keep her quiet?"

Uh... what? "Brock... Hana's... I'm not a field agent."

"That's covered. I need a face she trusts. That's you. It would make the job a lot easier."

"Me?"

"Or I go in and grab her, and she's scared and probably bites the shit out of my gloved hand. But word is out there that you're looking for a job. This is a gig. Want it?"

"Hell yes."

"There's the Cole family blood I know. Details will be texted to your phone before we hang up. Plan to get moving within the next thirty minutes. Other than that, radio silence."

"Okay."

"No Javier. No Colin."

"Understood," she said.

"See you in thirty."

Sophia ran out the front door, rain splashing in her face and her car keys in hand. A black Suburban with tinted windows zoomed down the quiet street. It veered across the road, locking brakes, making the screeching, splashing noise that Sophia was sure would result in an accident. But instead, the massive SUV came to a stop as though it had been choreographed by an expert stunt driver. It blocked the end of the driveway, and if nothing else, the timing was absurd. Intimidating vehicle blocking her path? Right after she got the call about Hana?

Drenched and uneasy, her adrenaline spiked. At times like this, she needed a little bit of Delta style. A gun on her hip? Yeah, that seemed like it'd be a good idea, though no one would call her a marksman. Still, she could fire the dang thing.

Maybe the better course of action was to get in her car, drive through the yard, and just flee. But reason wasn't happening as she, soaked through to the bone, moved to the SUV and the driver's window rolled down.

A near mirror image of Sophia, tack on a couple decades, looked back at her from the driver's seat. No makeup, hair tied back in a tight ponytail, dark shirt to match the dark windows, and overbearing car that seemed to dwarf *her mother*. "Get in the car, Sophia."

"Mom?"

Her mom smiled. Like, *smiled*. A genuine smile that said this was who she was, welcome to the club, a smile that both changed Sophia's entire world and made her question everything she'd ever known about her mother.

"Hop in."

"Uh…" In what world did the ambassador's wife say *hop in* while not wearing makeup and with her hair tied back? "I can't."

Whatever midlife crisis was happening with Mom, Sophia had places to be. Time ticked, and the seconds lost didn't bode well for Hana. If there was a chance to help her friend survive, there wasn't time for this mother-daughter bonding session, as much as her heart seemed to want to get in the car. "I have to go—"

"Get Hana. I know. *Get in the car*, Sophia."

Her jaw hinged open. Mom knew about Hana? Well… okay. Sophia had no idea what was happening, but her gut said go, and her mom knew about Hana. *Go to Honduras, Sophia Marie. Take the job.* The conversation at the breakfast table and her mother's words all came rushing back to her. Sophia ran to the passenger side, slopping the strings of wet hair off her face, and threw herself inside the SUV, not at all like the lady her mother had tried so hard to raise.

Running her hands across her wet face, Sophia didn't have a second to turn and say *what the hell* before Mom shifted out of park, slammed the gas, and made the engine roar as they sped down this quaint corner of suburbia.

"You know about Hana?"

"She knows everything about Hana."

Sophia spun in her seat to face Brock Gamble, who had a phone to his ear and a laptop taking his attention.

"Wait—I just talked to you."

"Yup," he mumbled.

"You didn't mention you were with my mom."

"Why would I?"

"Why would he?" Mom piped up. "It's not like *this* is how I foresaw our conversation going."

"This? What is this?"

"My involvement with Titan's contract with US intelligence."

"I'm sorry, *what*?" With a spinning mind, Sophia had no idea what to ask next. All she could do was stare at her mother, who wasn't driving like a lady and was very much acting as though she too were an operative.

"We all have a job to do," Mom continued. "Mine was to publicly be your father's wife."

"You're not Dad's wife?"

"No, sweetie. Calm down. Of course I am. What I mean is my public role was to be an ambassador's wife."

"Not…? Uh, and your private role?"

Mom's eyes danced as though she couldn't take hiding her secret any longer. "I've been on the CIA's payroll for years, even before I met your father."

They made a right and accelerated up an entrance ramp. "Holy. Shit."

"Mouth, Sophia."

Brock chuckled in the backseat.

Mom clucked. "Brock Gamble, don't pretend I didn't say the same thing to you half an hour ago."

Brock's amused chuckle became an even more amused grin. Sophia bounced between the two bantering *operatives* and couldn't think.

He cleared his throat. "Sophia, look, everything we discussed is still a go, but when I found Irene was available, we opted to swing by and pick you up."

Irene. Brock and her mom were on a first-name basis. She'd reprimanded him on his mouth, and he apparently did things like *swing by to pick me up*. How had Sophia missed this part of her life?

"When Brock called and said it was you, honey, I thought this would be great. Plus, spy-games carpool." An unexpected, unfamiliar, *awesome* trill of excitement tickled her mom's voice. "Far more fun than preschool pickup ever was."

Sophia swung her gaze back to her mom. "Are you kidding me?"

"Jeesh, it's like you just found out that your parents had sex more than twice in their life."

"Mom!"

Brock laughed again. Even her mom laughed.

"You guys, this isn't funny." Though it was slightly amusing. And gross. Why would Mom have to make the sex-spy connection? Easy, because neither were believable. Whoa.

"As much fun as this is…" Brock cleared his throat. "You going to have your head in the game in a few minutes?"

"Of course I will," Sophia snapped, pushing her wet hair off her shoulders and squaring back in her seat. But out of the corner of her eye, she watched her mom. There was another smile. This time it wasn't amused or free; it was proud, and *that* warmed Sophia in a way that she never could've expected.

CHAPTER THIRTY-FOUR

THEY WERE THE three unlikely amigos: Sophia, her mom, and Brock. In what world this was happening, Sophia had no clue, but her mom palmed a .22 as gracefully as she might a couture clutch. Brock jerked his head, Rambo code for "go that way," and Mom read him loud and clear as if it wasn't her first day out of designer heels.

Their intel had been deemed as accurate as possible. They had all but a live visual of Hana. Other than breaking into a hot facility, probably monitored by an underground terrorist cell, the op was a piece of cake, a simple smash and grab. Literally. There wasn't time for sophisticated security dismantling even with Delta's tech genius in their earpieces scrutinizing their every move.

Javier was in their earpieces, too. Brock, who had an eye for relationships or at least tried to insert himself into them—gruff and dickish though he was—wanted to know if that would make her nervous or not.

And her mom had asked as well. Another stunning shock, maybe even more shocking than the fact that Irene Cole was on Uncle Sam's armed-and-dangerous payroll, was that she seemed genuinely interested in their relationship. She even went as far as prying, whereas Brock pretended he was *not* listening when he *most certainly* was.

The plan was simple: Brock would do the dirty work. Sophia would never see any of that. Mom might see some of that—a fact that Sophia was still coming to grips with—and Sophia's only job was to be the friendly face that Hana needed to see to keep quiet.

Brock estimated the job should take less than two minutes, which included jumping out of the running car into the rain and returning with their high-value target. Hana. Her friend.

Between her friend, her mother's involvement, and Brock's oddball answers to hypothetical questions, Sophia was left chewing the inside of her mouth.

"What if someone steals the running car?" she asked.

"No one would be that stupid."

"But what if?"

"Then, kaboom."

Her jaw dropped. "You'd blow up someone who stole your car?"

"Sophia, don't gape." The mother she knew came out, reprimanding, and Sophia snapped her mouth closed.

"Trust me," Brock grumbled. "In our world, it's not the worst thing when something gets blown up."

"Doesn't sound great." Sophia glanced at her mom.

"Better than some*body* blowing up."

Sage advice from Mom the spy.

"Tango one." The low whisper of Brock's voice tickled in her earpiece. "Subdued—Irene, behind you."

A quick jostle of noise, and an unexpected second enemy made bile slosh in Sophia's stomach as she quickly ran to the room Hana was determined to be in. She'd memorized the blueprints in the car on the ride over, but even as her feet moved with purpose, Sophia was waiting for her mom's confirmation that everything would be alright.

"Second man down," Mom announced.

Sophia's heart jumped, then she opened the door, hoping to find an unsuspecting Hana. She put a finger to her lip, in case her friend needed shushing. Hana startled, but when she caught sight of Sophia's face, she stood up without a word. The two of them took off.

Mom came into sight, heading out the door they'd initially breached, Brock following. The rain hit Sophia's face, slapping cold and hard. But the sudden jolt was a taste of near freedom.

The SUV was still running, still in place, just as Brock had promised. Doors flew open. Hana and Sophia piled into the back, Brock took the driver's seat, and Mom rode shotgun. The tires squealed as the people at Titan HQ hooted their approval of the job well done. Several voices were on the line, but Javier's was the only one Sophia heard or cared about. She sank back into the seat, relaxed and dripping wet, freezing and head-over-heels in love, needing to tell him before she did anything else.

The earpiece was of no use anymore. She pulled it out, and Mom was doing the same.

Hana reached over and grabbed her hand, resting her head on Sophia's shoulder. "Thank you, my friend."

Sophia squeezed her, their soaked clothes and hair doing little to warm or soothe one another. But it was nice to actually have her safe. "I told you I would get you to the US."

"You also told me that I'd get a date with your brother."

"Haha." Sophia tossed her head back, laughing hard. "Let me introduce you to the team. Front passenger, my mom. Meaning Colin's mom. And Brock Gamble, his boss."

Hana laughed as hard as Sophia had. "Fabulous. *Mi amiga* is a black ops ninja girl now too?"

"Apparently, it runs in the family."

"Apparently," Mom said then turned to face them. "You know what else I heard runs in the family?"

"Hmm?" How many more surprises could she take that day?

"Falling in love with military men."

"Mom!" Who was this woman? First she was a spy, and now she wanted to gossip about Sophia's love life. "How would you know?"

Mom's head tilted toward her source.

"Brock!"

The man didn't turn around, but Sophia could see his cheeks flex as though he were trying not to smile.

"I swear," Sophia mumbled. "Men are almost worse than women."

"With what?" Hana asked.

"Gossip."

"Oh, this isn't gossip," Hana said. "It's fact."

"Hana!" Sophia pulled back and gave the stink eye as though she hadn't just been part of the rescue to save her friend's life.

Hana shrugged to Mom. "She won't say *I love you*. She says she wasted it on her waste of a groom."

Oh. Shit. Sophia's eyes flew to her mom, having no idea how the ambassador's wife—spy or not—would take *any* comment like that about the good doctor Josh.

Mom hummed, lost in thought, and for every rain-sloshed moment Brock continued to drive down the highway, Sophia wondered if her mom might accidentally turn back into a society lady and implode.

"Then," Mom said, "don't say it how you said it before."

Sophia's brow pinched as she tried to figure out if that advice was code from her mom, a spy, or a society lady. "I'm… sorry, wh—what?"

"A word is a word is a word, Sophia. Get new words."

Ha. "*I love you* is pretty much *it*, Mom."

"Or is it, sweetheart? There's more than one way to say many things, especially when English *is not* his language."

Hmmm. Discounting that this was their first personal mom-daughter conversation, and that Brock was eavesdropping, Sophia turned to Hana, who nodded as though it made sense.

"*Adoro su hija, la señora Cole.*"

Mom's gaze held onto Hana. "Exactly."

Hana's native tongue was Spanish, most of which Sophia could pick out. She adored Mrs. Cole's daughter. "Cute." But Javier was Brazilian Portuguese. "How do you say—"

"Tell him, *eu te amo.*" Mom's words were like a hug that they'd never shared. *I love you.* In Brazilian Portuguese.

This *I love you* offered Sophia a way to bridge her gap with Javier and brought her and her mom together more powerfully than sharing their first day in the field together ever could. "Thank you."

CHAPTER THIRTY-FIVE

T HE MATERNITY WING wasn't the way Sophia would have imagined. She would have guessed there'd be pinks and blues, teddy bears and balloons. She hadn't thought about it before, but walking into the security zone, she realized there was a high level of surveillance and protection in this place.

Hand in hand, she and Javier were buzzed in, passing Colin as he signed them in at the visitors' station. The waiting area was down the hall, but Jared Westin, *the* boss of Titan, had put all their names on a list of people to be sent in when they arrived. With a quick show of ID and a name on a form, Sophia and Javier were directed to a private suite.

Javier rounded into the room first, and Sophia's steps went heavy as she saw Jared, holding a very tiny newborn.

"Oh," was all she could whisper.

"Hi."

Sophia pulled her gaze from the tiny baby and the man who was normally almost scary looking but at the moment was just… a proud daddy quietly shifting his weight back and forth in his boots, soothing a sleeping bundle of blankets—his wife and other child. "Hi."

Javier used their joined hands to point as he made introductions. "Sugar and Asal."

Sugar smiled. "And that's Violet."

Jared walked over, quietly saying hello. Javier offered congratulations, and Violet was slipped into Sugar's arms. Asal curled around her mom. The Westins were a family of operatives—badasses, often irreverent and always interesting to hear about. From the little that Sophia knew, that clan led an exciting life. But at the moment, this was their bliss. Wow.

Jared cleared his throat quietly. "You heard about Rodrigo Moreira?"

Javier's grip in Sophia's hand flexed. "Yes, sir."

"The team found a ton of actionable intel. Enough to smoke out the last of the top dogs in the Primeiro Comando."

"Yes, sir. I heard."

Jared nodded to Sophia. "You made the right decision on which job to choose."

He raised his chin as though preparing to walk into a firing line. "Thank you, sir."

Jared continued. "I heard you two had come out of the closet. Though changing an op midstride was already a neon sign of an announcement." The baby stirred, waking and quietly flapping its mouth open and shut, turning its head side to side.

"I think Vi-Vi's hungry." Asal leaned in, inspecting the infant.

Sophia took a step back. "Do you want us to leave?"

Sugar shook her head, readying to nurse. "Nah, it's okay. I'm sure it'll become easier—"

"Because we can leave."

Knock, knock.

"There you go." Sugar ignored the door and blew out a breath as a doctor walked in.

"I'm Dr. Josh Ject, the pediatrician on rotation. Just a quick stop to check on…" He picked up the clipboard at the end of the bed. "Violet. How's everyone doing?"

Josh looked up from the chart, catching Sophia's eye. "Oh." It was the first time they'd set eyes on each other since she'd walked away from the altar.

"Hi," Sophia said. "We'll step out."

His gaze dropped to Sophia's hand, which was clasped in Javier's. Javier's other arm was around her protectively as he leaned into her from behind.

"Funny!" Sugar, who seemed highly amused but was moving slowly because of the baby on her breast, tossed her head back against the pillow. "I don't need introductions to know we've got an ex in the room."

Josh cleared his throat. "Mrs. Westin—"

"Sugar," she corrected.

Sophia's ex-fiancé smiled awkwardly. "Sugar." He stepped forward as Jared moved closer to her bedside.

"We'll step out." Sophia tugged Javier behind her. "Thanks for letting us visit."

"Just come back in a few." Sugar snuggled Violet to her.

"It was nice seeing you, Sophia," Josh said.

"We should go." Gripping Javier's hand with more force than needed, Sophia wasn't sure if her vehemence was because she wanted to strangle Josh for the hell of it or if because he'd ruined something she wanted to give to Javier. She *still* hadn't told Javier how much she loved him. Whatever the case, Javier didn't react to her ex. He simply guided Sophia through the semi-open door and into the hallway.

"Waiting room." Javier tilted his head toward the sign. "Let's go." Nothing fazed him.

"I need a candy bar. Or a balloon bouquet. Something over-the-top to erase the last few minutes from my mind."

He laughed. "You okay?"

"That was *so* awkward." They entered the small area. A few couches and chairs, a couple piles of magazines, and a row of vending machines awaited her. "So. So. So awkward."

He shrugged. "Could've been worse."

"Ha. How?"

"It could've been you lying in bed, holding our baby, when random ex-slash-doctor-on-duty rolls in."

The simple casualness of his words didn't take away from the monumental suggestion he'd just made. Between her spinning head and her swooning, Sophia managed to close her gaping mouth and not pass out. "*Our* baby?"

"You don't want kids?" A slight concern showed on his face.

"Are we having this conversation?" Eyes peeled wide, Sophia fumbled for a couch, still clinging to his hand.

"Do you want to?" he asked as though it were that simple.

Sophia nodded, head in a haze, thoughts of little Javier Almeidas making her dizzy. His children would be so beautiful... *their* children? God. She couldn't breathe.

"Remember that thing I said to you?" he asked, dropping to the spot next to her on the plastic couch.

There was no question what he was speaking about. He asked her that whenever he wanted to remind her how much she was loved. "Yes."

Whether Javier could hear her response or not was another question. It came out on an unbelieving breath. Could she *ever* forget the words "I love you" from him?

"I assume we're on the same page, and kids and a future come with *that*."

God. *God!* This man. She melted into the crook of his arm. "Really?"

Javier pressed his lips to the top of her head, wrapping her protectively in his hold. "Yes, paixão. Really."

Sophia pulled back enough to prop her chin against him. "Thank you."

"You want to have my babies one day?"

She nodded. More than anything. But that he wanted that too and had suggested it? There was no greater feeling than knowing Javier, who had a rough family life and a need to never be tied down, would want a situation—a relationship—like that in his future. All the words didn't matter. *I love you*—the words wasted on exes—and the fear that he'd never find a calm in his cartel-hunting inner storm all faded away. Javier wanted a family with her.

"Good." His smile made the rest of the world pale in comparison. "You will be a great mother. You know that?"

"*Eu te amo, Javier.*" She loved him from the very bottom of her soul. The words flowed, and nothing held any meaning except him and her, together.

The quietest catch of a breath. He'd heard and understood.

Javier froze then gathered her into his arms in the middle of the waiting room, burying her against his chest. "Ah, paixão, *my passion*. I love you too."

EPILOGUE

JAVIER SMOOTHED THE edge of the bedspread that Sophia had dragged from their first night together to their first apartment to their bedroom in the house they were calling home. "Sophia!"

Everything to her had meaning, especially that bedspread. His eyes ran over the bed and the chair with everything in place the way he wanted. His heart slammed in his chest, tension and excitement knotted in his shoulders. This would be something worth remembering and reliving.

He smiled, speaking to himself. "Paixão, love you."

There was no sound of footsteps heading up the stairs. Javier ran his fingers through his hair then smoothed his T-shirt as though it had bunched because his muscles and mind were jumping. "Soph? Can you come here?"

"What?" she called faintly from downstairs.

He walked to the hall, leaning over the banister. "Sophia, I want to show you something."

"Now?"

He laughed, making a face for the camera. "Yeah, gatinha."

"I'm almost done with the dishes. Hang tight."

Alright. Hanging tight. He chuckled, but he couldn't wipe the grin off his face and couldn't wait to see hers when she walked into their bedroom. He wanted to remember today because he'd never tried harder than at this moment to make her smile, make her fall in love with him again, and make his world spin as only she could do.

The water shut off, and footsteps sounded from the kitchen. He moved to the stairs, waiting.

"Coming," she mumbled, but when she saw him at the top of the stairs, her beautiful grin reached her sweet eyes.

"Come faster."

"What?" She laughed, maybe sensing he was up to no good.

"I need you in the bedroom."

She batted his chest when she reached the landing. "You *had* me in the bedroom earlier."

He took her hand, linking their fingers together and squeezing. "Need you again."

"You're insatiable."

Javier laughed, pulling her close. "Never complained before."

"Won't start today—" They rounded the corner into the bedroom, him leaning against the doorjamb, her gaping as he'd prayed she would.

"Javier, what is this?" Her hand squeezed tightly as though she couldn't let him go, couldn't believe what she saw.

"You said you wanted to marry me but to hell with planning a wedding."

"I did." She nodded, her voice tight and quiet. Beautiful. And awestruck.

"I planned it for you."

"You planned…" Tears slipped down her cheeks, and he pulled her in front of him, wrapping his arms around her, walking them closer to the bed.

On the bed, in front of three white dresses for her to choose from, was a bouquet of white calla lilies, a diamond ring, and a letter. Just as he knew she would, Sophia picked up the letter before the diamond, making him fall in love with her even more.

Paixão,

I've had a hundred dreams, a thousand wishes. To turn back the clock and hold you sooner, love you longer, give you everything that makes you smile.

I fell in love with you over and over, and each time, you had no idea just what you were doing to me. The feisty girl with the cake and scissors? I never had a chance.

I can't promise that life will be without problems or that you won't hurt when the world does. But I can promise you I will be by your side.

When we met, I didn't know if you were ripping my soul and slicing my heart or making me stronger. You were making me stronger.

So much stronger.

Sophia Cole. I love you, and I do not care how it is said. Or if it's said. I know we have love.

Here is a dress, or three. Take your pick. Put my ring on your finger. Our friends and family will be here today. You do not have to plan a thing. I'll be the man wearing the smile you gave me. Find me at the end of the aisle. Please be my wife.

Love,
Javier

She trembled as she read his words while in his arms. Sophia was everything. There was only one answer, and he had no doubt that it would fall from her lips.

Sophia turned, wrapping him in a hug. "You did this for me?"

"For us." Her touch made him feel unstoppable, and he knew why he'd been put on his life's path: to get to her.

"I love you, Javier." And as her head tilted back, her hair sliding back, she pressed her mouth to his and kissed the answer *yes*. "*Eu te amo.*"

Sophia tasted like sugar and smelled like sunshine. She held onto him as though she couldn't survive without his touch, and his tongue tangled with hers because he knew it was true. He'd be lost and gone without her.

Her lips slowed, and his stilled. "Thank you."

Emotion clogged his throat as he held her. "You are why I exist."

"God…" she whispered against his lips. "I love you."

Javier inched back. "Ready for today?"

Her soft brown eyes danced. "Like *today* today?"

"Yes, ma'am. Everything is planned." He pulled her attention to the nightstand. Printed on the same thick ivory paper as his letter was a schedule of their day, aptly named "Javier + Sophia's Agenda."

"Just choose your dress. Nothing poofy or that will require scissors to be removed from. Only decision you have today."

"That's it? You planned *everything*?"

He smirked playfully. "I get it. Bullets and ballistics are more my thing. But I had some help, you'll be happy to know." *A Titan amount of help from Marlena and Emma.*

"I'd be happy anyway…" Her gaze swept the room as a curious grin played on her cheeks. "The food?"

"Done. Janella is in charge of that. I had no say—"

"Really?" Sophia squeaked.

He nodded. "*Everything* is covered."

"Everything." Her eyebrow rose playfully. "You know what you're wearing?"

"Yes. *And* it's been pressed." He smiled. "Bonus points, right?"

"Absolutely." She beamed. "Guests?"

"Of course."

Then her eyes went wide, and she bit her lip. "My mother?"

Javier pulled her against his chest, letting his hand thread into her hair, and stroked her with the promise that *everything* would be perfect. "Today has her blessing."

Her arms squeezed as she melted into him. "Oh. My. God."

"Any other questions?" He kissed the top of her head.

She moved her chin onto his chest, letting their gaze lock and hold. "You're serious?"

"Like the mortar strike that took out the last of the PC, paixão. Read your agenda. Do what it says for one nonplanned, flawless wedding that I promise you'll remember forever." He dropped to one knee. "Will you marry me, Sophia Marie?"

She dropped beside him with a smile that touched his heart. "Absolutely. Yes. We were meant to be."

THE END

ACKNOWLEDGEMENTS

Some books take a village. This was one of them. Thanks to everyone who believed that a Delta book could be as sexy and exciting as a Titan novel.

Team Titan, I dedicated this one to you. It's smart, sexy, and resilient, just like the men and women who make up our book club. Javier and Sophia are survivors no matter the hand they've been dealt. I learn something every day from you, and I'm lucky to have such amazing readers. #titanstrong

Thank you to the amazing Delta: Revenge production team! Adriano Silva is the English-Brazilian Portuguese translator and editor. He went above and beyond the call of duty for this book, and for that I will always be grateful. Thanks to Red Adept, and in particular, Sarah Carleton, for editing this story. I have to give a big shout out to the InkSlinger PR team. Thank you Tara Gonzalez and Amber Noffke for your nonstop creativity. Also, thank you to Sara Shone, who deserves a superhero cape for all of the times she saved the day while I was writing Javier and Sophia's fall into love.

My crit partners are a crucial part of my process, and I will forever be appreciative for their time and effort. I love you all dearly.

Finally, this book would not exist if I did not have the love and support of my family. Thank you.

ABOUT THE AUTHOR

CRISTIN HARBER is a *New York Times* and *USA Today* bestselling romance author. She writes sexy, steamy romantic suspense, military romance, new adult, and contemporary romance. Readers voted her onto Amazon's Top Picks for Debut Romance Authors in 2013, and her debut Titan series was both a #1 romantic suspense and #1 military romance bestseller.

The Titan Series:
Book 1: Winters Heat
Book 1.5: Sweet Girl
Book 2: Garrison's Creed
Book 3: Westin's Chase
Book 4: Gambled
Book 5: Chased
Book 6: Savage Secrets
Book 7: Hart Attack
Book 8: Black Dawn
Book 9: Live Wire
Book 10: Bishop's Queen

The Delta Series:
Book 1: Delta: Retribution
Book 2: Delta: Revenge

The Delta Novella in Liliana Hart's MacKenzie Family Collection:
Delta: Rescue

The Only Series:
Book 1: Only for Him
Book 2: Only for Her
Book 3: Only for Us
Book 4: Only Forever